QUIET MURDER

NANCY LIVINGSTON

D0004076

W RLDWIDE ®

TORONTO • NEW YORK • LONDON
AMSTERDAM • PARIS • SYDNEY • HAMBURG
STOCKHOLM • ATHENS • TOKYO • MILAN
MADRID • WARSAW • BUDAPEST • AUCKLAND

QUIET MURDER

A Worldwide Mystery/December 1995

First published by St. Martin's Press, Incorporated.

ISBN 0-373-26186-1

Printed in U.S.A.

---------------- ★ ----------------

Mr. Pringle licked his dry lips. "Where are we going?"

"To the police station, to answer a few questions."

"What precisely are you inquiring into, may I ask?"

"The unlawful killing of Ernest Clare."

Unlawful...? Behind dusty spectacles, Mr. Pringle's eyes were owl-like with shock. "People assumed it was a heart attack."

"We cannot be responsible for what people assume, Mr. Pringle. Our interest is in the facts. We shall require a full statement as to your movements yesterday."

Indignation swept through him. "Surely you do not intend to apprehend *me?*"

Hard cynical eyes regarded him. "Move it."

---------------- ★ ----------------

For The Famous Five!

Diana
Alan
Sue
Brian
and...what's'isname

ONE

CHRISTMAS DAY WAS the following Sunday. The Thursday before, those who'd succeeded in ignoring the event were verging on panic, tripping over slow-moving pensioners, stretching credit to the limit. The big London store had removed every distraction: even the crib was outside. Beneath it, elderly shoppers sheltered from the drizzle so it wasn't entirely without a purpose.

Drizzle turned to rain. In a desperate bid to lure them back, the store turned up its muzak system. Those still sheltering were bombarded with synthetic, syrupy carols. It was almost a relief when someone shouted they'd glimpsed a bus.

The driver of an articulated lorry, Karl Gough, watched impassively as one or two stumbled across the road, too close to his wheels. Avoiding manslaughter was routine in London. Thank God he felt calmer now, able to cope. Since leaving Southend, the panicky feeling had gradually subsided. Its effect still lingered; the sweat-soaked T-shirt had dried against his skin, making him itchy.

Body odour disgusted him. Would his own frightened stink give him away? Karl swallowed. If there was a chance of a shower when he got to Lila's, he would certainly take it. He always carried a selection of unguents in his cab, plus a camping spray-pack for the Middle East: a clever gadget, foot operated, it didn't need much water.

Long distance you needed things like that. Dust, dirt, and smells that made your eyes water, that was the desert. With luck, he'd be heading that way tomorrow, after the initial drop in France. Which reminded him—he needed to confirm the pick-up time. He'd do that once he got to Lila's.

Beyond Turkey, the loneliness was great; Karl loved it. There was camaraderie when you needed it. Another driver would always stop if you'd got a problem. Artics tended to bunch together at night-time as well. Ignore that golden rule and you could wake up minus your load as well as your wheels.

At traffic lights, he stopped dreaming; today was still a sick reality. It wasn't his fault, he wasn't a violent man. But Sharon—he still couldn't get over it—filthy, dirty... It wasn't his fault, she'd goaded him over the limit!

Traffic wardens, glistening with rain, bellowed through loud-hailers, urging pedestrians to hurry. Stop thinking about it, concentrate on the future and it would be all right. Act confidently, that was the secret. Forget about Sharon, the way her mouth had twisted when—

'It wasn't my fault!'

Careful! A man passing in front of his lorry had glanced up, he must have heard the shout. Karl took a deep breath, his hands gripped the wheel. Provided he could be on his way first thing in the morning, he'd be OK.

With the engine at tick-over, the temperature had dropped. He shivered. Got to put as much distance as he could between him and ... Don't think about it! Stay calm. Concentrate on what still needed to be done, like the phone calls, filling up the tank, etc, etc. Stay very, very cool. But trying to change tapes in the cassette, his shaking hands fumbled and he swore.

The lights changed. Negotiating the awkward turn, he couldn't avoid sending a surge of rainwater over one pair of sodden elderly feet. Two fingers went up, injuring his professional pride.

'And the season's greetings to you, madam!'

She was lucky not to be strangled. Karl began to fantasise: why not? In this downpour he could leap out, choke her to death and be away in seconds. Headlines would describe an 'unknown assailant'. No one would guess and it would release the tension churning away in his gut. He sneered—that only happened in films; in real life you got caught.

His route through London continued westwards, skirting busy thoroughfares and threading through side-streets. This area wasn't fashionable although the trend had begun. A few deliberately bare windows revealed modernised interiors but, further on, paintwork was dingy and green dralon tightly drawn. It was along such a stretch Karl began to search for a once familiar front door.

When he'd spotted it, he drove past, turned sharply and bumped his lorry up on to a narrow patch of waste land between two pairs of houses. Air-brakes hissed. The space wasn't quite deep enough, the back of his trailer jutted out into Inkerman Street. It wasn't causing that much of an obstruction. All the same, in case there were busybodies anxious to report it to the police, Karl checked the rear number plate: splattered with mud it was almost illegible, which satisfied him.

The locals probably hadn't changed their habits. Street lights had been vandalised long ago, no one with any sense would open their front door after dark. Like a shadow, Karl moved silently down the pitch-black alley, round to the back of Lila Boyce's house.

They were all alike: narrow-fronted Victorian semi-detacheds, the white-pillared bay windows separated from the pavement by straggling privet and a low brick wall. Downstairs there were three rooms: the front parlour, the 'morning cum dining room' and finally the scullery. A steep staircase rose immediately inside the glass-panelled front door, parallel to the dark passage which led through to the back of the house.

There was a change of level in this passageway, a step down halfway along and those owners who were too mean to switch on the hall light were indifferently apologetic when visitors stumbled. The first time he'd stayed there, Lila had forgotten to point it out and he'd measured his length. The memory made him grin but his face was so taut the muscles cracked. Sharon used to taunt that he never smiled, he was too mean. She was a whore! She'd forced him to marry her because of his dad's bit of money. He'd been too thick not to see he was being conned. She'd been so pretty! Clean blond hair which smelled like fresh grass.

Once married, he'd refused to share his inheritance. He'd paid a deposit on the cheapest house he could find and gave her a weekly amount for house-keeping, telling her she'd have to manage on that. Sharon had screamed at him for being so mean. OK, so he kept a supply of ready cash locked away in his cab, it was necessary to grease many palms in his line of business. However many times he attempted to explain, she wouldn't listen. Nor did she believe how much the artic cost to maintain.

He was nearly there. Splashing through the alley, Karl groped along the grimy back wall as far as the wooden door and reached over the top for the bolt. It wasn't even thrust home. The door swung open as he leaned against it. Careless! People deserved what happened when they didn't take precautions. He stepped into the small back yard.

Familiar smells reminded him of the former WC and coal shed on his left, the new Wheelie Bin on his right. All along Inkerman Street, these yards were the same. Ahead, hidden in the deep black shadow of the house, would be the washing line. Memory made him stretch out until he'd located the wooden prop. Karl set it carefully against the wall. He didn't want its falling clatter to betray him. He told himself he wasn't really behaving furtively. It would be a surprise for Lila, that was all. The real reason, the one he wouldn't admit, was that he didn't want a rebuff.

Beyond the washing line, up three worn stone steps, was the back door. Beside it, the scullery window was dark. Lila must be on one of her habitual Christmas junkets, shopping up West. She couldn't stand the long dark afternoons cooped up here; any excuse and she was off to mingle with the crowds and bright lights.

Karl let out a long, slow breath. Unless the routine had changed, she'd be back in time to make tea for her lodgers, around six-thirty. Despite his earlier panic-stricken state he'd worked it all out and it really was going to be all right!

His mood changed again; nothing lasted long with him. Anxiety was replaced by bouncy confidence, his stance became cocky. He paused long enough to slick back his spikey mousey hair. Stop worrying, take a look around. Now he'd become accustomed to the darkness, he began to note the changes.

An uncomfortable wetness inside his back collar brought him back to the present and the need for shelter. Also, there were those phone calls he had to make. He was about to check whether the key was still in its usual hiding place when something made him hesitate.

Suppose Lila had moved away? He could be trespassing. After a moment's consideration, Karl shrugged: so what? A stranger who didn't recognise him wouldn't be a problem. Anyway there was obviously no one here. But supposing the stranger returned and found him using the phone...? Picturing the scene nearly made Karl giggle. Then memory jolted him in the stomach. Stop messing about! He had to organise his life and disappear for a while. Lila couldn't have moved away—where would she go, a widow with no family? She would be back soon, she was reliable and she could give him a bed for the night, so stop fretting.

The windows in the next-door semi were blank and dark. Was the old geezer there still alive? He must be older than God if he was. Memory was returning in waves. Rumour had it the stupid git kept his savings tucked down the side of his armchair. Maybe he had gone Christmas shopping?

Karl was skint. He could do with a few tenners, not enough to make the old boy suspicious, just to pay for the ferry crossing. What would an old fool need money for, anyway, apart from his funeral? And if you hadn't any savings the state would take care of that. It wouldn't take above a minute... Moving stealthily, Karl eased himself through the crack in the fence.

THE WINDOWS IN the handsome stone church further down Inkerman Street had been boarded up. The social hub these days, the Bricklayers, was nearer the junction with the main road and surrounded by a few small shops: it drew a regular, much more faithful congregation. The peeling sign swung in the squally wind. A string of bobbing red and yellow lights reminded passers-by of the pending Christian festival.

Inside, a darts match was in progress. In the saloon, the imitation log fire was switched to 'High Heat' and pinned to the door a hand-written sign offered customers today's equivalent of gold, frankincense and myrrh:

Christmas week: 6-7.00 p.m. Happy hour: all drinks half price. Tonight 7.30 p.m. Christmas club & Bequest payout.

The elderly man who lived at number 8, Inkerman Street, next door to Lila Boyce, spend his days in the middle ground-floor room. Here the sash window overlooked a blank wall. Even in summer, daylight scarcely penetrated. Despite this he preferred the room because of its privacy. When he'd first arrived, he'd spurned the front parlour, putting up thick lace curtains for added protection.

His few bits of furniture were shabby. A second-hand armchair had blankets covering the cracks in the leather. Odd dining chairs flanked the scratched oak table. This was usually heaped with old newspapers and magazines, with only a small space left for his meal tray, but tonight the table top was bare. All his belongings were strewn on the floor. The bookcase was empty, its glass doors splintered and the contents trampled among greasy broken supper plates.

The old man stared above his gag, his neck cords rigid. He hadn't spoken as he'd watched the room being torn apart, nor when angry feet thudded through the overhead rooms, nor afterwards, when he'd been tortured. The gas fire, which had been left switched on, revealed eyes which did not waver. The only sound was a frenzied breathing but this didn't come from the old man, his chest barely moved. He didn't utter a word although his mouth opened instinctively as his tormentor relaxed the pressure of the gag.

'For the last time, where's the money?'

There was despair as well as fury but any reply that formed in the darkening mind was left unspoken. The old man had caught the words, 'last time'. This hell must be nearing its conclusion: all he had to do was hang on, he could manage that.

Fear filled the silence. Sweat fell despite the chill as, standing behind the old man, the intruder cupped the skeletal jaw in both hands. He was committed to this now. His palms were slippery and old thin loose flesh slid over the bones. He gripped more firmly, braced himself and took a deep breath for the effort. There was a tremendous heave, a jerk, then another, but despite being attenuated, sinew and blood vessel didn't part that easily.

Sweat was pouring from him, spilling on to the victim, mingling with follicle and eyelid, tracing a course over those begging, pleading eyes. Faces inverted, intruder and victim stared at one another. Above the gag, the gashes still bled and caused inexplicable anger: the old bastard should have died long ago, he deserved to die! That thought gave enough strength for a further mighty effort followed by a curse: 'Sod you!'

A crack signalled the rude exit into eternity. The body sagged and the weight of it tipped over the chair to which it was bound. The intruder rubbed bloody, sweaty palms on a handkerchief and stuffed this deep inside his jacket. Seconds later the room was empty. This time the silence was profound.

THE SIGHT OF Karl sitting at her kitchen table when she switched on the scullery light made Lila Boyce scream.

'Where the hell did you spring from?'

His mind was numb; he made a ghastly effort to sound jokey. 'Evening, Lila. Popped up like a bad penny—you always said I would. I thought I'd give you a surprise—'

'A surprise!'

'Didn't you spot my wagon? I thought that'd be a dead giveaway.' Why use that word!

'Where? I never noticed.'

He remembered, the bus stop was in the opposite direction. She was panting, she must have run all the way.

'It was pissing down and the key was in its usual place, so I thought, Lila won't mind if I get out of the wet.'

Karl's mind began to function faster. Why the hell had he stuck to his original plan? Why not hit the road after what had happened? The trouble was, his brain was in shock. He'd made his plans first thing today and after what had happened he'd behaved like an automaton.

His body stank and his hands were still wet—if only she'd let him have a hot shower, it might, just might, wash the terrible memory away.

Lila tugged at her headscarf and shook the worst of the rain out of her thick grey fringe, her eyes never leaving his face.

'I've been up West,' she said. 'After all this time—you've got a nerve. Turning up. Sitting here in the dark—'

'You deserve to be done,' he snapped back. 'The bolt was undone, the key was where anyone could find it—where everyone *expects* to find it. Doesn't anyone change their habits round here?' She didn't reply. 'Burglars don't mess about these days, you know.'

She repeated, 'How long have you been here?'

'About half an hour.' Did she believe him? 'I was just thinking of making a pot of tea only you beat me to it. Didn't put the light on—I was going to shout the minute I heard the key in the lock—how was I to know you'd come crashing in like that.' It wasn't convincing but it was the best he could do. He asked, 'Shall I put the kettle on now?'

'If you want.' She watched him as he moved about the scullery, his confidence returning as he remembered where everything was kept. Finally she asked, 'How long is it since you were last here?'

He shrugged. 'Over three years, nearer four.'

'So... what did bring you back?'

He was ready for this, he'd got his answer pat. 'A row with Sharon, what else?' He began another circuit of the kitchen, stocky body moving lightly, shoulders hunched inside the bomber jacket, his eyes as guileless as he could make them. She guessed what he was searching for and pointed to the sugar bowl. 'Oh, ta.' He overdid the nonchalance, glancing slyly to see if his words had registered.

'Yes, Sharon threw me out this morning. Wasn't the first time we'd had a row. My own fault. I've been away so much and she's got herself this new boyfriend. She admitted she had. So...when she told me to go...' He hugged himself tightly inside his jacket. 'No point in hanging around if you're not wanted. Might as well earn some dosh. There's plenty with extra loads they want shifted and not many willing to work over Christmas. I made a couple of phone calls while I was waiting—local—hope you don't mind. I've left money by the phone.'

'So long as you didn't call Southend.'

He shook his head, tried to laugh. 'What for? Wish her a Merry Christmas? I'm off first thing tomorrow. Got a pick-up, then travelling via Felixstowe. I thought I'd treat myself to a proper bed tonight, that's why I've come. It's bloody cold this weather, sleeping in the cab.'

With Lila, it was impossible to read her thoughts. She didn't question him. Her eyes still followed wherever he moved but she had relaxed enough to hang up her coat. He'd done all he could; he didn't *have* to tell any more about Sharon, or what had happened since... He wished he could stop shivering! Stay schtum, let her work things out for herself.

He tried to act casual so she wouldn't notice the trembling. This morning had been bad enough, but now... The kettle whistled. His hands could scarcely stuff the teabags into the pot. Earlier when he'd worked out what he would tell Lila—that he had left home at Sharon's request—it had seemed so simple. That was before he'd arrived in Inkerman Street and let curiosity get the better of him.

If he kept his head, if he didn't elaborate, he could still be all right. If only he hadn't been tempted by those darkened windows. Or by what he'd spotted on the table. It had been an automatic reaction—then he had caught sight of those eyes, staring accusingly...

He'd been unable to think straight when he finally stumbled in here. Of course he should've followed his instinct to run like hell: then again, maybe not. That would have damned him. His wagon had been outside long enough for any passer-by to notice it even if Lila hadn't. Far better pretend he'd been sitting here all the time, waiting for her to return.

'You in trouble?'

'No!' Steady, steady. 'Why d'you ask?'

Without replying, Lila moved her handbag to make room for her tea cup. The overhead light glinted on the clasp of her purse.

'Not much of a way to spend Christmas.'

'Oh, I dunno. Out of harm's way. If I'm not wanted at home... Better let Sharon make up her mind between us.'

'What about the kiddie?'

'Sarah. She was going to Sharon's mum for Christmas. Right old bitch, she is.'

Karl could see the plastic credit card protruding from the stained leather purse. Unconsciously, his brain registered it was just what he needed. He tried to push this knowledge to the back of his mind but it refused to stay quiescent: he was being shown a way out, an opportunity to look after number one. It was fate; he knew he would succumb if she gave him the chance.

'Just the one night?' asked Lila.

'Is my old room free?'

'I don't take lodgers no more.'

This brought an easing of tension and made him careless. He sniggered, 'Come into money, have we?'

She was curt. 'Don't be stupid. And mind the stairs. The bulb's gone and the carpet's torn halfway up.'

He was regaining his confidence with every second. Was it imagination or was Lila looking nervous now? He grew bold. 'I'll be careful. Wouldn't do for me to trip and break my neck, would it?'

Immediately, he could have screamed at himself for being so stupid!

She said flatly, 'It'll be fifteen quid if you want a cooked breakfast. In advance.'

He was going to need every penny. To distract her he suggested, 'Fancy a drink? For old times' sake.' She never drank much, it was bound to be cheaper than rent. At the pub, he'd promise the money at breakfast time then he'd slip away before daybreak. He was bulletproof, he knew he was, it was all going his way!

When she went upstairs to make up his bed, he moved quickly. Even if she was tempted to buy a round, she wouldn't use her Visa card. Another idea occurred. He unzipped the inner pocket of her bag. He hadn't been mistaken, fate really was on his side tonight. He set the bag back in the middle of the table, making sure the purse protruded exactly as before. By the time she came downstairs again, he was rinsing the tea cups. 'Thought I'd make myself useful.'

She said laconically, 'Times have changed. Or is it your wife's influence?'

'Sharon doesn't influence me. Nobody does.'

Lila examined him from under thick eyebrows. His gut was beginning to thicken. Apart from that, he was as jumpy as a cat. He made her nervous but he looked as if he could fly off the handle altogether if she tried to throw him out.

'Just the one night then. I've given up B and B. Lodgers are damned hard work.'

'I've said, haven't I?' Calm down! That had been far too loud. Act natural. In a coaxing tone he pleaded, 'How about a bite to eat before we got to the pub?'

TWO

It was the worst time of year for those living alone. In Inkerman Street several of them were preparing to take part in unwished for conviviality rather than watch television bonhomie. From the hallway of her ground-floor flat at number 13, Mrs Betty Fisher called up the widower, Reg Wolfe, in 13a, to ask whether he was ready to leave.

Two houses further along another lonely man, John Hines, ex-sergeant major and retired security guard, having shined and reshined his shoes, struggled with a drawerful of socks in an attempt to find two that matched.

In the area of Inkerman Street, where landlords had divided property into a myriad bedsitters, Miss Rebecca Posner added blusher to pallid cheeks and tried to convince herself it was an improvement. Through thickish spectacles, she saw in her mirror it was not. She stopped fiddling with her cuffs to draw a finger along the deep lines on her forehead, the shadowy cavities of her cheeks. Why bother with cosmetics when you were nearly eighty? Then again, why not? She had been beautiful once; many men had told her so.

Another year almost over. This time last year, she hadn't felt too bad for her age. Since then, things had changed. Would the next twelve months bring peace of mind, at least? She sighed. This was being overly optimistic. Frailty was increasing, the GP had issued his warning. The greatest dread of all was bearing down on her: the possibility that she could no longer manage. But supposing, just supposing, a miracle occurred and there was enough money? If there was, she could stay here and employ a home help. As things were, she was faced with one of those terrifying nursing homes.

'Parking lots for those who should have died long ago,' Rebecca whispered despairingly to her mirror. She trembled at the thought of death, yet perhaps it would be better if it came soon.

There had been money once. Because of it, she had never learned to cope. Her childhood had been lavish, not a training for old age on a pittance. At this time of year the Christmas tree would be laden. She remembered her dear dead brother reaching up to detach the last present from the topmost branch: that small velours box containing a string of beautiful coral. Knobbly fingers shook as Becky Posner traced in memory the line where the beads, long since sold, used to lie against her neck.

Her tiny flat was cold: time to go. No point in keeping the paraffin stove on when she didn't intend staying in. Her grandparents' house had had a huge porcelain stove that used to stay alight throughout the winter.

'I must stop thinking about the past!'

She had supported herself once, as a translator. The salary had been minimal but she hadn't minded. She had enjoyed sending letters to places she'd once visited as a young girl. Nowadays, nineteen years into retirement, inflation had eroded her tiny pension so deeply she realised how naïve she had been.

'If only something had survived,' she whispered. Yet all had been swept away. The mirror reflected the wetness of defeat before she found a handkerchief and carefully obliterated the tears.

AT THE BRICKLAYERS, with Christmas bonuses burning holes in various pockets, no such fear existed among those still at work. Flustered by the noise, Miss Posner paused in

the doorway of the smoky bar. She clutched her coat where
the button was missing, clamping her worn leather bag under an elbow, and looked round anxiously for her friends.
Her generation was unaccustomed to entering a public house
alone, especially one as unusually raucous as this. Fortunately the barmaid spotted her.

'Evening, Miss Posner. Come over here and get warm.
Nice to see you—it's perishing out tonight, isn't it?'

Rebecca wobbled slightly in her old-fashioned lace-up
shoes. These were kept for best, the heels higher than her
usual slippers. She nodded politely to the lorry driver, now
leaning against the bar, his attention on Lila on the far side
of the room. Given such proximity, she strove to be sociable but her voice faltered with the effort.

'I—I don't believe we've met.' All he gave in return was a
cursory nod and the barmaid came to the rescue.

'His name's Karl, dear, Karl Gough. He drives a lorry,
long distance. He used to lodge with Lila at number six before he got married, that right, Karl?' She was dragging him
into the conversation but she felt the old lady deserved politeness. 'This is Miss Rebecca Posner, Karl. Say hello.'

'Evenin'.' Karl's self-confidence had faded. He felt uneasy, not sure what to do for the best. Perhaps this whey-
faced old girl was another opportunity to reinforce his alibi? Might as well make use of her.

He announced brashly, 'Biggest mistake of my life, marriage. My wife threw me out this morning. She's found herself a new boyfriend, see. A big bloke with a Ford. Very
macho, he is. Brags about it.' He paused to brush the froth
off his mouth with the back of his hand. Rebecca thought
he looked nervous. 'She's welcome to him. Me? I'm back
where I started. A bachelor boy again. Got to practise chat-
ting up the birds, haven't I? So, Rebecca, what'll it be?'

'Oh . . . goodness.'

The barmaid was also surprised. As far as she could remember Karl Gough wasn't famous for splashing his money
around. Maybe it was Christmas goodwill? She put it to the
test before he could back out.

'Miss Posner usually has a stout but what I think she'd
really like tonight would be a black velvet, right, dear?'

Rebecca Posner shivered gratefully.

What a bloody liberty, Karl thought angrily. Trying not
to let his temper show, he announced, 'Black velvet it is
then.'

Mavis Bignell began to draw the draught Guinness. Miss
Posner had her worried. Several elderly customers looked as
if they wouldn't make it through Christmas but this one
appeared especially frail. There was a virus about; that and
the weather might finish her off.

'You on your own tonight, Miss Posner? What's happened to Reg and Betty?'

'They're coming later, with Ernest. Because of bringing
the money.' Mavis nodded that she'd understood. 'I wish I'd
waited and come with them.' Rebecca Posner sounded unhappy. 'There's too many prowlers nowadays. I saw a
strange man making off down Inkerman Street as I was
coming along.'

She'd caught Karl's interest. 'A prowler, eh? What sort
was he? A black bloke?'

Perhaps she didn't hear. Instead she asked the barmaid,
'Has Mr Tucknell arrived?'

'I haven't seen him.'

'I'm sure he said he was coming. If there's no one to walk
me home I shan't be staying long, Mavis, I daren't.'

Mavis Bignell sighed. Thursdays were the worst night of
the week. Pensioners had been mugged for their pathetic bit
of cash before now. It was too bad they couldn't even walk
abroad at Christmas. She set the glass down carefully.

'Here we are. Enjoy yourself. And try not to worry. Charlie Tucknell's bound to turn up and if he doesn't, we'll find someone else to walk you home.'

It was an empty promise; most of her customers were so doddery it would be the blind leading the blind, except for John Hines, of course. The ex-sergeant major might be in his seventies but he'd kept himself fit. He was cussed enough, contrary about most things. He might not agree to it.

Mavis looked about, irritated. Where had all the young men gone, those good-looking, virile chaps she remembered from her youth? She gazed at one group of unfamiliar faces in the corner—strangers, rough-necks every single one—and made a mental note to point them out to the landlord.

Arthritic hands clutched the glass and Miss Posner gave Karl a timid smile of thanks. 'It's very kind of you, Mr Gough. I don't come here all that often. I'm a pensioner, you see.'

As if that wasn't bloody obvious. It was Karl's turn to pretend to be deaf. He needed to concentrate. The beer was stiffening his resolve to continue as he'd originally planned. If only that stupid old git had been shopping up West like everyone else! Careful. Keep your head and behave as though nothing had happened. Act innocent—no one knew he had been there. Above all, stay cool.

'Ready for another yourself, Mavis?'

'Hang on to your money, Karl, it'll be full in here shortly.' She indicated the two notices pinned to the wall. 'I might indulge once the rush is over, if you're not skint by then.'

He wandered across. ' "Would all participating members in the Bricklayers' Christmas club kindly present themselves in the saloon bar on Thursday 22 December at seven-thirty p.m. when repayments will be made. Signed: G.D.H. Pringle, Hon. Treasurer.'' So…it's loadsamoney night, eh?'

'Not at 50p a week,' she protested, 'but Mr Pringle makes sure they get a share of the interest as well. It helps toward a bit of Christmas cheer.'

'What's this one about?' The second notice was crabbily written. Karl stumbled over the words. ' ''The Sarah Beaumont Bequest … Annual dis-tri-bution''. Bloody funny handwriting.'

'It's Ernest. You remember, you must do? Lila's next-door neighbour? He's foreign. At least, he was before he came to live here. Don't you remember the bequest? It must have been on the go when you lived round here—five pounds six and ninepence three farthing split between twelve elderly people of the parish.'

'You're joking!'

' ''Six pious women and six men of virtuous character''—you can read the rules. Ernest has attached them underneath. Takes his responsibilities very seriously, bless him.'

Karl's laugh was too loud. 'Who bothers to turn up for five measly quid?'

'Plenty of us do.' Behind Miss Posner, another elderly woman pushed her way into the conversation. 'Ernest makes up the amount, you see. To near enough what it would have been if Sarah Beaumont had been making her will today. How are you Becky? You're looking peaky. I tried to phone you this afternoon, had you gone shopping?' The two old ladies wandered away.

'I know it's not a fortune,' Mavis said deprecatingly, 'but Ernest makes it worth everyone's while because he adds to it. And he does it out of his own pocket. A solicitor used to distribute it, someone from the firm who ran the trust, I think. He added a few quid but it never came to much.

When Ernest took it on, he was really generous. There's usually twelve pounds for each of the old dears and that means a lot if you've only got the pension.' She leaned forward, the pearly bosom deepening to pink at the base of her cleavage. 'I once asked Ernest how on earth he could afford it—he looks as if he's not got two pennies to rub together himself—but d'you know what he said? He said, "It is a small thank you to my adopted country." Wasn't that nice?'

She waited for a response. Instead, as Karl raised his glass, beer slopped on to the bar.

'Careful! Not coming down with flu, are you? There's a nasty virus about.'

'No, no.'

She mopped up the spillage, her attitude brisk. 'Can't afford to catch flu, me. We're doing Christmas dinner for the over-sixties tomorrow, and on Christmas Day I've got four coming over to my place.' There was a pause. He watched her replace the drip mat, searching desperately for some inane remark to keep the conversation going. His mouth was tight as he forced out the question, 'I still can't put a face to him—Ernest who?'

Mavis Bignell was surprised. 'You *must* remember, dear. Ernest *Clare*. Hungarian, I believe.' She frowned. 'I can't think how you've forgotten—he's lived next door to Lila since the war?'

Karl said quickly, 'Oh, him! Of course. Couldn't remember the name. I never saw him that often, he kept himself to himself.'

'He still does,' Mavis told him. 'Shy, like one or two round here.'

'So... how does he decide who to give the bequest to?'

'You have to be over sixty so there's plenty round here who qualify. He's not fussy about the pious bit. As long as you don't beat the wife or go for your husband with the carving knife, that's good enough for Ernest. People suggest names. They have to be on the voter's list, that's what "of the parish" means these days. He keeps it all a secret and announces who's won when he hands out the envelopes tonight, which is why there'll be standing room only in here. Excuse me, I'm wanted. Yes, dear, what'll it be?'

Karl had felt the draught each time the street door opened but hadn't bothered to look. Now he saw a fair-sized crowd milling behind him, mostly grey-haired. He thought he recognised a former drinking partner but pretended not to. The man might start asking questions and he'd said all he intended to.

Rebecca Posner was threatening to become a nuisance. She reappeared with another old biddy in tow. 'D'you remember Karl who used to stay at Lila's, Ellie?. He bought me a black velvet.' Anticipatory rheumy eyes regarded him. With mistletoe pinned to her old felt hat, this one had been stimulated into recognition.

'I'm sure I remember you... Didn't you go away for a while? Then come back?'

Shove that for a laugh! Stepping aside, Karl said loudly, 'Here, darlin', have my stool. I've just seen someone I know.' Beer in hand he began to make his way toward one of the tapestry-covered benches against the far wall. People who remembered he had a prison record weren't going to get a drink out of him!

Where the hell had Lila got to? His gut began to churn when he realised he couldn't see her. It had been a mistake after all. These old cronies had long memories. Dare he risk staying the night in Inkerman Street? Suppose Lila thought of checking her bag?

He was confused now, his ideas in turmoil. This morning he had one story firmly in his mind, but everything had changed and his brain wasn't working at all. As for that handbag—it had been automatic.

What the hell was he doing, hanging about here? It was all very well telling himself to stay calm and stick to his tale but, for Christ's sake, he should be on the road, distancing himself. If he'd pushed a bit harder, he could've picked up the load this evening and travelled overnight.

Once he was out of the country he could lie low. Earn a bit out east with his wagon. His plan to involve Lila had been to leave the impression of his calmness of mind but that had gone up the spout! After that little bit of thieving, it was madness to stay. Nevertheless Karl still hesitated. It was too late to pick up the load now, the yard would be closed.

At the bar, Mrs. Bignell was fully occupied serving halves and lemonade shandies. Despite the urge to disappear, he was distracted. She had worn well. The titian hair hadn't faded, the flamboyant figure was still buoyant. How old was Mavis? It didn't matter. None of it mattered. Karl breathed deeply to steady frayed nerves. He'd finish his pint and go: that was final. The decision made, he looked round for somewhere to sit and wandered across. 'This one taken?'

The bloke at the table looked up. 'Not at present.'

Another paid-up member of the geriatric brigade, slightly stooped, baggy suit with a Fair Isle waistcoat beneath, old-fashioned moustache and cool grey eyes behind the spectacles.

'Various people will, however, wish to occupy that chair once tonight's proceedings begin.' G.D.H. Pringle was nothing if not precise.

Karl spotted the cash box. 'You playing Santa?'

'I am honorary treasurer of the Christmas club.'

'Carry on, mate, don't let me interrupt.' Perhaps it was the difficulty in sliding behind the small round table that made his hand shake a second time. 'Whoops!'

Mr Pringle moved the accounts book to a safer position and began checking a list of names.

'Quite a business, sorting that lot out.' The forced laugh was overhearty. Mr Pringle's pen hovered uncertainly before returning to the top of the list to begin its work again. 'I said—'

'Yes, I heard you.' Mr Pringle put down his pen and waited for the lorry driver to finish. Karl could again smell his own acrid sweat. He had an urgent desire for human contact. It was necessary for even this stupid old fart to be a friend, just for a minute or two, while his nerves stopped twitching. He picked up the small empty glass.

'Ready for another whatever it is?'

'No, thank you.'

Bugger him then. 'I used to live round here.'

'Really.'

'With Lila Boyce.'

Mr Pringle sighed inwardly. It was the fate of so many in Inkerman Street to take in lodgers. Pray heaven his pension would keep up with inflation and he not be forced to share his home with a similar smelly young half-wit. He sat silent, noticing the various unattractive details. A nervy young man, with the sort of leather jacket airmen used to wear. His light brown hair was cropped very short—yet surely he was too old to be a bovver boy? Mr Pringle had heard of the breed but his knowledge was sketchy: weren't they usually in their late teens? This one was older than that.

He had pulled out a handkerchief to mop his forehead but Mr Pringle could see several disgusting brown stains. His disapproval was obviously apparent because Karl immediately shoved the offending article out of sight.

'People round here *used* to make you feel welcome,' he said aggressively. Oh lord, he expects me to buy him a drink, thought Mr Pringle gloomily.

The arrival of Miss Posner carrying another pint of beer and a small dry sherry was a welcome interruption.

'Mavis says these are on the house and the landlord wants to know if you're ready to start?'

Mr Pringle greeted her civilly. He raised his glass toward the bar. Behind it, Mrs Bignell returned him a demure smile, full of promise and expectation. Seeing it, Karl found himself wondering what on earth she saw in this decrepit old fool.

'Are you ready?' Miss Posner repeated.

Mr Pringle frowned. 'Oughtn't we to wait for Ernest?'

'Betty and Reg were going to collect him which is probably why he's late. Anyway, he always gives out the bequests after you've distributed the club money.'

'Of course he does. Well, here goes...' Mr Pringle cleared his throat. 'Ladies and gentlemen, if I could have your attention.' No one took any notice.

The lorry driver crashed his fist on to the table. 'Listen all of you! Father Christmas is talking!' That silenced them. 'Come on, Santa, don't keep them in suspense.'

Mr Pringle was reduced to an embarrassed mumble. 'The same procedure as last year, ladies and gentlemen. In alphabetical order. If I could have the first lady on the list...Mrs Ellie Bugg?'

Before Mrs Bugg could stir, the street door opened. They turned, a confident expectation of seeing Ernest and his companions. Instead, a police constable stood there, the rainwater trickling off his protective black coat. He was young. The face beneath the uniform cap was pasty with a lick of sandy-coloured hair beneath the cap. He glanced about. Mr Pringle found the pale eyes focused in his direction and felt awkward. Behind the bar, Mrs Bignell became very formal. 'May we be of assistance?'

'I'm looking for the driver of an articulated lorry.' The constable consulted his notebook. 'F159MJF. Is he here?'

Karl was filled with panic: he'd hung about when he'd had the chance to escape—he must be crazy! He cleared his throat.

'It's my wagon. What's it about?'

The officer addressed him across the sea of grey heads. 'We need you to shift it so the ambulance can turn round.'

Ambulance? There was an anxious rustle. Someone asked, 'Has there been an accident?' but the police officer was suddenly deaf. He jerked his head at Karl. 'Right away.'

'Sure.' Karl was moving swiftly now, his keys already in his hand.

Mavis Bignell asked conversationally, 'If it's not an accident, I hope it's not more of that virus, not so near Christmas?' No answer. She called out as Karl hurried past, 'Did you park on the bit of waste ground near Lila?'

'Yeah.' This made it easier for them.

'It can't be number four. Mr and Mrs Parker have gone to their married daughter's for Christmas.'

'Ernest is number eight.' Anxiety deepened suddenly. People eyed one another.

Mavis's voice was sharp. 'Is it number eight, officer? Is he poorly? I mean, are you taking him to the hospital or what?'

As the next of kin hadn't been informed, the constable's lips were sealed but the rest had their answer soon enough. The street door opened once more and a woman stumbled inside, clinging to a man's arm.

'Betty? What on earth's the matter?'

'Here, Reg, bring her over here where there's a chair—'

'It's Ernest,' Reg Wolfe interrupted. 'Betty and me found him. Get her a brandy, will you, Mavis? We went round like

we'd arranged—he didn't answer so we tried the back. The
door was open a crack. That's when we realised something
was wrong. We called the police as well as the ambulance in
case he'd been burgled.'

'Burgled? Poor soul! How is he?'

Betty gazed wild-eyed at Mavis Bignell.

'Ernest's dead.'

THREE

THE FESTIVE ATMOSPHERE had vanished. Members of the Christmas club, hopeful recipients of the bequest, regulars and casual customers alike, huddled in groups. None noticed when Karl failed to return. Instead they remained in the bar, frightened, telling one another of the last time they saw Ernest, the last conversational exchange or trivial remark, as if by retelling they could conjure him back to life.

Betty and Reg had been led away to the snug by the constable who reminded them sharply of the need to keep certain aspects of the matter secret. Out of general earshot, he repeated the official warning and quietly requested fresh instructions from his superiors via his radio mike. The reply was prompt and when the constable reappeared, he was alone and informed the company that Reg Wolfe had taken Mrs Fisher home.

There was general agreement this was for the best. After that, one or two tried to rearrange the few known facts into a more acceptable form. Received wisdom decided it must have been Ernest's heart that had failed him.

'Watching it happen, that's what probably did it. Ernest never left that room except Thursday mornings to get his pension and do his bit of shopping, when he could manage it, of course. If he couldn't, Lila got it for him, didn't you Lila?'

Mrs Boyce nodded confirmation. 'If Ernest had been sitting there, watching those villains wreck his home, it could have triggered an attack.'

Fellow pensioners agreed. They wanted to be brave but they shared a common dread and hearts continued to flutter. Unspoken questions hung heavily: was the thug still about? Was he waiting to pounce a second time? Worst of all, was he already wrecking another fragile nest?

'I can understand why Betty didn't look too good, finding Ernest dead. It makes me queasy just thinking about it,' said Ellie Bugg. The landlord took the hint and produced the brandy bottle again. Pouring another two measures, he said resignedly to Mavis, 'On the house.'

A quavery voice piped up, 'I wouldn't mind one, neither, Joe.'

People became garrulous. Finally, when departure could no longer be deferred, they moved outside en masse, each tipsy customer being escorted home, the door unlocked, the house checked from top to bottom as brave voices called to one another from every room. Then bolts, keys and chains were pushed back into position and the rest of the group, minus one, reassembled outside.

Finally, when the crowd had dwindled to two persons, Mr Pringle and Mrs Bignell went home together. Their route led them down Inkerman Street, past the house where death had visited earlier.

As they approached, they commented on the lights still on behind the thick lace curtains and the voices speaking loudly over the radio in the car outside.

Mavis said absently, 'I suppose it takes time to search for clues and fingerprints. I wonder where Karl disappeared to? The policeman said he only need move his lorry, to let the ambulance turn round.'

'They may have changed their minds and suggested he remove it to a more suitable spot altogether.'

'It wasn't in the pub car park. I know Joe charges five quid but it's the only other place where Karl could've left it.'

Mr Pringle wasn't interested. They were level with number eight now and, heads bent, their strides quickened.

Mavis muttered, 'Poor old Ernest... He used to like a glass or two of slivovic at Christmas. We kept a bottle specially for him. If it had to happen, I wish it had happened *afterwards.*'

'Pardon?'

'If he'd had a chance to announce the winners and give out the money, he might've died happier.'

In Mr Pringle's opinion, distributing the Sarah Beaumont bequest was unlikely to have eased Ernest's passing but he remained non-committal; he could feel the tremor in the hand tucked under his arm.

The rain had stopped and their footsteps sounded unnecessarily loud on the wet pavement. When they turned into the cul-de-sac where sodden leaves formed a carpet, both slowed thankfully. On Thursdays their habit was to stay at Mrs Bignell's home, a modest dwelling whose vibrant colour schemes never failed to make Mr Pringle blink. Tonight she regarded the floral wallpaper in the hall fondly.

'There... you couldn't be gloomy in here, could you?'

Mr Pringle agreed it would be well-nigh impossible.

His companion stroked the scarlet geranium pattern, saying casually, 'You wouldn't care to take a look around while I get us a hot drink?'

He knew what she meant and climbed the stairs, mentally girding his loins to face a dragon, or alternatively a masked, armed raider. His search was extremely thorough, however, and when he returned to the yellow and blue kitchen, he gave her a squeeze.

'Everything secure, no intruders, not even a mouse.'

'Thank God for that!'

'And I have put the electric blanket on.'

She picked up the two mugs. 'Let's have our cocoa in bed, shall we?'

To be beneath the plump pink satin eiderdown and rose-coloured blankets was often the beginning of silken dalliance. Tonight, however, Mrs Bignell couldn't be beguiled, nor did he wish to disturb her sombre mood. They had both known Ernest for several years. Mr Pringle regarded him more as a nodding acquaintance, a lonely outsider, one of the many refugees who had fled to Britain in the late 1930s but had never succeeded in being assimilated into another culture. Perhaps if Ernest had come over as a child, he thought; a child who would soak in the atmosphere and language until he was indistinguishable from his peers, but Ernest Clare had remained forever formal and separate.

'I wonder if he had any family.'

'Ernest?' Mrs Bignell's thoughts had already wandered back to Karl. 'I never heard mention of any.'

'He didn't chatter. He was a good listener,' Mr Pringle observed judiciously. 'I've heard his opinion sought, but about himself he divulged very little.'

'No.' She shifted uneasily. 'I wish Karl hadn't vanished like that. He was supposed to be seeing Lila home. I hope he hasn't done anything silly.'

'Was it his habit to do so?' Mr Pringle recalled again the jerky tension.

'He'd been in trouble before. Twice. Then his dad died and Karl inherited the money from the sale of the house. Bought himself that trailer lorry, set up in business on his own. He was doing quite well until he married Sharon. I don't know why he did, I don't think he really liked her and they'd hardly known one another five minutes. The rows those two had!' Mrs Bignell shook her head piously. 'They used to rent in Inkerman Street before they moved to Southend, you see, so we heard all about it at the Bricklayers. There was a baby on the way by then. Too impetuous by half, that was their trouble.'

As he and Mrs Bignell had achieved their present happy status after a very short period several years previously, Mr Pringle forbore to comment. They had been older and wiser, of course; at the peak of giddy middle age.

Latterly Mrs Bignell had exhibited the occasional lapse of memory when describing that first encounter. On that occasion, as Mr Pringle recalled with great happiness, she had been stark naked. These days when describing the event the location had been shifted from an art class to an unspecified tea room where, it was implicit, both participants were fully clad.

A smile played about Mr Pringle's lips as he remembered the true facts but he could not bring himself to speak of them just yet. There was another sigh: 'Poor old Ernest.' It was better to allow melancholy to take its course. But after a prolonged period of silence, he ventured to speed the process a little by offering a penny for Mrs Bignell's thoughts. Listening to them, he realised he had been rash.

'The thing is, whoever burgled Ernest might not have found the bequest money. If he didn't, it must still be hidden in the house.'

With an insight developed over several years, Mr Pringle anticipated what was coming: 'No.'

'You could just nip round and have a look. He must have written the names on the envelopes before he put the money inside.'

'My dear girl, if the burglar didn't succeed in finding them, what on earth makes you think I should be any more successful?'

She stared at him.

'*We* know where Ernest has hidden them.'

'We do?'

'Of course. He told me, once he divided up the money he always put the envelopes under the step, together with his pension book and his building society book.'

Mr Pringle looked at her blankly. 'The front door step?'

'No, silly. The houses in Inkerman Street, they're all the same. You go through the front door, the stairs are in front of you and the passage runs right the way through to the back.'

'Yes?'

'There's a step halfway down the passage before you get to the scullery door. Unless you live in the same sort of house, you wouldn't know how useful it is. The burglar probably didn't. You heard the policeman: "An opportunist", he called him. A stranger who'd found Ernest's back door unlocked—'

'Precisely—whoever it was *didn't* break in,' Mr Pringle reminded her. 'And when we enlightened the officer as to Ernest's regular habits—a cautious man, who never forgot to lock both doors and windows—'

'Yes, I know—'

'*He* then suggested, if you recall, that Ernest could well have admitted the burglar himself. It might have been someone *he* recognised.'

This was disquieting. Mrs Bignell said heatedly, 'He didn't know that many people. It's ridiculous to think any of his friends would do a thing like that! No, it must have been those kids you read about. In and out in five minutes. A casual burglar who kidded Ernest into unlocking the door and didn't know he was as poor as a church mouse.'

'Whoever it was, Betty described how thoroughly he had "turned the place over".'

Mavis was quiet when she said, 'I know Ernest had withdrawn the money. Yesterday lunchtime he popped in on his way home and told me he'd visited the building society. I was surprised to see him. He was looking shaky so I gave him a coffee. He never kept cash in the house in the ordinary way, only at Christmas when the bequests were due. And *we're* not going to let him down, are we?'

Mr Pringle quailed. 'Mavis, I cannot creep in and steal—'

'It's not stealing. It's money he intended to give away. There's no point in telling the police about it, they'd only nick it or hand it over to a solicitor. You'll be doing everyone a favour if you turn up with it tomorrow. It's not as though you'd be benefiting personally,' she added kindly. 'I've never heard anyone suggest your name when they were discussing who should be on the list.'

Suddenly he realised there was a way out of the dilemma. 'I won't be able to get in. The police will have ensured the house was secure before they left tonight.'

'You can use the key that's hidden beside the coal bunker.'

'Pardon?'

She explained patiently, 'Ernest left it there in case he had an accident, so that a neighbour could let themselves in. We all knew about it. It's under the brick.'

It was Mr Pringle's turn to stare. 'Mavis, you do realise what you are saying?'

'Not a burglar, I don't mean someone like that. I mean us. His friends. We knew.'

'The key to the back door?'

'Yes.'

'The door which was standing ajar when Betty and Reg called this evening.' The tone was accusatory.

'Oh, don't make such a fuss. It was only for use in an *emergency*.'

'Perhaps the house-breaker explained it to himself in similar fashion. My word, he said as he kicked the brick aside and discovered the key, I must not let opportunity pass me by. Ergo, I will enter this establishment and mayhap replenish my pockets with silver and gold.'

'Burglars don't talk like that, they read the *Sun*,' Mavis said contemptuously. 'Look, are you going to fetch that money or not? I'd go myself only I haven't the time. I'm busy at lunchtime tomorrow as well as collecting your Christmas present. They said they'd have it in by the afternoon. I only hope you like it.'

His heart sank even further. He said feebly, 'Mavis, I hope you haven't been wasting your money.'

'More than likely.'

'It's not another waistcoat, is it?' He'd revived a painful memory.

'As if I'd make that mistake a second time.'

'It would have suited a younger man. I fear it was yet another instance of my inability to live up to your expectations.'

She ignored this. 'I can tell them lunchtime you'll be bringing the envelopes, can I? If I put the word out, they'll all be there.'

He recognised an ultimatum: he had no real choice. 'I will do my best. Provided the key is under the brick...'

'Which it will be.'

'And the envelopes are still concealed beneath the step...'

'You have to lift the carpet and slide the breadknife behind the riser, that's what people usually do. It comes out easily enough. There'll be cockroaches and beetles, of course, those old houses are riddled with them. Try not to let any run up your arm.' And with this encouragement Mrs Bignell settled herself for sleep.

Mr Pringle had planned tonight to introduce a passing reference to *his* Christmas gift. Indirectly, naturally. An amusing quip as to the price of lingerie being inversely proportionate to the amount of fabric involved. Not that he begrudged a penny, of course, but it was French lace, it had cost an arm and a leg and it would have been pleasant had Mavis been given some idea of the *extent* of his outlay, reflecting as it did his deep affection ... Beside him, his companion gave a faint snore. The moment had obviously come and gone. Given Mrs Bignell's present intransigent mood, he doubted if it would return for some time.

FOUR

In the commercial car park alongside the ferry terminal, curtains were drawn in various cabs. Through some, their owner's private world could be glimpsed. In nearly all there was the mandatory photograph of a nude priestess with obscenely swollen breasts, plus a small television set with the equally inevitable football match in progress. There were photos of wives and girlfriends; in one, a child's colourful drawing of Daddy.

Karl's was a different world. He had parked away from the rest. His curtains left no chinks—his privacy was total—nor were there any mementoes. Here he revelled in the luxury of being alone. The cab was bare except for the neatly written notice declaring it to be a no-smoking area. More than anything else this had irritated Sharon with her habit of knocking ash into any handy receptacle.

The heater still whirred to keep the temperature high. Karl had stripped, enjoying the fragrance from his cleanly anointed body. It had been warm like this in the maternity ward the day Sarah was born. Sharon knew how he felt about the sight of blood but she had insisted Karl stay with her. To share her agony, he thought bitterly. The hated sweat began breaking out as he remembered.

Being forced to watch Sarah emerge had been purgatory. The midwife had wiped away some of the mucus and slime and tried to hand the baby to him but Karl had backed away to the sound of Sharon's derisive laughter.

Blood and dirt, that summed up birth; the same as death. Smells, sour fear and unspeakable body fluids. He reached automatically to turn up the fan and sprayed the air. Inhaling synthetic pine calmed him. The music was loud, to insulate him from all outside contamination. Eyes closed, Karl steadied his mind, the better to concentrate on assembling the components of his 'office'.

He'd never been with a woman before he met Sharon. Men, yes. In prison it was the only way to avoid being badly hurt. Afterwards, the feeling of being dirty inside as well as out had made him physically sick. Gradually, he'd learned to detach himself from what was happening. He'd stand under a hot, hot shower, letting the heat wash away his shame along with the blood and bile, all of it disappearing in the swirl of suds down the drain. That way he could emerge, reborn; not like Sarah's filthy birth but *clean*. Sharon had fooled him properly, though: she was as depraved as those buggers inside.

Stop thinking about her! He could feel the madness crawling in under his skin and penetrating his brain. Near panic, he squeezed his head between his hands to try to force it out.

Assembling the lap-top computer and printer helped him regain control. This equipment had been costly but worth it. He had splashed out on a battery as well as the adaptor so that he could use the computer anywhere. The technology still excited him—all those tiny vaporised bubbles of ink controlled by a finger to produce such dense black letters!

He could issue professional-looking invoices—he'd learned the basics of typing, plus much else that was useful, in Chelmsford. Compared with other one-man businesses, his was the smartest paperwork around.

Karl giggled as he realised just how far-sighted he'd been: choosing a printer with a variable font, for instance. Not that he'd had tonight's little business in mind, which was to match the printed name on a cheque.

At Chelmsford, the advantages of being able to add such information had been explained, plus a demonstration of how to achieve success using a child's printing kit. There the operation had taken several hours but there they had had all the time in the world. Tonight he intended to produce a much better result in minutes.

Whistling quietly, Karl ran through the typefaces, rejecting pitch 12 subscript in Sans serif and Courier, settling on pitch 15 subscript Orator. It wasn't a proper match—the print was slightly larger—but unless the cashier was sharp-eyed, it was near enough.

He checked the spelling of Lila's name on the plastic card and wondered idly what the initial E stood for. He printed it several times, deciding finally on pitch 12 instead of 15. Using a smaller version, the difference between the two print sizes was less obvious.

He focused the beam of his torch to a white pinpoint of light to check the density. Even using Bold, it wasn't as black as the name on the cheque. He changed the ink cartridge for a new one. Finally, when he was satisfied nothing more could be done, holding the cheque with a tissue, Karl tore it out of the book and inserted it into the printer.

He took great care with alignment. Following ERNEST CLARE he typed an ampersand. Rolling the cheque one and a half line spaces down, he typed the second name beneath the first: LILA E. BOYCE. He then began to practise the signature.

He'd been schooled in the various points to look for in handwriting: the changes of pressure, the flourish given to initial and final letters. It made him smug to recall how his tutor at Chelmsford had praised his ambidexterity, pointing out what a huge advantage this gave him. Karl sniggered: who says people don't learn anything in prison? It had turned him from an amateur into a true professional.

Karl selected a narrower pointed biro than the one he'd been using. Exercising his newly honed skill he coped Lila's signature on to the cheque. He repeated the process with two more, telling himself he would use the best and destroy the others. After what had happened in Inkerman Street it was dangerous to use even one, he knew that perfectly well, but he needed ready cash. He daren't use his own plastic, not here, not if he wanted to get away and lie low. Using his card could alert the police by morning if the bank clerks were sharp.

It wasn't in his nature to think further than the next couple of days although Karl acknowledged it was now virtually certain he would be intercepted before long. Communication was so simple nowadays. However, if his alibi held, why worry? He'd be going about his lawful business by the time the law caught up, nothing wrong with that.

Lila would guess it was he who had taken her card but when she discovered it wasn't costing her a penny, she wouldn't hold it against him. It was easy enough to get a new one. Being without would stop her wasting her money for a week or two, he thought primly. It occurred to him that perhaps he should have paid her the fifteen quid but he shrugged this off. He hadn't stayed, only used her shower. Anyway, it was too late.

The tape had finished. He fiddled with the radio instead. Nothing but sodding Christmas music, which reminded him of one vital fact: banks closed down for Christmas. Therefore there was even less risk in what he was about to do.

Karl sat perfectly still and considered the significance. Today was Friday—01.20 hours to be precise. Because Christmas fell on Sunday, banks and most businesses were tacking an extra day on to the holiday weekend. Everywhere would remain shut until nine a.m. next Wednesday morning. Brilliant! Any cheques would be lost in the system till then.

He'd got five whole days in which to deliver his present load to Orléans, find another for somewhere in the East if possible and stay out of sight. He'd already put Lila off the scent by hinting at Felixstowe instead of Dover. As he sat there, revelling in his quick thinking allied to good luck, a distant tannoy brought him back to earth. He had work to do before he could catch the next ferry.

The change in his fortunes made Karl bold. Suppose he kept Lila's card instead of chucking it away and kept a lookout for another careless Barclay customer? Maybe not; it would be tempting providence. No brief could argue him out of that.

He began to scold himself: he wouldn't need a brief, not this time, because he wouldn't get caught. But the surge of cockiness was doused by a sudden flash of memory: the scene in that dreary room, those terrible staring eyes. 'Oh, Christ!' He'd use one cheque. He would ask for a hundred because the card didn't guarantee more. With what he'd already picked up, it should be sufficient until he was clear of Europe.

As methodically as before, Karl dismantled the computer and printer, replacing them in the stowage. Instinct made him swap the cartridges, tucking the new one back in its box. Attention to detail, that's what the con at Chelmsford had always taught him; it's what keeps you out of trouble. That and staying cool.

INSIDE THE ferry terminal, lethargic back-packers sprawled on plastic benches. Neon lighting left deep shadows between. Karl walked through them to the cashier's window. He was hyped up, pulse racing. 'My girlfriend has endorsed this on the back. She's in the car trying to get the kiddie to settle.'

The clerk was bored. 'Any proof of identification? Passport, driving licence?' Karl pretended to fumble through his pockets. He shoved Lila's driving licence under the protective glass.

'Here, this is hers. Will it do?' Don't sound so bloody eager! Pretend you're as bored as the rest. Fortunately the man only glanced at it cursorily.

'I need your endorsement as well.' Karl signed *Ernest Clare* and pushed the cheque back. 'How d'you want the money?'

'Tens.'

In a sleazy gents once the ferry was under way he disposed of the shredded remains of the cheque book. He'd hang on to the card and driving licence, he decided. So far everything had worked beautifully, luck was running his way and he must take advantage. The coastline was disappearing as fast as his fears. His volatile mood changed again. Waste not, want not: one of those two remaining cheques tucked inside his wallet might come in handy after all.

LATER THAT SAME morning, certain terrifying details concerning Ernest's demise reached the Bricklayers. They were in the midst of serving lunch. The little-used dining room had been hastily aired, the table laid with crackers and jolly serviettes. Paper streamers dangled from the ceiling, and in the grate the first real fire since the previous Christmas struggled to stay alive.

Round the table, those over-sixties—most of them in their seventies or eighties—who had survived the perils of the previous night were now looking forward to turkey and mince pies. The Dread Reaper had called but it had not been their turn! By now, relief had given way to truculence.

They had paid 30p a week since the summer and for seven pounds fifty were entitled to three courses plus a cracker. They had drunk their soup, they had read the mottoes and were wearing silly hats. Since then, nothing. A few had launched into 'Why are we wa-iting?' as the landlord struggled to serve them single-handed and Mrs Bignell poured busily behind the bar. As he hurried past her, he hissed, 'Tracy phoned in to say she'd caught the virus, that's why she isn't here. I reckon she'd heard what happened to Ernest.'

'He couldn't help dying, poor old thing!'

'He didn't die, that's the whole point.'

'What?' But he'd rushed back to the kitchen before reappearing with a single plate and the next instalment of news.

'Betty had been told to say nothing last night. The police arrived at her place this morning, to ask more questions ... That's when Betty and Reg knew for certain what had happened to Ernest; the police gave them the details, or rather they had to explain because Reg insisted.' He paused, advancing on the nearest pensioner. 'Excuse me, Charlie, are you the vegetarian?'

'No, I'm bloody not. I ordered a proper dinner, not rabbit food.'

'All right, all right, keep your hair on.'

Given the bald pate, this remark was unfortunate. Its owner announced in hurt tones, 'Stop being personal, Joe. I'll have another pint of Special seeing as it is my only chance at turkey plus the trimmings.'

'Mavis, another pint for Charlie.' The landlord bawled to the rest of the room, 'Will the vegetarian put his or her hand up, please! I-thank-you!'

When he next went past, Mrs Bignell murmured, 'Why did Reg insist? And why did the police tell Betty not to talk?'

'It wasn't a heart attack. Ernest was murdered.'

'Never!'

'They wanted to know why she and Reg had moved him nearer the fire.'

'Why would they do a thing like that?'

'The police say Ernest was tied to his chair and someone had pushed it over.'

Mrs Bignell was bewildered. 'Tied to his chair—what for?'

'To stop him fighting back. I told you, Ernest didn't die, he was killed.'

'Mavis! Where's me drink?'

'Coming up.'

The bald one, Charlie Tucknell, had decided to treat his friends. 'Hang on, I've got a shipping order. Another port for Mrs Meredith for a start. Arthur! What are you having? Stout? And a milk stout for Arthur. Wait a minute.' Mr Tucknell examined the collection of coins in his old-fashioned purse. 'How much will that be? Have I got enough, Mavie?'

Shock had slowed her mental processes; Mrs Bignell stared at the loose change but couldn't recall what she should charge.

'Give me two seventy-five, we'll call that square.' Both of them knew it wasn't enough; he looked at her gratefully.

'I want you to have a drink as well. I want to catch you under the mistletoe, Mavie. I'm coming back here tonight because it's my celebration today, see. *Christmas* Day, I'm always invited to me sister's, as you know. She's so bloody mean! Last year it was home-made wine. Plum. I was sick after.' Mavis sympathised, her mind racing. 'You have to go though, don't you? You can't let them down. She might not be here next year, with a bit of luck.'

Watery bloodshot eyes gazed fondly at Mrs Bignell. 'I was planning on getting you tiddy tonight... A couple of G and Ts and you might've fancied me, you never know. If I'd qualified for the bequest money, I could've afforded to have you at me mercy.'

She flashed him a sympathetic barmaid's smile. 'I don't think Mr Pringle would approve.'

'Bugger Mr Pringle.'

'Tut-tut-tut! He'll be bringing those envelopes tonight, I hope. He's gone to Ernest's place to see if they're still there. Spread the word, would you, Charlie? And keep your fingers crossed the burglar didn't find them.'

A wobbly cheer followed this news as she hurried through to the kitchen. The landlord was hurling sprouts on to the last four plates.

'Why haven't Betty and Reg turned up for their lunch?' she wanted to know. 'The police can't still be asking them questions.'

'By the time they'd finished Betty was so upset she couldn't face coming here this morning, according to Reg.'

'Poor thing.'

'She might feel well enough by tonight. We'd better save two helpings of turkey. What worries me, Mavis, the police told them they want to interview *everyone* who might have visited Ernest yesterday.' He jerked his head at the dining room. 'That lot are always in and out of one another's houses, several of them probably visited him—they'll all have to answer questions.'

'Oh, dear! But what about—' Mrs Bignell was about to mention the prowler who had so disturbed Becky Posner but the bell on the bar tinged. A female voice demanded, 'Two Babychams!' She responded automatically, 'In a minute, dear,' and shook her head, still unable to accept what she'd been told. 'Are the police quite sure? That it wasn't a heart attack, I mean.'

'He'd been strangled apart from being tied up and gagged.'

'My God!' Mavis Bignell suddenly looked her age.

'That's what upset Betty so much. Last night, the light wasn't on so they couldn't see properly. They didn't realise. Reg saw that he was dead and hustled Betty back into the hall. He could see ropes round his arms, he'd no idea what was going on. When the police arrived and took a look, they told them to keep quiet about it.'

'Who'd do a thing like that to an old man?' Could it have been the prowler? Mrs Bignell tried to recall what Becky Posner had said about him as the landlord eased past with another load.

'We'll keep it a secret until this lot have finished their meal, eh?'

'Oh, yes... Definitely. Some of them have only just got over last night.'

They arrived in the dining room together in time to hear Mr Tucknell airing his views on society's current mores. 'If Ernest hadn't died last night, he'd have been invited to go soon enough. We all will now they've done for the Health Service. Euthanasia they call it, to make it sound posh. It's telling you when your number's up. There's too many of us older ones nowadays and the young ones don't like it.'

'Oh, give over, Mr Tucknell!'

'They've already started in Holland and America. Injections. Telling you they can't bear to see you suffer then, wham, in goes the needle. What they really mean is *they* don't want the bother of looking after you no more. They'll be building gas ovens next, like 'itler, to make it more efficient.'

'Shut up!'

'Aah!'

'Oh, my God—'

'Now look what you've done. Don't listen to him, Miss Posner.'

'Nor you, Mrs Norton. He's a silly old fool, doesn't think before he opens his mouth.' Mrs Norton was puzzled rather than upset.

'I know he's being stupid, he always is, but why is Becky in such a state?'

'She lost her brother in a camp.'

'Oh, dear! I'd forgotten.'

The ex-sergeant major, beefier than the rest and now red-faced, was towering over the culprit, hands clenched. 'Charlie Tucknell, you're a miserable old sod. Look what you've done to Wilf as well. Get Wilf a brandy, Mavis, he looks like he's going to throw up.'

'Not in here, he's not!' Despite his bulk the landlord moved like a gazelle to seize the withered arm. 'Hang on, Wilf, there's new carpet down in here. Give us a hand to get him into the toilet, John.' John Hines took hold and together they carted him away.

Through the frightened babble, one voice piped clear above the rest: 'Where's me mince pie and rum sauce then?'

It was later that afternoon, as she was fighting her way down Oxford Street, that Mavis realised Mr Pringle might not have heard the terrible news.

FIVE

MR. PRINGLE WAS full of misgivings over his mission. He paused on the corner of Inkerman Street as if seeking a character witness to accompany him but at this hour, when most were still at work and the elderly snoozing in front of the television, the street was empty. Leaden-footed, he moved forward. At the gate he glanced about so often that the two CID men, left to clear up after Scenes of Crime had finished, spotted him.

'Hey, look. Must be the neighbourhood prowler we were told about. What's he up to?'

'He obviously doesn't intend to knock. Looks like he's going down the alley.' They moved from the front to the back bedroom and stared down, waiting. 'Yes, here he comes, right on cue. Opening that gate like Inspector Clouseau...'

Once inside the yard, it disturbed Mr Pringle to find the key precisely where Mavis had predicted. To his added dismay, it also fitted the back door. This opened as he turned the handle and, under surveillance from upstairs, he entered the scullery.

Finding a breadknife wasn't difficult, Ernest's collection of kitchen gadgetry was minimal. Holding it away from his body as though fearing contamination, Mr Pringle opened the door to the hall. The atmosphere was dank. He shivered; it wasn't entirely due to the chill. Halfway down the passage, the door to the middle room was ajar. He daren't close it. It was dark in the passage and he didn't fancy switching on the light.

All the same, he tried to avoid looking inside the room and cleared his throat, loudly. He waited: there was no response. He scolded himself: how could there be? Death had come and gone, there was no one else about. It was only imagination which made him think a board had creaked upstairs. The sooner he finished this senseless farce, the better. Naturally the burglar had found the wretched envelopes—burglars were experienced in such things. But he hadn't done his duty until he'd examined beneath the step. Mr Pringle went down on his knees in front of it.

The first thing he noticed was the brass stair-rod holding the strip of carpet was not nearly as dingy as the brackets which supported it, and was easily removed. He set it aside. Mrs Bignell's inside knowledge was correct here also; this action had obviously been performed many times before. It was a matter of seconds to fold back the flap of carpet. He realised he should have provided himself with a torch. The winter afternoon was already drawing in but by peering closely he could make out score marks at one end of the loose riser. Presumably this was where the breadknife was normally inserted as a lever. He wished he didn't keep hearing those imaginary noises above. Anxiety made him exert too much pressure. The piece of wood sprang out and a couple of splinters hit him in the face.

The space beneath the step was black as pitch. Mr Pringle's nose twitched. Could he smell death under here as well? It was an extremely unpleasant odour, gaseous even. Was it a dead mouse or merely cockroaches? Forewarned by Mrs Bignell, he drew on gardening gloves. Lying on his side, he probed tentatively. The space went beyond the extent of his fingers, presumably as far as the threshold of the front door. There was rubble and bits of what he hoped was rubbish, not the corpses of rats. Oh, thank heavens, paper! Something like it anyway. From the feel he couldn't be sure. Not envelopes but small scraps, possibly cardboard. He tried to pick one up as evidence that he had accomplished his mission, albeit without a result.

The gloves made his fingers insensitive. Cursing, Mr Pringle withdrew his hands and shed them. He realised, in Ernest's shoes, he would have pushed the envelopes as far beneath as they would go, away from a thief's casual probing. He couldn't claim to have searched properly unless he did the same. There was nothing for it; Mr Pringle took off his jacket, rolled up his sleeve and with a great effort thrust one arm at full stretch under the step. Ah! He could feel the shape of a plastic cover containing a slim book, possibly a building society—

'Stay right where you are.'

'Aaah!' Pinned by his shoulder, he could only half-turn on to his side and stare upwards. A powerful torch directed at his face dazzled him. As the beam began to travel slowly over his body, he noted the muscular arm to which it was attached and the two unsmiling faces looming over the banister rail. Mr Pringle's heart thudded, he was suffering severe dyspnoea and, as he struggled on to all fours, causing one of the two men to yell, 'I said, stay there!' he knew beyond a shadow of a doubt he had made a complete fool of himself.

HE WAS ALLOWED to pick up the gardening gloves. He stood, with one police officer firmly grasping his elbow as the second shone his torch into the void beneath the step. When they told him there was nothing there beyond the building society book, Mr Pringle agreed sadly that it was all he had expected to find. He walked meekly between them out to the police car and saw, with growing horror, bystanders, who not only recognised him but pointed excitedly.

The two policemen obviously didn't believe his story. Worse, they kept saying incomprehensible things to do with Ernest Clare and Mr Pringle's wits were refusing to function.

Ernest had died of a heart attack but when these two kept repeating, 'the deceased is now the subject of an inquiry', he couldn't make head nor tail of it. He offered no objection when they suggested he accompany them to an incident room, although he didn't understand what this meant.

'The interview room next door,' one suggested to the other. 'We'll take him in there.'

What 'incident'? It still didn't make sense. Maybe if he took a few deep breaths to steady himself, his brain would begin to act on his behalf once more. The police car shot forward.

Mr Pringle licked dry lips. 'Where are we going?'

His companion on the back seat spelled it out as if to an idiot. 'To the police station. To answer a few questions. To help us with our enquiries.'

Mr Pringle's interest had suddenly been stimulated. 'What precisely are you enquiring into, may I ask?'

'The unlawful killing of Ernest Clare.'

Unlawful…? Behind dusty spectacles, Mr Pringle's eyes were owl-like with shock. 'Ernest died of natural causes, surely?' he stuttered. 'Mrs Betty Fisher and her friend Reg Wolfe found him lying in front of the gas fire, they said so last night. People assumed it was a heart attack.'

'We cannot be responsible for what people assume, Mr Pringle. Our interest is in the facts. We shall require a full statement as to your movements yesterday.'

They had turned into a parking area behind a building and high metal gates clanged shut. Mr Pringle was helped out, the grip on each of his arms tightening. He found he was facing a blank brick wall with small barred windows.

Stunned, he realised these were probably police cells. Indignation swept through him.

'You surely do not intend to apprehend *me*?'

Hard cynical eyes regarded him. 'Move it.'

THE COFFEE MACHINE in the incident room, which was on the first floor, had run out of brown powder, milk powder, sweetener, boiling water and plastic cups. Doggedly, the receiver, Detective Sergeant Bramwell, tried to fill one of the fragile drinking-fountain paper cups with tomato soup. Hot red liquid leaked over his shoes.

'Shit! Are you trying to tell me this old bloke, who simply wanted to find if the bequest envelopes were still there, was the same one who *murdered* Ernest Clare? What's he like—big, hefty?' Wiping his scalded fingers, DS Bramwell sat at his terminal and punched up the post-mortem report. 'Strong enough to break the fourth and fifth neck vertebrae with his bare hands, like it says here?' He read aloud the particular phrase: 'Such a fracture . . . equivalent to injuries sustained during violent activity, i.e. a rugby match or car crash, required a considerable degree of strength and determination.'

Detective Constable Cass tried to fit Mr Pringle into the mould, and failed. 'Maybe not. We haven't found the envelopes, either,' he admitted. 'This was all there was.'

'Did we expect to?' Taking the building society book from him, DS Bramwell was sarcastic, 'Maybe those envelopes were nicked, Cass. Maybe they were just what one of our chums was looking for.'

'One?'

'Latest thinking is there must have been two of them.'

'I thought the bequest was a hundred and forty-four pounds, top whack. Not exactly a fortune, especially divided in half.'

'Suppose the two of them didn't know that. Saw the notice in the pub—it's been up for the past week—and assumed it referred to a fortune.'

'In that case, whoever they were, they weren't local,' Cass retorted promptly. 'Everyone we've talked to knew roughly what the amount would be.'

'True.' The receiver idly flipped through the book to the final entry. 'Uh-huh...a total of one hundred and sixty-eight pounds withdrawn two days ago by the deceased.'

Cass did the necessary arithmetic. 'Fourteen pounds for each of the recipients this year?'

'Looks like it.' DS Bramwell's attention was still on the book. The balance remaining in Ernest Clare's ninety-day account astonished him: it was close to the maximum amount permitted. He closed the book without comment. A slip of paper fell out.

'What's that?'

Bramwell stared at it. It wasn't the amount of the balance. 'A six-figure number...a word. German? Here, take a look.'

Cass frowned. 'Could be. Looks like a name.'

'We'll enter it under Miscellaneous.'

When Bramwell had finished with his keyboard he gave his attention to Cass. 'This Pringle character, have you checked his story?'

'He *says* he was out comparing the prices of Christmas trees yesterday afternoon. Didn't buy one. Wanted to consult with his girlfriend first.'

'And she is...?'

'That part-time barmaid down at the pub. Mavis Bignell. She's as old as my gran,' DC Cass added callously. 'Mind you, my gran never had a figure stacked like that. He refers to her as "my friend Mrs Bignell", like she was a proper girlfriend.'

It disquieted Cass that a man of G.D.H. Pringle's age should continue to show an interest in the opposite sex. How disgusting to think there might be a reason behind it, like, like . . . He threw out the idea because it was too ridiculous and said, 'Pringle claims he hadn't heard Clare had been murdered.'

'Which is reasonable. The information was only released at ten o'clock this morning.'

Cass nodded. 'And he wasn't listening to the radio, if what he claims to have been doing is true. Last night Bignell told him which tree to buy and to take it round to her place today. He says it took him most of the morning to do just that. After he arrived at Bignell's house he found she'd put the Christmas tree lights on the kitchen table and he decided to try and decorate the tree with them. They weren't working and he's not very handy. He had two goes before he managed to replace the fuse. After that, he made himself a cheese sandwich again as per her instructions and set off for Inkerman Street.'

The receiver yawned. 'Which is what you would expect from a doddery OAP. If the rest of his story's true, let him go. We know where he lives. He's not likely to disappear.'

'Has the driver been found?'

The yawn stopped abruptly. 'Karl Gough needs his head examined. Apart from doing a bunk, that woman he used to lodge with, Lila Boyce, she reported her cheque card is missing. She used it yesterday and she's positive she had it when she came home. Remembers leaving her bag on the kitchen table when she went upstairs to make the spare bed. Karl Gough stayed in the kitchen while she did that.'

'What about her cheque book?'

'That was still in the bag but her driving licence has gone. Gough's got form and it looks like he's been up to his tricks again.' DS Bramwell gave Cass a significant look. 'So far we haven't turned up a cheque book belonging to the deceased.'

He wondered if Ernest Clare's bank account was as flush as his building society one and whether the manager would come across with the information or demand a warrant. With Christmas so near, pernickety officialdom could be a pain. Realisation had dawned for DC Cass.

'Karl Gough intends helping himself to deceased's cash, is that it? How could he do that with the wrong bit of plastic?'

The receiver was half-annoyed, half-pitying. 'Don't they teach you anything at Hendon? Work it out for yourself. We may be lucky, though. We put a stop on deceased's bank account this morning. The only snag is if Gough found a bank open last night.' DS Bramwell grimaced. 'The call didn't go out to Interpol till 0-eight-hundred today, he could be anywhere in Europe by now. We'll have to wait till he resurfaces. And if they work over there at the same speed as our records department, that might not be till the New Year.'

'D'you reckon it was Gough who took those bequest envelopes?'

'Him or his associate, whichever of 'em killed Clare. It's probably been spent—doesn't take long to get through a hundred and fifty quid. Gough's used more than one method to acquire cash in the past but he's always managed to give himself away. He never stole much, usually tiddly amounts so he's no Great Train Robber. He's been in the clear for the past three years, ever since he set himself up driving long distance. We've sent someone round to check with his wife—maybe she can tell us where he's headed.'

'Who was he working with before?'

'No one. He's always been a loner.'

The break in the pattern was disturbing but one DS Bramwell knew the Senior Investigating Officer was prepared to ignore. The SIO wanted the case sewn up quickly, before Christmas if possible. 'Gough may have chummed up with a proper villain during his last stretch. He already knew Clare, remember; he used to lodge next door.' The receiver swallowed another yawn. It was the lack of excitement which made him tired. A pathetic burglary that had gone badly wrong, that's what it looked like—except for those burns and gashes on Clare's face and neck, which didn't make sense. They were hoping that Forensic could come up with a few suggestions.

None of it added up for Gough though, he had never been known to attack anyone. His speciality had been tills when the owner's back was turned or, following his second spell in prison, cheque books from open briefcases or bags. It must have been the accomplice who was responsible for the violence. 'He must be mixed up with a real pro,' Bramwell said aloud, to convince himself as well as Cass.

He parked the known facts in a part of his memory where they would simmer gently until they re-emerged to fit into the pattern. It was a habit which had worked well for him in the past. No doubt Records would oblige with Gough's file eventually. Maybe in one of those detailed reports would be the missing link: a minor incident, a friendship, a shared cell during his spells in prison.

For the present, Bramwell banished the lorry driver from his mind and wondered instead about that building society account. According to Lila Boyce, Clare had existed on his state pension alone. Had they stumbled on a wealthy recluse who'd fooled everyone? Was this hitherto unknown wealth the reason he had been killed? If it was, if Gough had known, why hadn't he found the building society book? The hiding place beneath the step was obviously well known.

Bramwell glanced round the incident room. On a TV monitor, another member of the team was re-running the cassette Scenes of Crime had made of the murder site. Clare's room was pathetically bare, no knick-knacks or decent furniture. Why had such a wealthy man not made himself comfortable? From their checks so far, he had no family to inherit. Presumably he'd had to leave his wife behind when he became a refugee. That must have been when Clare was in his late twenties, according to the interviews so far.

Bramwell checked statements on his terminal, reading, re-reading, hammering every single fact into his dull brain—the lack of oxygen was sapping his concentration. All the neighbours agreed Clare had moved into Inkerman Street during the war. None knew much more about him than that.

Bramwell caught sight of the clock. Damn. They were only waiting for Gough's finger marks to be confirmed and that would be it for today. More routine interviews were in hand and once Gough was detained they could call a halt, or at least take time off over Christmas.

Bramwell thought of his wife's reaction if he had to tell her he was working again this year. She'd threatened divorce last time and it hadn't been entirely a joke. He swallowed more yawns and re-dialled Records: engaged! Everyone was at a bloody office party so they had taken it off the hook! Back at his computer, he entered up the building society balance in the file of Clare's personal details, underlining the total. So much for a penniless old-age pensioner.

Bramwell almost hoped the money didn't have a bearing on the case. If Gough had been after the book, if Clare had surprised him searching for it, surely the driver was far more likely to try and talk his way out of the mess, certainly not kill the old man? And you couldn't describe that broken neck as accidental. Whoever set out to do that must have been full of intent. No, whichever way you looked at it, the perishing facts didn't add up, which increased his irritation.

On the video screen there was a shot of the fireplace area. Bramwell already had black and white photos of the dead man. The gag was still in place, the bulging eyes were haunting, they were still so full of—what? Anger? Despair? The receiver couldn't decide. What was certain, the villains could have knocked him out, maybe even left him to die beside the gas fire instead of choking the life out of him. It was a really vicious act.

But it was pointless to speculate further at present. Confirmation from Records was needed, then a further fax to Interpol, to speed up the interception of Gough. The driver would no doubt give them his accomplice's name, which would save more wasted man hours. Solving an OAP's murder was a low-budget priority. They would have a more precise idea of Gough's movements once Southend responded—if only someone, somewhere would deign to answer either the phone or the faxes!

Fuming again, Bramwell rechecked the autopsy report. The condition of the body confirmed under-nourishment and the usual thickening of joints due to arthritis, nothing more sinister. They were waiting for the results on the contents of the stomach but these would no doubt prove routine. Death was obviously due to the broken vertebrae and asphyxiation. But it was that niggling final sentence about those gashes to the head which made Bramwell uneasy. Medical opinion was divided as to whether these had been caused by the same hand. Had both villains had a go? If so, that was odd too.

He called across to where Cass was now entering his report. 'You've run a check on this guy Pringle?'

Cass understood what was meant: two clear prints had been found beneath Ernest Clare's jaw. One partial one on the door jamb.

'No match. No record. Nothing known.'

It was a long shot but it was all part of the routine.

Cass called back, 'What about Gough? Do we know anything more?'

DS Bramwell practically ground his teeth. 'I am *still* waiting to hear from Records.'

Unaware of the tightness, Cass said casually, 'I'll pop round to the Bricklayers later, shall I? Have a chat with Pringle's inamorata and check his story?'

The reply was terse. 'You know where she lives—go there now when you've finished your report. No need for any unnecessary expenditure on alcohol.'

Jeez-us, thought Cass indignantly. At Christmas? What's the bastard like when it's his birthday? He remembered one more unanswered question.

'What about our unknown prowler?'

'See for yourself, it's on file.'

Cass typed a command and read the details.

The man had been seen by Mrs Lila Boyce and Mr Reg Wolfe as well as Miss Rebecca Posner. None could agree on age or height because of the inferior street lighting. A white man with darkish hair wearing the inevitable jeans, mid-blue denim jacket and trainers. All three agreed that the man appeared young, athletic-looking and had moved quickly down Inkerman Street. 'Young,' thought Cass derisively. 'For that mob, it could mean anyone under sixty—might even *include* a sixty-year-old if he'd kept his hair.' All the same, a stranger had been seen; he couldn't be discounted. In all likelihood, if he was the one, he and Gough had done a split and Gough had returned to Lila Boyce, in order to set up an alibi.

Which was what? And why nick her card? Did he expect
the body to remain undiscovered? That didn't add up, either. It was the one night of the year when Ernest Clare was
definitely expected to show up at the Bricklayers. Cass
sneaked a look at the receiver, sitting glaring at his screen,
arms folded, and knew how he felt. This one was getting
worse, not better.

He decided it was time to go and visit Mrs Bignell. If he
was lucky, she might offer him more than tea.

SIX

CROWDS PLUS a breakdown on the Central Line meant that Mrs Bignell arrived home in a fractious frame of mind. She was also extremely worried about Mr Pringle's present. Ordered by phone from a glowing description plus golden-tinted photograph in a brochure, it wasn't quite as she had imagined. Nor, she was sure, was it a surprise Mr Pringle would be keen to receive. It was also extremely heavy and tiring to carry. A police car parked outside her gate, the sight of the dark-haired young officer obviously lying in wait, added to her irritation.

'Yes, what is it? I'm late. I'm due at the pub in half an hour.'

'Might I come inside, madam? A few questions concerning an acquaintance of yours, Mr G.D.H. Pringle.'

Fright meant she didn't notice the smirk.

'He's not been murdered as well?'

'He's been caught breaking and entering.'

Mavis put two and two together and was outraged. 'If you mean what I think you mean, he was doing everyone a favour, trying to find those bequest envelopes. Breaking and entering, my aunt Fanny! Were they under the step?'

'No.'

She looked at him severely. 'Your lot hadn't taken them?'

'Certainly not!'

'There's no need to act the innocent, not after the Birmingham Six. I presume it was the villain who found them. Poor old Ernest, he probably had them ready on the table. It would be the easiest thing in the world for someone to take them. Oh, come inside then.' She was impatient as well as indignant. 'I'm dying for a cuppa after those crowds.' He followed her into the exuberant hall. 'The kitchen's through here. You put the kettle on while I get rid of this package.'

When she came downstairs having shed her coat, in her green patterned dress with the red hair flaming above, Cass was reminded of an angry poppy. She began thumping cups, saucers and teaspoons on to a tray.

'The old folks will be disappointed a second time when they come to the pub tonight.'

He listened patiently as she explained before asking, 'So it was your idea? That Mr Pringle go round and see if he could find the envelopes?'

'Of course it was. Where's the harm? It was not,' she said fiercely, 'as if *he* couldn't be trusted. A more honest chap never lived—but he was reluctant. I had to bully him into it.'

'How many people knew about that back-door key?'

'*He* didn't. I had to tell him.' Mrs Bignell thought for a moment. 'Lila knew, of course. She's been good to Ernest, helping with his shopping when his arthritis began to cripple him. The other side, they aren't neighbourly, they wouldn't know about it. Anyway, they're away, staying with their married daughter. We knew at the Bricklayers. People are very confiding once they've had a couple.'

So it was general knowledge; Cass made a mental note.

'Did Mr Clare drink much?'

'He couldn't afford to. Once, maybe twice a month. Not more. He used to save up to treat people to the bequest. I don't know how he managed it when he only had his pension. Generous to a fault, that was Ernest. Once he'd handed out those envelopes, Joe would stand him a drink on the house. He'd have a second, from whoever offered, and that was his limit. Strict, you see. That generation weren't given to indulging, were they?'

'It would be one of those to whom he'd awarded the bequest presumably?'

Mavis hesitated. 'Not necessarily. More likely Charlie Tucknell. Treats everyone does Charlie, then can't pay his gas bill.'

'Who were Mr Clare's special friends?'

'I don't think he had any, not that we knew of,' Mavis said frankly. 'Ernest was a very private person, kept himself to himself.'

'What do you know about Karl Gough?'

'Not much. Used to be one of Lila's lodgers till he got married. He and his wife live Southend way, I think. Here…' She stared in disbelief. 'You don't think *he* did it?' Cass's face was impassive. 'You must be joking! Young Karl? He hadn't got it in him.'

From Cass's viewpoint there were several reasons for thinking he had. 'He'd been inside.'

'For stealing, yes. We knew about that. He admitted it to Lila. First time he was only a kid, later on he was stupid. Someone in prison showed him how to fiddle but when he was caught doing it, Karl confessed to everything. Cleaned the slate. That's why Lila agreed to let him stay when he came out. Then he came into money and was able to buy that lorry. He's been on the straight and narrow since. Apart from marrying Sharon, he's behaved very sensibly. He was never a real *criminal*. Not the sort you're after.'

'Any idea what your friend got up to yesterday?'

Mrs Bignell became extremely frosty. 'If you mean Mr Pringle, he was looking for a Christmas tree. Today he bought the one I wanted, fetched it here, decorated it and unless you're blind you'll have noticed it standing in the pot in the hall. Very kind and helpful, as always. I'm only sorry if I've been responsible for him being in bother. I hope you lot didn't upset him?'

'He's been assisting with our enquiries.'

Her eyebrows rose. 'You don't mean . . . you took him to the police station?'

Cass became formal. 'This is a murder inquiry, madam.'

'Don't you "madam" me. Out.'

'Now look here—'

Mavis had marched across and flung open her back door. The poppy had been transformed into a red-hot poker.

'You can see the tradesmen's entrance. No wonder the gaols are full of innocent people when fools like you are in charge. Too stupid to see what's obvious, that's your trouble.' Anger and emotion threatened to undo her. 'If you've harmed one hair of that dear man's head—'

'Calm down! When he's completed his statement he'll be told he can go.'

'Go! I want him brought back here in a car, not thrown on to the street. And I want an apology from whoever's in charge. You get back there and tell them. Double quick.' As DC Cass tried to exit with dignity, she shouted after him, 'And don't bother asking me to assist with any enquiries— I wouldn't waste my breath!'

Keeping his temper in check, DC Cass got into his car. 'You already have, thank you, madam. You already have...'

She was so apprehensive by the time Mr Pringle finally arrived, she forgot to check whether her orders concerning the provision of transport had been obeyed. As he faced her across the kitchen table, she did her best to placate him but his expression did not soften.

'Mavis, I must remonstrate. Today I have been utterly humiliated. As far as the local constabulary are concerned, my name is high on their list of possible suspects to a murder. I have been forced to give a record of my finger prints. I have had to sign an undertaking not to leave the country, I have been threatened with confiscation of my passport. In short: my reputation has suffered the most grievous indignity and my liberty has been severely curtailed.'

'I'm very sorry, dear. If I'd had the slightest notion Ernest had been strangled—'

'He wasn't strangled, his neck was broken and I have been under suspicion of committing that offence for the entire afternoon...' He caught sight of her grey face. 'Surely you knew?'

'Reg Wolfe told Joe Ernest had been strangled.'

He could see that a broken neck was far worse. 'I'm sorry to be the one to break it to you,' he'd had time to get used to the idea, 'but I insist it was not a wise suggestion on your part that I break into his house. The police placed the worst possible interpretation on my actions—to be perfectly honest, I do not blame them.'

'The police are fools. They think Karl did it.'

'That nervy young lorry driver? Then why the devil did they let me go on believing ... ?' Wrath had been diverted.

'I told you they weren't very intelligent.'

'That young man behaved very oddly if indeed he was responsible. He seemed in no particular hurry to leave the pub yet it was obvious Clare's death would be discovered at any moment.'

'Of course he didn't do it! I'm sorry, dear, but you summed him up perfectly: highly strung, that's Karl. And daft. A petty crook maybe but to kill someone? He wouldn't have the bottle.'

Mr Pringle was silent; desperate men had been known to behave out of character before now.

'When I rang Joe to say I'd be late, he told me the police had been round at the pub, making a nuisance of themselves, asking questions. Lila has been complaining to them that her credit card had been pinched—now that was more Karl's sort of thing.'

'You mean he was a thief?'

'It was a while ago. He was only a kid the first time. He nicked silly amounts from the newsagent's in the arcade and stole one or two purses and wallets but then they put him in prison which did him no good at all. He shared a cell with a lot of clever old lags. When he got caught the second time, he asked for ever such a lot of things to be taken into account. He did fifteen months that time. Lila took him back because she thought he'd turned over a new leaf but she admitted he seemed to know more than was good for him about fiddling cheques.'

For Mr Pringle, a former Revenue man, this was more heinous than murder. 'You mean he emerged better equipped to commit fraud?'

'If you like to think of it that way. But he was never a *real* criminal, not compared to some of our customers.' Mrs Bignell was more tolerant toward human aberration. 'Karl only ever took small amounts, enough to see him through the weekend. He wasn't big time. That's what I mean when I say the police are being stupid. All that boy ever did was take a few quid, he's never been *violent*.' Her voice wobbled. 'He'd never break an old man's neck. Besides, he knew Ernest.' She remembered the conversation in the pub. 'At least, he did when I reminded him, he remembered him after that.'

'Karl Gough also knew Lila Boyce. If your surmise is correct, that didn't prevent him from stealing her credit card.'

Mavis shrugged. 'That was silly, I agree. Especially as he'd asked if he could stay the night. Perhaps that's the reason he scarpered once the police arrived, because he'd pinched her plastic.' She sighed. 'Personally I blame the Conservatives. Too much greed. Karl never used to steal from his *friends* before they took over parliament.'

'Mavis, whatever the scale of young Karl's fraudulent activities, we are avoiding one unpalatable fact: yesterday Ernest Clare was murdered. However mistaken the police are as to the identity of his killer I fear the possibility exists it may be someone known to you and I. Ernest would not have unlocked his back door to a stranger and the spare key was under the brick, no one had disturbed it.'

Mrs Bignell shivered. 'It gives me goose-pimples even to think of it. Look, let's have our supper. I promised Joe I'd be there by nine o'clock and I need something hot inside me first.' An idea took hold. 'While I do the veg, why not try and work out who it was? They'd be very grateful at the Bricklayers. It would stop the police ruining everyone's Christmas.'

Her complete faith in his powers mollified him a little.

'I may not be able to produce such a quick result,' he offered modestly, 'however, I can but try. Unfortunately I am not entitled to question people with the same freedom as the authorities.'

'No, but you know them better than they do.'

'Perhaps. It would help if you could cast your mind back to yesterday; you may have heard the odd remark which could be a pointer?'

Mrs Bignell produced pencil and paper and settled him at the kitchen table while she began the potatoes. Mr Pringle wrote down ERNEST CLARE, deceased, and underlined it neatly.

'What do you want to know?' she asked.

'I think we ought to begin as the police are doing and list all those who visited Ernest yesterday. These will not necessarily be people we suspect, I simply want to fill in every verifiable detail. What can you remember?'

Mrs Bignell considered. 'Lila popped in the pub at lunchtime. She hadn't time for a drink. She just wanted to tell Joe she'd seen Ernest, that Betty and Reg were calling for him that evening and to warn Joe they might all be late because it was Reg's indoor bowls night.'

'This was when?'

'About twelve-thirty. Lila was off up West as per usual, for the afternoon.'

Under a heading 'Visited by' Mr Pringle wrote, 'Seen by Lila Boyce at 12:15 p.m. approximately'. And in a column labelled 'Miscellaneous information' 'Reg Wolfe attended indoor bowling club from' . . . He looked up.

Mavis said promptly, 'From six to seven, I think. It's in the old community centre so add on a fifteen-minute walk in each direction. Reg would be back at his flat by seven-fifteen, then he'd want to change. Everyone looks smart on Bequest Night.'

'Can you remember what other people were doing?'

'Lila told us that Becky Posner had offered to take Ernest his tea. His hands were bad because of the damp, he couldn't manage a pan and it wasn't the day for Meals on Wheels.'

Mr Pringle was a little surprised. Miss Posner was not one of those renowned for being neighbourly, due, he was sure, to her natural reserve.

'Who normally performed that function?'

'Tuesdays Betty Fisher did, Thursdays Lila; but you know what Lila's like once the lights are on in Regent Street. She spends every afternoon up there if she can. Ernest wasn't neglected, though. She always arranged for someone else to do it if she was going out and Mondays, Wednesdays and Fridays he had the WVS.' Mrs Bignell sighed and shook her head. 'This Friday he would have been at the Bricklayers for his turkey and plum pud with the rest of them, of course, if some bugger hadn't broken his neck.'

'Quite. What time would Miss Posner . . . ?'

'Five-thirty, sixish. Lila used to take it to him when she did the meal for her lodgers. Since she stopped having them, it varied, but she would have suggested the same time to Becky Posner.'

Mr Pringle entered the event in the column and put the time at 5:45 p.m. approximately. He tapped the table with his pencil.

'I think we ought to list what everyone was doing. It will tell us where everyone was and eliminate several, I feel sure.'

'We can eliminate Becky, Lila, Betty and Reg for a start,' Mavis said practically. 'Why not start a separate list of those who couldn't possibly have done it? Like all the neighbours in Inkerman Street.'

'Perhaps.' G.D.H. Pringle had spent his life being methodical and refused to be rushed. 'We don't yet know the precise time of Ernest's death. Perhaps by this evening that fact may be known. The murder will, I imagine, be the main topic of discussion.'

'They can't always tell when you were killed, not exactly.' Mavis was suddenly knowledgeable. 'I read an article once. It depends on the state of your stomach. Would you like custard with your apple pie?'

'Er, no, thank you.'

'Why not ask the police if they have any idea?' she suggested. 'They're asking enough questions of us.'

'I fear they could withhold information on the grounds of confidentiality. Did Ernest have any other visitors?'

'Oh yes, plenty. Thursday morning he always paid his milkman, Damien. So do the rest of us, of course. And Thursday afternoon was football coupon day.'

'You're not telling me Ernest Clare did the pools!'

'No, Lila. He used to give her money to Charlie Tucknell if she was gadding about somewhere. It was just a little thing Ernest could do for her in return. I don't think he enjoyed it, mind. He was very private and Charlie being such a gossip. *He* used to complain Ernest never invited him inside.'

Nor would Mr Pringle who considered Charlie Tucknell a garrulous nuisance. Being comparatively self-sufficient, he commented he had no idea how often members of the local community were in and out of one another's houses.

'We all need a helping hand eventually,' Mavis announced ominously. 'You will soon, I expect. If you're spared.'

By THE TIME THEY had finished supper, Mr Pringle had plumbed the extent of Mrs Bignell's knowledge. If correct, Ernest had been visited at intervals throughout Thursday culminating in the call by Charlie Tucknell.

'Charlie told us last night that he'd been,' Mrs Bignell assured him, 'and that Ernest had seemed much as usual. Came to the door when Charlie knocked and handed over Lila's money with the coupon. Charlie complained Ernest was the only one who ever asked for a receipt.' Another reason why Ernest Clare had earned Mr Pringle's respect.

'And this was after Miss Posner had delivered Ernest's meal?'

'I think so. We'll have to check with Becky but Charlie said Ernest had his serviette tucked in his collar.' This brought back a memory which nagged Mr Pringle but which he couldn't pin down.

'Will Charlie be at the Bricklayers tonight?'

'No. He had to go over to his sister's because of the restricted train service tomorrow.'

'Bother.' In answer to her unspoken query, Mr Pringle explained, 'I was wondering what sort of serviette Ernest used.'

If she was surprised Mrs Bignell gave no sign. 'I'll ask Becky. She'll have made sure it was with his tray before she left. Likes everything to be just right. She even uses doilies when she's on her own. Lacy ones.'

'I didn't realise you had ever visited her?'

'Once. It's only a little flat; two rooms, kitchen and bathroom. She won the Over-Sixties Raffle, a bottle of whisky. She hardly ever comes to the pub so I took it round.'

He was intrigued. 'What's it like?'

'Her flat? Nothing special. She acts la-de-dah about it like people do when they want you to think they were posh once upon a time. It was spotless, I'll give her that. She's like Ernest, never enough cash to buy decent furniture.'

Mr Pringle considered this unjust. For him, Miss Posner was the genuine article; an example of a woman of gentle birth, now in her eighties and stranded forever in poverty. She had once consulted him privately about a worrying income tax return. As a result, Mr Pringle had a shrewd idea her inability to live within her means was due to a lack of practical experience of budgeting.

He finished adding to his list. With quiet satisfaction, he commented to Mrs Bignell, 'We seem to have accounted for the entire day beginning with the milkman, ending with Charlie at approximately six p.m.—perhaps that can be confirmed by one of your customers?'

Mavis nodded. 'Charlie sometimes visits Mrs Norton after Ernest. She'll remember.'

'Which means a gap of an hour and a half, probably a little more, from the time Ernest was last seen alive to the moment when Betty and Reg entered the premises and found him ... Ample time, I fear.'

'Yes.'

'Can you recall anything else?'

'When Lila came home she nearly had a heart attack when she switched the kitchen light on and saw Karl sitting there. He'd come in the back way...he knew where she kept her key, of course. He said he'd been in the house about half an hour. If he hadn't scarpered, we could have asked him if he saw anything suspicious.'

Mr Pringle judged that the police had come to the same conclusion. 'I fear it looks very black for that young man.'

'Oh, pooh,' Mavis countered vigorously, 'but I suppose we'll all have to stop leaving the spare key outside. The older ones did it so someone could get in, in an emergency. The absent-minded ones depend on it for when they lock themselves out. It's terrible to think we can't trust people any more.'

Throughout his working life, Mr Pringle had never trusted anyone: it was a sound principle when working in taxation although it made for hostility among those whose attitude to expenses was particularly creative.

It was ten to nine, they were preparing to leave. He finished fastening his coat and thrust his hands in his pockets in search of his scarf. Instead he found the gardening gauntlets.

'Leave those on the hall table, dear. What's this?' Mrs Bignell stooped to pick up the small scrap of paper.

'A souvenir from Ernest's hiding place,' he said shortly.

'It looks like something he tore up.' Mrs Bignell held the paper under the light. 'Perhaps it got swept through a crack in the floorboards.'

Mr Pringle remembered the carpet. 'I doubt it. It may have been caught up when he tucked his building society book away.'

'There's a number. Part of one, anyway. The rest is missing. Seven . . . four . . . nine.'

Mr Pringle examined it more closely. The figures were written in a Gothic script.

'It's Ernest's style of writing.' Mrs Bignell turned the scrap the other way up. 'Perhaps it was a PIN number?'

'Perhaps.'

'Come on. We'll be late. Hey! What about the prowler?'

'What about him?'

'Why are we worrying ourselves silly—or imagining Karl could have done it—when there was that stranger wandering about. Didn't you think to remind the police when they were bullying you?'

Mr Pringle hadn't felt the slightest inclination to remind the police of their duties.

'Mavis, I am quite sure they are capable. Enquiries will be in hand—'

'Becky knew he was a stranger.'

'Miss Posner isn't acquainted with every frequenter of the Bricklayers. It could have been someone hitherto unknown to her but with a perfectly valid reason for being abroad.'

'Becky knows most people in Inkerman Street by sight,' Mavis insisted. 'She's lived here long enough. She wouldn't go describing anyone as a *prowler* unless he was. If the police come bothering me tonight, I shall ask them what they're doing about it.'

Mr Pringle sent up a silent, weary prayer for an undisturbed evening.

SEVEN

It was a street in Southend where during summer months landladies waged war against one another to entice the few customers. Drab frontages were adorned with exotic wrought-iron signs: Malibu, Sunnyside, Al'nBren and, more pretentiously, The Laurels. A poor season was at an end; NO VACANCY notices were up and their owners had retreated into winter hibernation.

The Goughs' house was squashed between two much larger ones. Small and squat with a solid concrete driveway big enough for the lorry, where once there had been a pleasant garden. To compensate, someone had filled a patio tub with flowers and then neglected it. From inside the police car, DPW Vivien Tunnicliffe observed the spindly dead aubretia and knew how they felt.

A second querulous fax had arrived from the incident room demanding to know why no reply had been received. Whatever information Mrs Sharon Gough could give as to her husband's whereabouts should be faxed back 'at your *earliest* convenience'.

Two days before Christmas, when she should have been off-duty an hour ago, the sarcasm was wasted. As she undid her seat-belt Vivien considered the house's façade from the point of view of a first-time buyer. Street lights emphasised the blotchy state of the concrete rendering.

'Some people just don't care, do they? I mean, if you were trying to sell that, Ian, what would you put in the advert?'

Her colleague leaned over the steering wheel to get a better view. 'Suit couple totally without ambition?' he suggested. 'More to the point, it looks as though no one's home.'

'If not, we're instructed to proceed to...' She consulted the fax on her clipboard, 'Mrs Sharon Gough's mother, surname understood to be Berryman, Berriman—or similar! Believed to live in Leigh-on-Sea. Why couldn't they sort out a proper name and address instead of bombarding us?'

'Sharon Gough has probably gone there already,' said Ian fatalistically. 'If her husband's away, what's the betting she's taken herself off to her mother's. Your turn.'

DPW Tunnicliffe eased herself out of the warm womb of the car and scuttled across the pavement. A vicious wind blew in from the sea. There was no knocker or bell. She rattled the letterbox and shouted through the flap. Next door, a moon face appeared at the ground-floor window and mouthed an unintelligible message.

'You what?' Tunnicliffe shuddered inside her coat. 'Could you come to the door, please? I can't make out what you're saying.'

It opened to the extent of the chain. Half of the landlady was visible. Out of season she obviously didn't bother to dress. Through the crack, DPW Tunnicliffe spoke to the one eye that peered at her over the dirty padded blue collar of a housecoat.

'Good evening. I'm looking for Mrs Sharon Gough. Do you know where she is?'

'I said—it's a pity you didn't come here yesterday. You might have stopped it.'

'Stopped what?'

'Him beating her up. It's a mercy the little girl was with her granny.' The detective policewoman ran through a mental list of yesterday's 'domestics' as described at the morning briefing.

'Were the police informed?'

'Oh, no. *He* come round here and asked me to call the ambulance.'

'Mr Gough?'

The eye expressed contempt. 'Her boyfriend. He asked me to do the phoning because *he* didn't want to get involved. He said he'd found her lying there but I don't know about that.'

DPW Tunnicliffe didn't understand. She seized the vital thread. 'Actually it was Mr Gough I wanted to see. Have you any idea where he's gone?'

The eye went in and out of view as the landlady shook her head. 'He's been in prison. That's not what upset Sharon. When he told her what they got up to in there, that's what did it. Wicked! She said she'd no idea... Men, doing things like that to one another.'

The wind was doing equally wicked things to DPW Tunnicliffe.

'Where's Mrs Gough now? Still in hospital?'

A shrug. 'How would I know? They've not brought her back, though, have they?'

Back in the car, the policewoman gave her colleague the new destination. 'At least the hospital's nearer than Leigh.'

FROM CASUALTY they were sent to Women's Surgical and there told to wait. When the staff nurse arrived, she bristled. 'Who told you lot about it?' Without waiting for an answer, she steam-rollered on, 'It's no good asking questions, Mrs Gough won't tell *us* anything so she's not likely to talk to *you*.'

DPW Tunnicliffe wondered why the woman was so defensive.

'We're making enquiries about her husband. Have you any idea where he is?'

'No.'

'Is she expecting either her boyfriend or her husband to call?'

'I've no idea. She hasn't said a word except to say we're not to let the boyfriend in. Which we won't, of course.'

The policewoman's eyes narrowed: what was behind all this?

'Can we see her?'

'I'll ask.'

When he arrived, the doctor said tiredly, 'Whatever you do, don't upset her. She's very poorly and I don't think she understands the full extent of it. A couple of minutes, that's all, and only one of you.'

Vivien Tunnicliffe went through the curtains. On the bed, above the thick white collar and tensioning cables, the swollen face was immobile. Her first thought was, bloody hell! Her second: why didn't you kick him in the goolies, girl?

'Mrs Gough . . . ? Sharon?'

Eyelids were raised momentarily. 'Go away . . .' The voice was slurred with pain-killers.

The policewoman bent closer, murmuring, 'Can you tell us where Karl is? That's all we want to know. We won't bother you with any more questions.'

Colourless lips formed the phrase, 'Piss off.'

'Have you any idea at all?'

This time, no reply. The curtains parted behind DPW Tunnicliffe. There was a bossy whisper. 'That's enough. She mustn't be upset. You heard what doctor said, she's still very poorly.'

Back at the nursing station, the policewoman demanded, 'What's wrong?'

'The fifth vertebra has been fractured, the spinal cord damaged and the kidneys. We don't know how badly, we haven't completed the tests. She's lost control of bladder and bowels. She'll never walk again. She doesn't know, of course.' The nurse snorted. 'She needn't worry about the boyfriend turning up, once he hears about the damage, he'll run a mile.'

'How did it happen?' DPW Tunnicliffe asked tersely.

'We don't know, she refused to tell us. The boyfriend found her. She was lying near the front door so it wasn't too difficult to get her on to the stretcher, thank goodness. It might have been a fall, it looked as if she could have gone head-first over the banister.' The nurse's self-importance spilled out. 'My God, do I get fed up. In Maternity you look at those babies—a few more years, they'll be half-killing one another—'

'This incident should have been reported,' DPW Tunnicliffe said coldly. 'People don't fracture their necks even when they tumble over a banister. It would take a very heavy fall or a violent attack, which is much more likely. Mrs Gough may require twenty-four-hour protection. Which phone can I use?'

The staff nurse tried to re-assert her authority.

'This one is only for use in an emergency. There's a pay-phone in the day room—where are you off to?'

'To ask my colleague to stay with Mrs Gough.'

'Dr Harding won't permit it. Mrs Gough is his patient—'

DPW Tunnicliffe rounded on her. 'Listen. A pensioner was found yesterday. His neck had been broken and that woman's husband is wanted for questioning so don't try and interfere. We'll provide protection until our relief arrives. And I want to see your security officer. *He* might want to know why he wasn't informed as soon as this patient was admitted—you know perfectly well he should have been—but that's your problem.'

White-faced, the staff nurse retreated behind her only defence: 'Mrs Gough wasn't prepared to talk.'

'So she's being loyal? If her husband was responsible for trying to break her neck, why give him the chance to finish her off?'

When she returned from speaking to Ian, DPW Tunnicliffe picked up the phone and began to punch in the number savagely. 'And I'm using this...because it *is* an emergency.'

As MR PRINGLE and Mrs Bignell approached the Bricklayers, he said tactfully, 'It might be better if you didn't mention our discussion. If we are to solve this problem, one can glean more information by being unobtrusive.'

'You're better at doing that. Shall I try and find out the time of death?'

He knew she would be in the thick of speculation and gossip. 'If anyone has heard it as a *fact*, from a police officer's lips as it were, then it would be helpful.'

Did the time of death really matter? They knew approximately. Although they had accounted for the whereabouts of all those they knew, the truth was that most were having supper at that time. The majority lived alone, none were likely to have alibis but with the exception of Karl Gough all could be described as elderly. None, as far as Mr Pringle was aware, had the slightest reason to want Ernest Clare dead. 'By the way...'

'Yes?'

'How long had Ernest needed Meals on Wheels?'

Mavis considered. 'He had a fall last Easter when his arthritis got worse. I think that's when Lila first organised it for him.'

'Not long then?'

'About nine months'

THE BAR WAS crowded not just with seasonal revellers but
with those who needed to support one another. Home was
no longer a safe fortress. To be here, amid smoke and noise,
was far better.

Many had had a sleepless night followed by a day answering police questions. Neighbours looked to one another for reassurance. John Hines, less spruce following his
interrogation, invited Mr Pringle to join them.

'You don't want to sit on your ownsome tonight, Mr P.,
none of us do. Company, that's what we need after what
we've been through. Besides,' he added as an afterthought,
'as it's Christmas, what'll you have?'

Mr Pringle's usual small sherry appeared, embellished
with a festive coaster. A bucolic robin glared at him aggressively through the bottom of the glass. John Hines raised his
beer. 'Cheers.'

'Good health.' Mr Pringle took a tentative sip. 'Yes, a
very trying time...'

It was all it needed for the flood gates to open and their
fears to gush forth. Through the hubbub, Rebecca Posner
cried plaintively, 'Mr Tucknell has been grumbling for weeks
about having to visit his sister but he's been lucky. He hasn't
had the third degree.'

'The police talked to Charlie yesterday,' Lila Boyce reminded her.

'They talked to all of us yesterday but only for a few
minutes. Today they went on and on.' Reg Wolfe was indignant. 'Even though I told them all I could remember
about that prowler, they still kept asking.' Mr Pringle listened attentively to the complaints. Intimate details had
been required; no one's word had been accepted.

'When I told them I'd been to the library they made me
produce my ticket and actually telephoned to check the *time*
of my withdrawal,' Betty Fisher complained.

'How fortunate the computer can offer confirmation at the touch of a button,' Mr Pringle observed, 'probably quoting not only the hour but the precise minute...'

'I estimated half past five. It was just a bit before. I know I was nearly the last customer, one of the librarians was fastening her coat.'

And the building was a twenty-minute walk away, therefore Mrs Fisher must have been home by six. But why on earth suspect Betty? A genuine, kind-hearted woman who had been so distressed by the terrible discovery?

'Has anyone heard whether the police have reached any conclusion?' An avalanche this time, all of it indicating Karl Gough was being sought 'to assist with enquiries.'

'I was surprised,' Betty confessed. 'Especially after Becky and Lila and Reg had told them about that prowler. You'd think they'd concentrate on him rather than Karl. We know he'd been inside but not for anything *serious*. If he had, you wouldn't have taken him back, would you, Lila?'

'I would not.' She scowled. 'Mind you, I wanted to break his bloody neck when I found he'd pinched my credit card.'

Mr Pringle coughed. 'Mention of the prowler... There were one or two strange faces in here last night.'

Lila, Reg and Miss Posner shook their heads emphatically. Lila spoke, 'He wasn't one of them but whether they were all part of the same gang...? The police will tell us eventually, I suppose. Anyway, I could kick myself for leaving my bag where Karl was bound to see it. It was the sort of temptation he couldn't resist.'

'He let himself in unaided, I understand?' Mr Pringle was overly casual.

'He even scolded me for leaving the key on the hook in the outside lav, cheeky beggar! Said I deserved to be robbed.'

There was general agreement Karl Gough was too cocky by half.

'How long had he been waiting?'

Lila was irritated. 'The police kept asking me that—I don't know. He was there when I got back about half six. He *claimed* he'd been sitting there half an hour and he certainly hadn't got around to making himself a cuppa, which was odd. He was always one for putting the kettle on without a by-your-leave. It wasn't like Karl to sit there feeling thirsty.'

'And for him to disappear like that, the minute the police walked in here...' Mr Pringle shook his head disapprovingly.

'It's not really surprising when you think about it,' Betty Fisher retorted. 'Seeing the police walk in here and with that card burning a hole in his pocket, Karl obviously panicked.'

'Especially being told about the ambulance,' John Hines pointed out. 'Karl must have realised they'd suspect him straightaway.'

Mr Pringle frowned. 'The constable explained the *reason* for moving the lorry, not why the ambulance had been summoned.'

'Wasn't Karl still here when I shouted Ernest was dead?' Betty asked innocently. 'Had he gone by then?'

'Mrs Bignell will remember.'

The group looked toward the bar. Mavis was enjoying an exchange of *badinage*. It wasn't that Mr Pringle was jealous, heaven forbid. But it was galling to see her enjoying ripostes from an exhibitionist wearing a nylon shirt.

'I suppose the police could have told Karl about Ernest when he went outside,' Betty suggested.

Mr Pringle wondered. If not, if the young lorry driver knew more than he should, perhaps the police were right to suspect him after all.

THE POLICE CAR was parked outside an attractive bungalow, one of a row close to the sea front in Leigh-on-Sea.
Normally, DPW Tunnicliffe would have passed the time
assessing the property's potential and asking her colleague's opinion of the selling price. Instead, four hours into
her rest day, she was finding it difficult to control her temper.

'I don't believe it... Why does this have to happen tonight? How can the phone in there be disconnected?'

'Plenty of people can't afford to pay the bill,' Ian reminded her. 'OAP? Happens all the time. We have to help
out with my nan. Anyway, it makes no difference, Mrs Berriman isn't in.' He rubbed salt in the wound.

'Why does she have to go out tonight of all nights?'

'You know why. Her neighbour told us she's gone to see
the panto at the Palace Theatre, Westcliffe-on-Sea. *She*
doesn't know her daughter's in hospital. Nobody could tell
her, could they, because of the phone. The kiddie is being
looked after at number forty-eight but the woman there
doesn't know of Gough's whereabouts.' Ian yawned. '*She*
thought it unlikely Mrs Berriman would, either. Still, we've
got to hang about until she gets back.'

DPW Tunnicliffe leaned back and closed her eyes.

'What time d'you reckon? Eleven, eleven-fifteen? My
turn to break the glad tidings, I suppose?'

'Takes a woman's touch, Vivien.'

In a mock-official voice, she announced, 'I'm afraid your
daughter's neck is fractured. She'll never walk again, she'll
always need a colostomy bag, her kidneys are on the blink—
we believe your son-in-law could be responsible. He's also
wanted for questioning in connection with a murder committed in London yesterday.'

'We bloody well don't say that!'

'I know!'

'Karl Gough is wanted for questioning and that's all. You watch your step, Vivien.'

'I was only joking!'

There was a pause. They listened to the tide sucking in the shingle at the end of the road. Finally, he said, 'It's bloody odd if Gough was responsible. Two murders? Well, one attempted one. Two broken necks? I mean, there are easier ways.'

'He might be psycho.'

'There aren't too many of them about. There's plenty *pretend*, to get off the hook. Not the genuine article.'

She said pointedly, 'Someone was responsible.'

'Granted. What you should be asking yourself is how, not who.'

'Pardon?'

'You told the nurse it was difficult to break someone's neck. You were right. I've never come across one, except via the condemned cell.'

Vivien Tunnicliffe sat up straighter. 'I don't know why she didn't defend herself.'

'It would still take one hell of a punch to crack a vertebra.'

'She *could* have fallen over the banisters, I suppose.'

He pulled a face. 'Where's the rest of the damage? The fractured skull? Mrs Gough didn't have any of the *signs* of having fallen like that.'

'So what do you think happened?'

'I don't know. It looks bloody odd, that's for sure. Unless Gough has a track record for incredible violence, in which case, we'd have been told.'

'I wonder why she refused to tell that nurse.'

'Stupid old busybody. She's bound to tell *us* eventually, they always do.'

She might tell you, thought Tunnicliffe. Ian had a way with difficult witnesses although Sharon Gough didn't look the confiding type, never mind 'interviewing techniques'.

She sighed. 'Guess what Gordon and I were planning to do tonight.'

'It's no good complaining. You knew the conditions when you joined.'

'We intended to announce our engagement, that's all. The table was booked, our parents were coming, his mother had had her hair done specially—that was only to outdo my mum, of course. I rang from the hospital to tell Gordon to cancel. He was furious.'

Her colleague wasn't unsympathetic, 'He'll have to get used to it unless you plan to quit.'

Vivien said flatly, 'No, I don't. Gordon finds that difficult to believe, apparently.' She swivelled round to face him. 'He's always boasting at Rotary—my fiancée in the police—then when this happens, he says I should hand in my resignation.'

'Uh-huh.' This was dangerous ground. 'Maybe he was very upset.'

'Not too upset to tell me I was responsible for the cancellation charge at the restaurant.'

'Uh-huh.' Ian kept his thoughts on that to himself. To divert her, he said, 'I spent my silver wedding night having my eye treated after a West Ham supporter stuck his thumb in it.'

There was another pause before she spoke. 'I'll tell you another odd thing about this case.'

'What's that?'

'The toddler. Where was she while her mother was being knocked about? Did Mrs Berriman pick her up before-hand? If she did, if Karl Gough was still in the house, she must have noticed what sort of *mood* he was in. Unless he was one of those karate freaks. Five seconds of hype and he can chop a brick wall with the side of his hand.'

Ian was relieved to have her attention back on the job so quickly. 'If Berriman had gone to collect the kiddie, there has to be a reason for that as well.' He stretched his stiff back. 'So hurry back, grandma. We've got plenty of questions need answering.'

IN THE INCIDENT ROOM overhead lights shone down on the shiny patches of ground-in dirt, the permanently wet patch beneath the drinks dispenser. The air was fetid. Everybody's recycled breath, thought Bramwell despairingly. It was becoming impossible to stay alert. He felt poisoned by carbon monoxide, his body inert, every molecule of oxygen consumed long ago.

He should have felt stimulated. The fax had arrived from Southend notifying them of the attack on Sharon Gough. Further information would be despatched once Mrs Berriman had been interviewed. Meanwhile, lines of communication to various parts of France, Belgium and Spain had been re-established, greater efforts demanded: Gough must be found and returned. One quiet murder had taken on a different dimension.

Addressing them now, the Senior Investigating Officer, DI Kevin Crombie, emphasised the need for urgency and with an effort Bramwell forced his eyelids to stay apart.

The clock on the wall above the SIO's head showed seven minutes to midnight. This meeting, called abruptly, had caught those still foolish enough to be on the premises. Bramwell was willing to bet everyone there with young kids was aware of that clock. Six and a half minutes to Christmas Eve. How many were in the same boat, without a present for the wife and those for the kids still unwrapped?

He forced his mind to concentrate: this SIO was a humourless sod, renowned for his insistence on a quick result. At the beginning, Bramwell would have agreed this was possible. Then the doubts about Gough had begun. These were apparently unfounded but he still wasn't happy. There were too many unreconciled facts. The SIO was summing up.

'So, we have the full details of Ernest Clare's movements up to seventeen-thirty yesterday.'

Bramwell coughed.

'Yes?'

'We haven't been able to check again with Charles Tucknell. He was the last person known to have spoken to the deceased. He didn't enter the house according to the woman who lives opposite, he'd only gone there to collect a pools coupon. Clare chatted to him on the doorstep but we don't yet know details of their conversation. Yesterday we only took a brief statement.'

'Why hasn't it been double-checked today?' The SIO was obviously exasperated.

'Tucknell is believed to have gone to his sister—address unknown but we're working on it.'

'So? She's not living in Alaska?'

'Kingston-upon-Thames, we believe.' Bramwell's eyes fell before the glare.

The SIO glanced at the white board. 'Send Cass first thing tomorrow. Tucknell's information may turn out to be useless but I want everything sewn up by the time we track Gough down. I'm aware the prints on the deceased's neck aren't Gough's and the only one that is, the partial one on the door jamb, won't stand up without additional evidence but he has to be our main suspect. Until we find our prowler, of course. Forensic suggested two people were involved: these two must be the pair. Where's Gough's file by the way?'

'It's been despatched,' Bramwell said smoothly. He'd create the biggest stink Records had ever known if it hadn't arrived by tomorrow.

'Tut-tut-tut. Anyone would think it was Christmas.' The laughter was polite. Everyone recognised when the SIO had made a joke.

'About the so-called "prowler", sir...'

'I was coming to that.'

'Sir.'

'To ask *you* what progress has been made?'

Bastard, thought Bramwell. He replied evenly, 'We should be able to issue an identikit tomorrow. The three witnesses are coming here at nine. I think our best bet is Lila Boyce. She's the youngest, by a couple of years anyway, and her hobby is shopping. She notices things. She was the first to tell us what the man was wearing, Miss Posner and Mr Wolfe were vague.'

'I want him identified by the time we interview Gough.' It was arrogant but Bramwell agreed it would make life easier; Gough was more likely to crumble. 'I want the whole thing wrapped up quickly as soon as Gough *is* brought in. We oughtn't to waste man-hours on something as straight-forward and sordid as this.'

Not at double time and a half over Christmas.

MR PRINGLE SAW Mrs Bignell to her door, waited until she'd unlocked it, offered to search the house once more and then announced he would prefer to return to his own home that night.

'I wish to think,' he explained simply. 'Being with you is too much of a distraction.'

Mrs Bignell dimpled. 'Have a cocoa before you go?'

'Forgive me, no. I need to resist all temptation.'

She reached up to plant a kiss. 'Don't forget to switch the electric blanket on. What time will I see you tomorrow? I want to nip out early and do some last-minute shopping.'

Mr Pringle arranged to phone before he set out. He listened until she had bolted the door and switched off the outside light then set off for home in the cold, dark sleet.

To be Mrs Bignell's accredited lover was to be envied, yet at this time of year, when he had forgotten to put on his galoshes and the distance between their two dwellings seemed to increase rather than diminish, he found himself wondering whether he should try and persuade her to renounce romance for matrimony. Her principal objection was valid: as relict of the late Herbert Bignell, Mavis did not wish to relinquish her share of his pension.

'It's only a tiddly little sum, dear. But he was so mean with cash while he was alive it would be a shame to lose a penny of it now he's dead. If I remarry, they stop paying altogether. I use it for things I know Herbert would dislike,' she chuckled. 'The minute I saw that living-room wallpaper, I thought if he were alive those yellow roses would give him the pip.'

They produced a similar (though loyally unspoken) effect on Mr Pringle. He pointed out that as *his* widow she would be entitled to a similar proportion of a much larger sum but Mrs Bignell could not be persuaded. She returned her to *leitmotiv*: 'Not being married gives such a lovely sparkle to our lives, dear. I wouldn't want it to disappear.' And how could any lover object to that?

He inserted the key into his own front door and entered the shabby drab hall.

Here the décor was muted. Mr Pringle wandered from room to silent room, absorbing the peace. He touched the furniture he and Renée had chosen together. They had been so shy of one another in those days. In retrospect, the world had seemed a much more innocent place.

He wished he could recall her face. There were plenty of photographs but these had become unfamiliar. Had the two of them really stood in the garden together? Who had taken the snapshot?

He replaced it on top of the bookcase, his thoughts sliding back to Ernest Clare. Had he had to abandon his wife? Like the rest, Mr Pringle really knew little. Ernest was part of the loose-knit circle of acquaintance that converged on the pub from this end of Inkerman Street.

'Until Lila arranged for Meals on Wheels,' Betty Fisher had explained that night, 'that's the first time Ernest came out of his shell. The WVS wanted to know details, you see. Lila went round with the form. Even then, he didn't tell her much.' Mr Pringle had looked expectantly at Mrs Boyce. The thick grey hair had been thrust aside so often, it rose in a tangled peak of thatch. Stubby square fingers revealed nicotine stains as Lila drained the last of her vodka and tonic.

'Ernest managed to avoid answering most of the questions,' she announced. 'He filled in his date of birth and address but that was all. I answered some of the rest after I'd coaxed it out of him.'

'He was a widower?'

She shrugged. 'He didn't deny it so I put down that he was.'

'How long had he been living over here?'

'They didn't ask that.'

'But he arrived in Inkerman Street as a refugee?'

Betty crossed her legs and leaned back against the banquette. 'I remember Ernest moving into that house when my sister was first married. Nineteen thirty-nine or forty that must have been. During the war anyway.'

Lila nodded. 'He was already there when I arrived. It's all so long ago, of course.'

It was Mr Pringle's turn to buy the round. He was at the bar several minutes and when he returned the conversation had moved on.

THE ABORTIVE MISSION to retrieve the bequest had been Mr Pringle's first visit to number eight. He thought it likely that very few people had been permitted over the threshold.

He remembered again the bare, bleak kitchen. Tonight, in the pub, more than one person had remarked on the miserable way in which Ernest spent his days, alone in that dark middle room.

On an impulse Mr Pringle had asked Lila if she had ever visited upstairs. She laughed. 'Into his bedroom, you mean? Once or twice. He didn't like it when I did. The furniture looked like a job lot from an auction sale. A bed, a chair, a chest of drawers. Oh, and a rug. I offered to wash that for him but Ernest wouldn't have it. It would probably have fallen to pieces it was so worn out.'

'No creature comforts?'

'None. The bed was one of those old army surplus things, with a couple of blankets and an eiderdown. Not a man worth robbing, really.' This had produced a silence.

'Perhaps,' Mr Pringle suggested idly, 'Ernest had other treasures tucked away.'

What on earth had made him say that? The circle of faces stared.

'Such as?' asked one.

'I—I don't know. Pictures, perhaps?' He effaced himself behind his sherry glass and listened as Lila described the lack of personal belongings.

'There was absolutely nothing. When he left Hungary, he must've travelled light.'

'Did Ernest have any close friends?'

This had caused embarrassment. Betty Fisher said softly, 'It was difficult to get to know him. We did try.'

Sitting in the dark in his own house, Mr Pringle tried to imagine what it must have been like, watching the room being torn apart, tied up, unable to barter for his life.

That bothered him—why had Ernest's killing been so grotesque? Surely a quick crack on the head would have been sufficient? As thoughts began to whirl the telephone rang, startling him.

He bumped his way across, stumbling into familiar objects which in the dark had become an obstacle course. 'Yes?'

'All your clean vests are in the airing cupboard, not in your drawer. I thought I'd save you hunting for one in the morning.'

'Thank you.'

'Everything all right, dear? You sound a bit odd.'

'I was thinking about Ernest.'

'Best not. It won't bring him back.'

'I know it won't.' He was suddenly tetchy. 'What I want to know is why break his neck? Most thugs would give you a smart tap on the skull.'

'You'd better ask Karl when they catch him.'

'I thought you'd decided he couldn't have done it.'

'I know, dear,' her yawn was very close to his ear, 'but as Lila said, the police know things we don't. They've been all over Ernest's place looking for clues, they must have a reason for believing it was him.'

Well I'll be blowed, he thought, annoyed.

'So my efforts at deduction are no longer required?'

'I don't think so, thank you. One or two of them were a bit upset tonight. Reg Wolfe guessed what you were trying to do. You look through the bottom of your bi-focals when you're listening hard, it's a habit you have. After the police grilling, they were a bit fed up when you started doing the same thing.'

But he'd been so subtle, treated them all with such infinite care!

'I refuse to accept I can have offended anyone.'

'Now don't be upset. Did you remember to warm your bed?'

The fact that he hadn't, that he would be sleeping between cold sheets added to his temper. How wise Rhett had been not to give a damn. Had he stayed, Scarlett would surely have emasculated him.

'I prefer a hot-water bottle.'

Mrs Bignell lit the blue touchpaper. 'You forgot, that's what it was. How can I look after you when you forget all the time? You'd better have a hot bath. Those sheets aren't flannelette—'

'Good night.' Mr Pringle banged down the receiver. He'd never done such a thing to her before. He marched into the kitchen to heat the milk for his cocoa. He sailed upstairs, switching on lights, blankets, the immersion heater.

He wasn't forgetful! There was nothing wrong with his memory. He had been applying his orderly mind to a most serious problem.

Relaxing in a scalding bath, Mr Pringle was addressing the bath taps, scolding them for speaking to him so rudely, when he began to smell the milk.

EIGHT

IT WAS Christmas Eve. Karl had delivered his load and come on a long chase south, following a tip which turned out to be false. He was in unfamiliar territory now, without a replacement. Worse, he was dog-tired. He'd not stopped since leaving the ferry. Now, in a busy container depot on the outskirts of Le Puy, he waited for a French driver to help him find a load. The Frenchman sat at a terminal of the national Minitel computer, used his password to enter the system and tapped in Karl's requirements.

'It doesn't matter where it's for... Turkey, Greece, Middle East...'

The man had stopped, distracted by a message which appeared at the bottom of the screen. 'Numéro?'

'What?'

'Numéro, numéro!'

'You mean the registration?' Karl scribbled it down. 'There, F-cent-cinquante-neuf-M-J-F. What d'you need that for?' He'd already given him all the relevant information. 'I don't want anything perishable.' He pronounced the words slowly so the foreigner would understand, 'No perishable goods, OK?' The man had gone back to the keyboard, this time punching keys rapidly. The information on the screen changed from questions and answers to the local weather map. Tiredness aggravated Karl's temper.

'Look, I'm not bothered about the weather—I don't mind Spain if there's no other choice...' The Frenchman ignored him, rose and walked away abruptly toward the depot manager's office. Before Karl could sit at the Minitel himself, a burly German driver had shoved him aside.

They could really piss you about in this country. What a road! Karl had come down on the N88 from St Etienne on some of the worst gradients he could remember. He should have stopped for a nap but his anxiety to drop out of sight had been too great. Now, even the weather was against him. Rain was sheeting down. He wandered across to stare at a wall map beside a mirror advertising Amstel. There was only the one terminal available, he'd have to wait until the German had finished.

The crowd of international drivers was thinning out. None would be here much longer, everyone had a bolthole for Christmas. Karl began to wonder how much longer the depot would remain open.

Lethargy dulled him. He scanned the map and spotted the name 'Tournon'. His mind began to clear. That was a name he knew. From Tournon he could pick up the autoroute and head for Lyons. Relief replaced tiredness. Lyons was a great place. For a man who wanted to hole up for a while, it was damn near perfect. Volatile optimism bubbled.

He knew a woman there, he'd stayed at her place. She had a few rooms over her restaurant not far from the hospital. On that occasion he'd needed a repair and her son had taken him to his workshop at the back of a coal yard. Karl remembered the large empty sheds. His artic could remain out of sight until it was prudent to leave. The woman might know of a load, she had contacts. Her name came back to him: Marie-Christine.

Tiredness vanished. He didn't need the Minitel. One more reviving cup of coffee then fill up and head for Tournon. Maybe he'd investigate the ablutions first? France definitely had the edge when it came to facilities. He'd clean up, have a shave. Karl examined his chin in the mirror. He ought to make himself presentable before knocking on Marie-Christine's door. Should he take her some flowers?

Why not cash the second cheque before he left? He'd seen a couple of the drivers approach the manager, he'd watched the transactions covertly. He glanced over his shoulder to check the manager was there. The French driver was still with him and both stared in his direction. When Karl nodded they immediately looked away. He felt in his pocket for one of the cheques. He wouldn't push his luck. If the manager objected, that was that.

He still faced the mirror alongside the map. He could see the reflection of the Minitel. The German was noting down the roadworks between Le Puy and Brioude but it was the message below which caught Karl's eye. Even backwards, the number was unmistakable: F159 MJF.

He was outside in seconds, dodging from one vehicle to the next, keeping these obstacles between him and the view from the office window. His breath came in sobs as he tried to calculate the amount of fuel remaining. Could he reach Tournon? The gauge was worse than he'd hoped. He'd have to find a garage off the beaten track, without a computer terminal.

He tried to recall details of the map. The direction was due east. He wished he could remember the road number; there were too many bloody mountains in this area. Windscreen wipers fought a losing battle against the storm as Karl nosed his way forward, behind a Belgian tanker.

Inside the depot office, the manager leapt to his feet and began to gesticulate as he shouted into the phone.

IN THE HOSPITAL WARD, the bustle of handing over to the day-shift was in progress but behind the curtained-off bed there was nothing but silence.

Mrs Berriman stared at the bed, at the collar and wires, the sinister machinery bleeping away, at the evil-looking tubes leading from her daughter's body. Doctors had tried to prepare her but nothing matched the reality. Sharon looked as if she'd been crucified. Her mother licked glossy lips.

'Sharon? Can you hear me?'

Eyelids flickered. The voice from the pillows was hoarse. 'Get out!'

'It wasn't my fault, Sharon—'

'It bloody well was!' The eyes were full of hatred. 'Why couldn't you have told me *sooner*?'

A terrible fear filled Mrs Berriman. She shrank back, instinct keeping her voice low so those listening couldn't hear. 'You're not trying to say...' She couldn't bring herself to utter the words.

Sharon said them deliberately, 'I told him Sarah wasn't his daughter.' She watched as her mother teetered on her high heels, the thick makeup unable to disguise the terrified face beneath. Full of scorn as well as hate, she hissed, 'Want to hear the rest of it?'

'No!' It was a shriek. Mrs Berriman glanced round waiting for authority to appear. No one came. She pulled the tightly fitted jacket close across her lurex body. 'It's wicked, trying to blame me—'

'What did you tell them about Lee?'

'Ssh! Nothing. What d'you take me for?'

'What did you say to them?'

'Nothing! They kept asking if I knew where Karl was. They told me you were, you know... in here... They gave me a lift over this morning.'

'Where's Sarah?'

'With Connie.' Mrs Berriman was shivering inside her thin clothes. 'Listen, Sharon...I can't—you know. I couldn't take her, not after...' Sharon watched her flounder, her face twisted in a bitter smile.

'Spit it out, Mum. You'll feel better, honest.' Mrs Berriman compressed her lips. 'Did they explain apart from breaking my neck, he's kicked me so hard my kidneys don't work no more? Did they mention that?'

Mrs Berriman's hands were out in front to fend off any more dreadfulness. She was desperate for a smoke. Sharon went on remorselessly as if it were normal conversation.

'Yes, I shan't ever leave this bed. The only thing that works is my head. A pity, really. I can smell my own shit. That's what all those bags are for, Mum. I've got no control.'

'Sharon!'

The hoarse, strained voice was suddenly loud. 'I'll never be able to sit up or walk, or screw. It's a living death, Mum. I can't even finish myself off because I can't *move*. I don't suppose you'd do that for me? As a favour?'

The last shreds of pretence were gone. Neither woman was aware of listeners now.

'You always said I was a mistake,' Sharon whispered pitilessly. 'So now's your opportunity. I'd be truly thankful, believe me.'

Mrs Berriman could barely speak. 'Sharon, don't, please.'

Sharon closed her eyes; the small amount of energy was ebbing fast.

'You'd better watch yourself with Lee. Do you know where either of them are?'

'No! I swear to God.'

'And you're not willing to take Sarah?'

'I couldn't!' The shaking had come back with a vengeance. Mrs Berriman clung to the chair for support. Sharon's breath came in gasps, she'd pushed herself too far.

'She'll have to go...for adoption.'

'Sharon!' The desperate shadowy eyes were full of anger.

'Stop pretending, Mum. What other choice is there?' Mrs Berriman made as if to speak but didn't. 'You'll have to sign the papers. I can't even hold a fucking pen.'

As her mother tried to slip away between the curtains, one last whisper followed her.

'Mum.'

'Yes?'

'Don't come back. I don't want to see you again.'

Outside, Mrs Berriman smoothed her short skirt automatically. Sharon had got it wrong. Technology these days, they could do transplants, fantastic things like that. She had to have some hope to cling to in this terrible mess—it wasn't her fault! She was so overwrought, she hadn't noticed that the police officer was speaking.

'What?'

'I asked if your daughter gave any details? We can't press charges until she does. Did she drop any hint as to where we might find her husband?'

'No, she didn't. I told you, neither of us knows.' Self-preservation was returning. Mrs Berriman straightened her shoulders. 'One thing she did say, though. She wants to put her baby up for adoption. I hope my neighbours don't think I'm responsible. And I'm not coming back. She doesn't want to see me and you can't do anything when Sharon's in that mood. I'll bring Sarah over and leave her in Reception, shall I? You and the nurses can tell the DSS. It's what Sharon wants.'

The officer watched her go, thoughts of murder coming unbidden into his mind.

THE FACT THAT Christmas Eve had fallen on a Saturday didn't deter Charlie Tucknell's sister: she always bought her

veg on a Saturday to make sure it was fresh, she would do
so again today. Charlie must carry the basket because her
long-suffering husband Godfrey had been detailed to clean
the silver.

'Why not use plastic knives and forks?' grumbled Charlie. 'The disposable sort? And why bother with veg? I like
frozen peas.' He looked at Godfrey for support but his
brother-in-law had learned the wisdom of silence. Charlie
glared. 'I said—I like frozen peas.'

'Well, we don't,' retorted his sister, 'and I'm ready so you
go and get your cap.'

'I'm not as young as I was, Violet. Ernest being murdered—it's taken its toll. Me waterworks let me down if I
have to stand too long at a bus stop. Can't we use the corner shop?'

'And pay their prices! *You* may be able to afford it, *we*
can't. Godfrey's pension hasn't kept up. We'll go into town.'

There was no arguing with her, there never had been, not
since they were children. He followed her outside into the
chaotic hell that was Kingston-upon-Thames.

MR PRINGLE was up early. His sleep had been troubled by
dreams. One concerned the small scrap of paper he'd collected from Ernest's hiding place.

He studied the figures. Behind him, the ancient gas fire
plopped sympathetically. There weren't enough numbers for
it to be a computer reference, the grouping didn't make
sense as a date. He tried various mathematical formulae but
none worked. He began to wonder if the conundrum had
any significance at all and found he had wandered in front
of his favourite picture, a crayon drawing of a northern
market scene.

Last night this too had been part of his dream. Because it
was so embedded in his subconscious, presumably this

meant his mind was striving to bring some relevant fact to his attention. He had been thinking of Ernest Clare, therefore the two must be linked. He was also convinced the inhabitants of Inkerman Street had been correct in their first assumption: Karl Gough was not the man to mount such a brutal attack.

The doorbell rang. Mr Pringle hurried downstairs. The milkman had collected his Christmas box, the postman his, surely he hadn't forgotten anyone? There were no spare gifts, such as Mrs Bignell kept for emergencies. His hand was already searching for his wallet as he opened the front door. A small unpleasant child challenged him.

'Compliments of the season.'

Mr Pringle had never liked this particular newspaper boy.

'I gave money to the newsagent, to be shared amongst the three of you.' A five-pound note was surely sufficient. The child's aggression changed to a self-pity.

'I never got my share. The others took it.'

'Rubbish.' At one time Mr Pringle might have been fooled but early-morning observation convinced him otherwise. 'I've seen you steal milk and yoghurt from the milk float. I've also watched you hit a smaller boy to make him give you his chocolate. In fact,' Mr Pringle said warmly, 'I have no doubt that far from being defrauded, you have probably seized their rightful money from your two comrades. Now, be off with you.'

The unpleasant child deposited a gobbet of spittle with deadly accuracy in the middle of Mr Pringle's best tie. 'A sodding new year. I hope you drop down dead.'

'And may I wish you the worst of bad luck. May your memory fail at the most crucial moments of your life, your organ fail to rise and...' Mr Pringle loomed menacingly, 'in the midst of any exam, may you never remember how many beans make five.' He stood back, full of pride at the obvious bafflement.

'All children should be exterminated!' shrieked a silent wicked portion of his brain. Mr Pringle didn't try to stifle the voice. Instead he changed his tie with composure. If the boy's father came to complain he would present him with the bill for cleaning it.

This new serenity caused his subconscious to surrender the connection between Ernest Clare and his drawing. In the picture the figures were all self-contained. It was as if each was wrapped in his or her own thoughts while continuing to perform their joint function within the market. In Inkerman Street, each guarded their privacy but banded together when the need arose, all except Ernest.

Mr Pringle ran through the rest: Betty Fisher and Reg Wolfe, divorcee and widower, they kept one another company and shared the cost of excursions. Charlie Tucknell lived alone, as did Miss Posner, John Hines and Lila Boyce, but all called on one another, doing messages, fetching pensions if another were ill. None had, as far as Mr Pringle was aware, any connection yet all played a part in one another's lives. Ernest Clare was the odd one out. Admitting Lila had been a penance, he had made that plain. However, was it possible there was a connection?

Mr Pringle pondered the annual uncharacteristic act of benevolence. Did that money really represent gratitude to the country of his adoption? There was only one other clue. He reached for a dictionary to check the source of a word but what he found didn't help solve the riddle.

He went downstairs to make himself coffee. Radio headlines about Catholics killing Protestants in Northern Ireland reminded him tomorrow was the birthday of the Prince of Peace. He needed to wrap up Mrs Bignell's present.

A carol service began as he fought a losing battle with gold string. It slithered away over the corners, developing mysterious kinks on the underside. 'Shepherds abiding in the field...' That had always bothered him: why stay outside when the weather was so bad? British shepherds always brought their sheep down from the hills. He'd once asked his Sunday school teacher but she had been very short with him.

'Blast!' Taut gold string had sliced through the paper. Mr Pringle cut away the torn part and attempted to join the pieces together. Sellotape wound round his fingers. The flimsy paper puckered, the pattern no longer matched. Christmas, with or without murder, was nothing but harassment. Far better abandon handiwork and pursue his enquiries instead. Despite Mrs Bignell's strictures, it still rankled that the police could even begin to think *he* might be responsible for such a terrible crime.

'OH, HELLO.' Betty Fisher undid the chain on her front door.

'I trust I do not call at an inconvenient time?'

Betty tried not to let her feelings show: to be in the midst of Christmas preparations and be asked that question! 'Not at all, come in. I was about to make coffee.'

How fortuitous, Mr Pringle thought complacently. He wondered if Reg would be invited to join them.

'Do you mind if we have it in the kitchen?' she asked.

'Not at all.' When he saw the bomb site, he began to have doubts. 'You are quite sure... I could call back later.'

Betty smiled. 'Sit down. It'll do me good to put my feet up for ten minutes.' He waited until she had set the cup down in front of him.

'You're most kind. I fear this must be extremely inconvenient.'

'Have a biscuit.'

'I came to apologise for my clumsy behaviour last night.' Her eyebrows went up. 'Mrs Bignell told me how I had offended.'

'Oh, that... It was Reg, not me, who grumbled. *I* thought it was a good idea. The sooner we get to the bottom of this business, the better.' She shivered, involuntarily, at the memory.

'It was most unfortunate you had to make the discovery.'

'Reg spotted what had happened, he held me back so I only got a glimpse of Ernest, lying there... and I managed to sleep last night for the first time, which was a relief. I must be getting over it.'

Mr Pringle hastened to change the subject. 'I believe it was Reg who also spotted the prowler? You weren't with him on that occasion?'

'That's right. Reg was on his way back from indoor bowls. He'd told me earlier he was going to nip home and change. When he was ready we both went together to collect Ernest... which was when...'

'Quite. And when did Reg mention seeing the stranger?'

She frowned. 'You mean was it while we were on our way to Ernest's? Yes, yes, I think it was. Not when we were in the pub. That's when Lila told us she had seen him as well.'

Mr Pringle said slowly, 'So conversation about him was general?'

'One or two wondered if they'd noticed him but it was dark by then and most weren't sure. Lila had been quite close, you see. She'd been looking in her bag for her door key. She glanced up and there he was, standing on the pavement.'

'And when she went indoors, there was young Karl.'

'Exactly.' Betty gave a relieved sigh. 'So it couldn't have been him outside, could it?''

'Even Houdini could not have managed that,' Mr Pringle agreed.

'More coffee?'

He took the hint and rose. 'I fear I also have the odd task to complete. Thank you again for allowing me to interrupt all this activity.'

Betty followed him through to the hall. 'It's chocolate truffles. Reg really loves them—we always have them on Christmas Day—and I enjoy making them but they do take time.' Mr Pringle glanced at the ceiling absently, as though expecting Reg Wolfe to materialise. 'It's a very convenient arrangement, having such a good friend in the upstairs flat,' Betty Fisher confided. 'I expect you and Mrs Bignell find the same.' She stopped abruptly and went pink. 'Not that Reg and I . . .'

Mr Pringle said quickly, 'Companionship at our time of life, in whatever form, is both a comfort and consolation.'

'I never wanted to remarry. Once was enough. But I do enjoy cooking—it's so boring when it's only for one person. In return, Reg helps me with the difficult jobs, like putting up shelves or when the rubber ring goes on the washing machine. I expect you do the same for Mavis?'

Mr Pringle was forced to admit Mrs Bignell would not let him touch any of her mechanical apparatus.

'We all have different talents, I suppose,' Betty Fisher offered vaguely. 'I must say I'm more than relieved to know Reg is upstairs when there's a prowler on the loose in Inkerman Street. Have you worked out who he could be?'

'Not yet.'

'We'll all be very thankful when you do. When Reg started grumbling last night, Lila told him to be grateful you were taking an interest. She said it was very reassuring. Merry Christmas.'

Mr Pringle raised his hat and listened as the chain rattled back into position behind the closed front door. Events were beginning to take on a pattern.

LUCK, THOUGH HE did not realise it, was on Karl's side. Because of the rain, he missed his way out of Le Puy and found himself back on the N88, staring at converging lines of poplars. Realisation came when he noticed the view seen earlier, of the hill like a pimple with the rose-red statue at the summit. This was pathetic! If the police were looking for him, it would be on this sort of road.

He changed direction, turning east to Yssingeaux. Anxiety to distance himself made him keep going, past the remaining garages, on a southerly bearing for Tence. Here the road was nothing better than a track. Karl was cursing his own stupidity when there was the dreaded sound of a deflated tyre.

He backed off the track into a field. The fuel gauge registered zero, the afternoon had already turned to dusk. At home, families would be gathering for tea. He wound down the window; dripping beech trees were the only sound in the silence. Whatever he'd done, he didn't deserve this: Karl had never felt so lonely.

NINE

'BRAMWELL, THAT YOU?'

'Sir.' All right for some, the receiver thought bitterly. At this time on Christmas Eve, with the memory of his daughter's tearful face when he'd had to tell her there wasn't time to buy Mummy a present, it was difficult to maintain politeness. Especially if this call was to check they were all still there.

'Cass come up with anything?'

'He's still over in Kingston, sir. He phoned in to say Tucknell had gone shopping with his sister. I advised him to wait.'

'Damn.'

'Which could be a long time, seeing as it's Christmas.'

'I am aware of the date.'

Careful, careful... The SIO wasn't renowned for his sense of humour.

'We've heard from the bank, sir. They are sticking to the rules so it'll be after Boxing Day before we find out about Clare's account.'

'Damn, damn, damn!'

'One encouraging item. That docket tucked inside the building society book. One of our lads thought it sounded Austrian or German and could be the name of another bank. We've found it listed and he's chasing it up.'

'Excellent. What about Gough?'

'No news so far, sir. Nothing from the hospital, either. We're hoping for a result after the broadcast, of course. Someone may have supplied him with a load. The plan is to include a head-on shot of a similar Volvo artic with the number plate superimposed. Might jog someone's memory.'

'Good. I trust the file has finally arrived?'

'It has but I'm afraid it hasn't been much use.'

'What about Gough's contacts?'

'Very few and none which help in this instance. He chummed up with an old con named Pearson in Chelmsford. They both worked in the laundry and kept a very low profile. Used to be employed by Coutts.'

The SIO wasn't impressed. Bramwell went on, 'I've got a call out to Chelmsford. They haven't come back to me yet.'

'There must have been other contacts?'

'Not according to Gough's file. He and Pearson seem to be two timid types who kept each other company...' Bramwell let the description linger because it had worried him. The SIO was silent. 'As far as we know, Pearson is still inside. That's one thing I still need to check. Even if he's not, he doesn't sound like our prowler. For a start, he's far too old.'

At his end of the line, the SIO cursed silently. It looked as if this straightforward case was going to drag on after all. God knows what the overtime bill would be. He asked abruptly, 'How many are in there today, Bramwell?'

Hello? Was one murdered OAP about to be quietly shelved and forgotten?

'Five, sir.'

'Five?' The reproach wasn't veiled enough.

'Apart from Cass over in Kingston and Dexter chasing up the bank, we have to finish the identikit in time for the bulletins. We had to wait for the last witness, Mrs Lila Boyce, to come in. She wanted to finish various messages—'

'What progress has been made?' interrupted the SIO.

Bramwell sighed, loud enough for it to register. 'Not much. It was a wet night, none of the witnesses have good vision and all are in their seventies or thereabouts. They described his clothes all right. They agree more or less about his height but none of them saw his face.'

The SIO wasn't having any defeatist talk, not at time and a half. 'It must be possible to put a name to him. If necessary, we shall have to rely on Gough to finger him. He doesn't sound the type to hold out, not when the charge is murder.'

When we find him, thought Bramwell wearily. He wondered how long it would be before the SIO admitted the facts weren't adding up.

'About Mrs Gough, sir.'

'Yes?'

'We're making no mention of her in the item.'

'No, I agree.'

'She's still refusing to talk—and shouldn't be interviewed according to the medical people—but I've had a chat with the DPW who spoke to Mrs Gough's mother, Mrs Berriman.'

'And?'

'When she finally arrived home in the early hours and was told of her daughter's accident, she expressed her opinion very vigorously indeed.'

'Which was?'

'That Karl Gough hadn't got the guts to carry out such an attack. Her precise words...' Bramwell spooled through the pages on his screen. 'Yes, here we are... According to DPW Tunnicliffe, Berriman stated, "If you told me Sharon had broken Karl's neck, that I could believe. I hope she does. Useless he is, nothing but prison fodder." And when asked if Gough had ever shown violence to her daughter before, Berriman said, "If he had, Sharon would have gone for him

with the bread knife. She's not shy, my daughter isn't."
Ends.'

The SIO gave a mental wriggle. 'It's ridiculous that we
should be kept dangling for a statement from Mrs Gough.'

'The doctors broke the news about her condition this
morning. She took it badly, which isn't surprising. She is
only twenty-five.'

The SIO had no time for sympathy. 'Was anything said
when her mother visited her?'

'They were whispering to one another but no one could
understand what it was about. Since then, according to the
ward sister, there has been a deterioration. This morning
when the doctors explained, Mrs Gough asked whether she
would be able to use a wheelchair, implying in an inde-
pendent manner. When told this was impossible, she became upset and had to be sedated. Afterwards, following the
visit of Mrs Berriman, medical opinion was heavily against
any further questioning for at least twenty-four hours.'

'I can't believe she hasn't said *anything* about the attack.
Surely she told her mother?'

'Mrs Gough certainly asked if her mother wanted to know
the details but Mrs Berriman declined.'

'Damned unnatural family.'

'There is a line I think we should follow up, sir. I've had
a chat with a contact of mine in Southend. Well, Leigh-on-
Sea, now he's retired. According to him, Mrs Berriman may
have form. He thinks she's a woman who was on the game
when he was a young copper.'

Up till now, in his comfortable home in Surrey, the SIO
had pictured Mrs Berriman as a standard advertiser's
C-class grandmother, with comfortable hips, grey hair and
an unnatural apple-cheeked complexion: 'Good grief!'

'If it is the same woman, she was shacked up for a time
with a member of an East End gang who killed a security

guard during a pay snatch. He got the maximum because he'd used a pick-axe to split the guard's head open. When he came out, he began knocking Sharon about—she would have been about fifteen—and social services were involved. There had been a Mr Berriman but he was dead by then. Mrs Berriman used *his* life insurance to buy the place where she lives now, and turned respectable. I don't know whether there is any connection, if she or Sharon have taken up with any of the gang, but I think we ought to make sure.'

'Not tomorrow, Bramwell.' Not at treble-time.

'We don't want to leave it too long, sir. It could be that Sharon provided the contacts. Her husband knew about Ernest Clare and Mrs Gough provided the rough stuff to help with breaking and entering. It would make better sense than Pearson. And we know Gough wasn't operating on his own.'

'We have a clear print on the door jamb of deceased's residence,' the SIO said flatly.

'Only a partial, sir,' Bramwell corrected. 'I doubt if it would be considered sufficient evidence. There are plenty of other prints about the place from neighbours who helped look after Clare, of course.'

'Nevertheless, I see no need for unnecessary expenditure on Mrs Berriman. Any connection between Gough and her mother's former companions is likely to prove extremely tenuous in my judgement.'

'Yes, sir.'

'We're not doing badly. Tell that DPW to keep her ears open if she visits Mrs Gough again, she's obviously a sharp girl. We may learn all we need to know via that source.'

'Yes, sir.'

It encouraged the SIO to hear the note of dejection; Bramwell needed curbing. 'Good luck with the broadcast.

Telephone me if anything develops. I can be over there in half an hour, you know that, don't you?'

'Of course, sir. Merry Christmas.'

'It is still Christmas Eve, Bramwell. No need to jump the gun.'

The receiver stared balefully at the receiver. No doubt the phone would ring at one minute to midnight, to ensure the incident room was empty before golden time began.

BUFFETED BY every passing stranger, his arms aching from the weight of the basket, Charlie Tucknell had reached the end of his tether. Anger throbbed as his feet were crushed by the crowds on the bus. This pain was in addition to the one in his bladder. Why did he submit to this ritual? He didn't have to, he had a perfectly pleasant little home. And why worry about being lonely when he was surrounded by friends and good neighbours? Clinging to the strap he mouthed at his sister in her seat, 'I'm fed up.'

'What? Speak up, you know I'm deaf on that side.'

'I said, I'm bloody well fed up with it!' The roar reached the length of the bus. It found kindred spirits among the packed humanity as well as those who were affronted by it. The argument had reached monumental proportions by the time Charlie and his sister descended, and continued unabated as they walked down the street. It was only brought to a halt by his sudden, 'Hey, look. That's a police car and it's parked right outside your house.' For his sister it was the final straw.

'Is that your doing?'

Charlie had no idea. Apprehension swept over him. He was tempted to drop the blessed basket and head straight back to those amorphous, anonymous crowds. The moment passed as quickly as it had come and his sister prodded him in the back.

'Don't just stand there—get rid of them. Tell the police to park somewhere else. I'm not letting you embarrass me in front of my neighbours.'

There was no one in the car. His sister entered the house and marched ahead of him into the kitchen where Charlie recognised DC Cass standing beside Godfrey. The officer put down his tea cup.

'Mr Tucknell, we'd like to ask you a few more questions.'

CHARLIE CLAIMED his right to the dregs in the teapot before consenting to retire to the privacy of the parlour. It gave him a chance to collect his thoughts but when the questions came, they weren't as bad as he'd feared. DC Cass wanted to know if Charlie had by now a more precise idea of the time of his visit to Ernest Clare.

'I can't be sure, to tell you the truth. I know it was around six o'clock because when I got home the news had finished on the telly.'

'Which channel?'

'BBC. Always is for me.'

Which meant the six p.m. bulletin. Cass asked, 'You turned the set on immediately you got back?'

Charlie reviewed his progress from memory. 'I let myself in, took me coat off and me cap. Hung them on the hall-stand. I went through to the kitchen and put the kettle on, lit the gas . . . then I went through and switched on the set. Wouldn't have taken me more than a couple of minutes to do all that.'

'And the news had finished?'

'Just about. They hadn't started the local news.' So about twenty past six, Cass decided. Charlie slurped the last of his tea. 'My God, I needed that. It's cruel making a chap go shopping on a Christmas Eve.'

'How long did it take to walk home from number eight?'

'You've asked me that before.'

'Tell me again.'

Charlie sighed. 'About fifteen minutes, unless I stop for a chat or visit Mrs Norton, which I didn't that evening.'

'You're sure?'

'Positive.'

'And Ernest Clare was alive when you left him.'

'Of course he was.' Charlie was impatient. 'He'd gone back in and slammed the door by the time I reached the gate, he didn't wait to see me go for once. I think he was a bit put out. I'd tried to get him to say the names of the bequest winners. I dropped a hint but Ernest didn't take the bait. Always very careful. You can't blame him. It was his money and he wanted to have the pleasure of seeing how chuffed people were.'

'So... allow a quarter of an hour for your walk, two minutes for letting yourself in, et cetera, and it was roughly twenty past six when you switched on the television—Ernest Clare was still alive at five minutes past?'

Charlie banged the cup down in the saucer in exasperation. 'Look, I don't see why it matters so much but I've said so, haven't I? He could've been alive at half past for all I know—why keep on asking the same bloody questions? Anyway, I wasn't the last person to see him alive. Becky Posner was.'

DC Cass froze. 'What do you mean?'

'She was still there, wasn't she? Getting his tea ready. I could see her moving about the kitchen.'

The police officer's expression became very cool. 'You never said.'

'Because you kept on and on about when *I* last saw him, you didn't ask me about her. And who knows, she may not have been the last.' Charlie gestured expansively. 'There may have been someone else call on him after she left.'

Of course there was, you great prat: the murderer. Fortunately DC Cass's face didn't betray his thoughts.

'The trouble with all you young fellas, you try and rush us,' Charlie explained kindly. 'We has to take us time, sorting things out in our minds.'

'So tell me now.'

'I was on the step and I rang the bell. When he opened the front door I could see past Ernest into the kitchen at the back. The door to that was open as well, you see. He's got one of those cabinets standing against the wall. He must have kept his plates and stuff in it because I could see Miss Posner open one of the glass doors as if she was looking for something. She doesn't normally see to his tea, you know. Lila does. *She* would have known where his things were.'

'You're sure it was Miss Posner? Not some other neighbour?'

'It was dark...he doesn't have much of a light in there...too bloody mean, uses forty-watt bulbs. Odd when you remember how generous he could be. But I've known Becky since she first came to Inkerman Street, I couldn't be mistaken about her.'

DC Cass assessed the thick bi-focals and began a new, fierce interrogation.

If he'd found the questioning tiresome before, this time Charlie was exhausted. His body ached, his mind was numbed by the constant repetition. He pleaded, 'I can't tell you any more because I don't *know* and that's God's truth.'

DC Cass repeated, 'If you're quite, quite sure you didn't see any stranger in the vicinity of number eight Inkerman Street between seven—'

'—and seven-thirty p.m. on Thursday. I know, I know. You've already asked.' Charlie's eyes were bloodshot, his top plate which had never fitted properly chafed against his gums. 'If I could help you, I would, but I never saw the fellow because he'd disappeared by the time I set out for the pub. I wish he hadn't. I wish I'd been there and taken a good look at him. I'd tell you what he looked like, what he had for dinner, what colour his eyes were—but I can't. Because I never saw him. I was late because of filling in the football coupon and sorting out the cash. Becky Posner was in the pub with a drink in her hand by the time I arrived. She was with Karl. Maybe he saw him? They must've been among the first ones there.'

There was no sarcasm in the remark, DC Cass was certain.

'Maybe,' he agreed non-committally.

'If he did you can ask him when he gets back. Have you finished with me?'

DC Cass nodded. 'We'll leave you to enjoy your Christmas, Mr Tucknell.'

His words set alarm bells ringing. Exhausted though he was, Charlie remembered he was about to face two solid days with Violet.

'Here...which way are you going in that?' He pointed to the police car parked outside.

'Back to the incident room, why?'

'Do us a favour. Give us a lift.'

'We're not a ruddy taxi service—'

'Just to the corner of Inkerman Street. I can walk the rest.'

'I thought you'd come over here to be with your sister?'

'Ssh! Keep your voice down. I'll just nip upstairs and get me things. If she wants to know what's happening, keep her talking. Ask to see her TV licence. I bet she hasn't got one. Too bloody mean to buy the stamps. I won't be more'n a jiffy.'

Despite his enervated state, Charlie fled upstairs and rammed his belongings into his zip-up carrier. He hurried down, grabbing his cap and scarf off the hallstand and throwing the two small presents beneath the dusty plastic tree which was Violet's idea of celebration.

His brother-in-law watched these antics, open-mouthed. 'It wasn't you who did it, was it, Charlie? Have they come to take you away?'

'No, you daft-head. I've cadged a lift. This packet's yours. I hope they're the right colour. And this is for her.'

Years of being married to Violet enabled Godfrey to predict his spouse's likely reaction. 'She won't like it. She won't like you dashing off, neither. You know what she'll say? All that work and he wasn't even grateful. She might not invite you next year.' Charlie couldn't keep his delight hidden. 'Besides, what about you?' demanded Godfrey. 'Where will you go? Everywhere's shut.'

'Home. Where else?' A fish and chip supper then the Bricklayers—sheer bliss. Charlie began to forget about the blisters on his feet.

'What about your Christmas dinner?'

'I shall throw meself on the kindness of me friends,' Charlie announced.

Violet appeared behind her husband's shoulder, her mouth tight as a trap. 'You're off. Well, good riddance! If that killer is still about, I hope he breaks your neck an' all.'

Charlie gave her a beatific smile. 'If it's between you or him, Vi, I'd rather be back in Inkerman Street.' He turned to Cass. 'Shall we go?'

'I think we'd better.'

In the incident room they were studying copies of the identikit picture. Bramwell broke the silence. 'I think it's pathetic that they couldn't agree about *something*.'

'Could I just have a look at Gough?' DC Dexter reached out a hand and Bramwell gave him the file. Dexter compared the black and white photograph with the identikit. 'It's not unlike him for build, is it? Apart from the fact that this'—he waved the identikit—'has no features.'

Bramwell sighed. 'We shall look fools putting it out, but what else can we do?'

'Perhaps it was delayed shock affecting them. They're all so old.'

'That doesn't help us. This was Reg Wolfe's effort. He said he only got a back view as he hurried home from his indoor bowls.'

Someone sniggered.

'Quite,' said Bramwell drily. 'So much for eye witnesses.'

'Perhaps it was the man come to repair someone's washing machine.'

'At six-thirty p.m.?'

'There's plenty go moonlighting nowadays.'

'Wish they did round our way,' Bramwell grumbled. He looked at the wall clock. 'Switch on. Let's see what sort of coverage we get.'

They crowded round the television which was balanced on a pile of phone directories. When the newscaster came into vision, someone asked, 'How does she keep those earrings on?'

'Araldite.'

'Ssh!' Bramwell leaned forward with a stop-watch.

The item, when it came, began with the faceless identikit picture which was held for a couple of seconds. The newscaster came back into vision replaced by a shot of the vehicle. One of the group in the incident room began reading the number aloud: 'F-one-five-nine-M-J—' He was too slow. The shot changed to the incident room telephone number. 'Blimey. Not giving us much of a chance, are they?'

It was over. On screen there was familiar footage of ter-
rorists annihilating civilians. Bramwell clicked off the watch.
'Eleven seconds. Thank you, press officer. I can't wait to
hear the old man's reaction.'

A phone began to ring. It was on the receiver's desk.
Bramwell picked it up, his stomach muscles tightening.
Sometimes, a genuine witness rang in. Someone with a re-
tentive memory and a vital piece of information. Could this
be such a one?

Around the receiver's desk, other phones sprang to life.
For the next half-hour officers moved from one to another,
taking down details, thanking the pompous, calming the
excited and, in one case, assuring the caller that if his vision of Gough's lorry in a south London parking lot had
indeed been inspired by Almighty God, his assistance had
been most valuable.

Eventually, when silence prevailed and the results had
been collated, Bramwell summed them up in a terse sentence:

'Karl Gough's artic has been positively sighted in Pen-
rith, Dumfries, on the road to Bratislava, in Carshalton and
Chorlton-cum-Hardy—'

'Where?'

'You heard. Our prowler, on the other hand, could be any
one of forty-seven people but...according to Ms Juliet
Hardacre of Nightingale Close, Pontefract, couldn't have
been in the vicinity of Inkerman Street at seven p.m. on
Thursday 22nd December because she has made a positive
identification from the identikit. She states categorically that
the gentleman concerned was in bed with her.' He topped the
cynical laughter. 'If indeed he was, then the lucky chap's
name is Paul James Crossman. So let's hear it again for Paul
James because he was on the job by seven p.m., lucky bastard—'

The receiver's phone rang and Bramwell answered it. They heard him say, 'Yes, sir. Yes, most disappointing. Er, eleven seconds actually... Er, quite a few. We'll check them out, obviously. Nothing that I would call *solid*. Oh, certainly. We're chasing every likely lead.'

The rest moved back to their terminals. There was much still to be done before they could go home. Joe Public might be unreliable but, even so, his evidence had to be checked.

Bramwell dealt patiently with the SIO. It had been three days now and there was every danger of the trail going cold.

DC Dexter slumped disconsolately in front of his screen. 'Gough has to turn up. You can't disappear in an artic, for Christ's sake.'

The fax machine began to clatter. He wandered over to it. As he did, DC Cass came hurrying in and began conferring with Bramwell.

'Hello...' Reading the message, Dexter perked up and shouted, 'Looks like friend Gough hasn't vanished after all. There's been a definite sighting at Le Puy. Confirmed, everything. Whoopee!'

'Where's that?'

'France, you pillock. Gough's vehicle was seen today around sixteen hundred hours local. Where's a map? Le Puy's got a cathedral with a black Madonna. My sister once went there on a school trip.' Dexter grabbed the fax and began searching among the reference books for a road atlas.

'Who did the interview with Rebecca Posner?' shouted Bramwell to the room at large. Faces stared at him blankly. 'Come on, it's important. She was one of our witnesses to the prowler. Apparently she visited deceased on Thursday evening and forgot to tell us about it. We need to talk to her again.'

'Wasn't it DPW Pullen, Jim? She's gone on leave. I think she said she was visiting her parents in Doncaster.'

'Shit!'

Cass knew what was in his mind. 'I'll go and see Posner. There's a knees-up at the pub tonight, we might find her there.'

But Bramwell hesitated. 'I wonder if we shouldn't leave it a day. She was a confused old lady by the time we'd finished this morning. Let's see what she said originally.'

He summoned Becky Posner's statement on to his screen, saying, 'She may have left the house only minutes after Tucknell. It was later when she saw the prowler.'

The statement, when it came up, was short. Bramwell read through it to remind himself. Cass did the same over his shoulder.

'You see. There's nothing to contradict what Tucknell said . . . apart from forgetting to mention she was still there when he left. Posner wasn't sure of the time. She warmed up Clare's supper and set the tray. The tray was still on the kitchen table.' Bramwell pointed to the sentence. 'So at that point, Clare hadn't carried it through to the middle room. Posner then puts on coat, hat, et cetera and leaves via the back door . . . when asked why'—he read the answer—'I returned Mrs Boyce's insulated bag to her back door step as I would not be making Ernest's tea the following day. She would be doing so. No, I did not see anybody about. I let myself out of the yard door and walked back down the alley into Inkerman Street.'

Bramwell leaned back in his chair. 'She obviously left without seeing the villains arrive. I wonder if we're making too much of this. If it's worth bothering her again tonight?'

Cass was keen. 'We were assuming Posner had left the house before Tucknell called but this makes it several minutes later. She may have noticed someone she *knew* close to the house.'

Bramwell pointed to the final sentence of the statement. 'She says categorically that she did not see Karl Gough.'

'We don't yet know who was with him. Suppose it was someone *he* knew from the time he was a lodger? Posner would simply think of him as an everyday neighbour and not include him when she was questioned.'

'Possibly.'

'If she wasn't aware of the significance,' Cass insisted, 'just as Tucknell wasn't until he came out with it, it might be that Posner does know something important.'

The receiver still looked doubtful.

'The Bricklayers isn't too much out of my way. I might just happen to stop by for a half.'

Bramwell's face cleared. 'OK. If she's there, don't push too hard. Go easy. We can always try her again.'

'Sure.'

'Hello, what's this?'

Dexter was handing him the fax plus the road map, open at the Aurillac-St Etienne section. 'A definite sighting of our elusive friend. Gough paid a visit to a loading depot situated approximately here, where I've marked it, at roughly fourteen hundred hours today... but apparently nipped off before they could nab him. Destination unknown.'

'Blast!' Bramwell read the fax rapidly.

'At least we know he's in France, sir.'

The receiver was staring at the wall clock. 'What time is it in France? One hour later?'

'Uh-huh.'

'So your average vigilant French cop will be at home by now, celebrating while his missus grills the frog's legs. The point I'm trying to make—this fax has taken three hours to get here. I detect a touch of seasonal delay. We'll send another asking them to beef up their efforts but I doubt whether anyone will study it before Boxing Day.'

'St Nicholas might,' suggested Dexter promptly. 'That's what the French call Father Christmas.'

'Thank you, Dexter. Perhaps you'd like to send the signal? Ask him to set up road blocks with his reindeer.' Bramwell addressed the whole group. 'That last phone call from the SIO, he's changed his mind about Mrs Gough. He wants one of us to be at her bedside when the doctors agree she can be interviewed. That should be early tomorrow morning. Meanwhile, I'm calling off the twenty-four-hour surveillance.' He waved the fax. 'Wherever Gough's headed, he couldn't get back tonight because the ferries will have stopped.'

'Can I do that, interview Mrs Gough?' To Bramwell's surprise Cass looked eager.

'Any particular reason? Not wanting the overtime, are you?'

Cass blushed. 'Relatives living out that way, sir. After talking to Mrs Gough I could occupy myself in the vicinity pending developments. At the end of a phone so to speak.'

Bramwell frowned: was Cass the right man? 'This woman is a tart's daughter. She's not going to be easy... We don't know why she's protecting Gough but there must be a damn good reason.' Cass's enthusiasm didn't waver. 'OK. Be at the hospital by eight o'clock. I'll ask Southend to send that DPW along to keep you company. And Cass, watch out for the mother. If she fancies you, run like hell.'

MR PRINGLE'S shy nature abhorred community singing. His vocal range fluctuated between reedy and gruff but tonight, with a Salvation Army trombone inches from his ear, he had no choice.

Sheet music had been distributed. They were to work their way solidly through 'While Shepherds' to 'O, come all ye' via 'God rest ye' and 'O little'. At the finish there was to be a collection. The SA major warned them what sort. 'We're singing ''Silent Night'' and what could be more silent than a five-pound note?'

Mrs Bignell, resplendent in bronze velvet and gold jewellery, circulated with mince pies. Behind the bar, the landlord was dispensing a hot fluid described as punch. Mr Pringle, his paper hat tucked firmly out of sight, took a deep breath and prepared to let himself go, just a little.

' ''The holly and the...'' '

Voices petered out altogether at the sigh of Charlie Tucknell shouting, 'I'm back... I've got here! Hello, Mavie... Where's the mistletoe? Joe, get Mrs Bignell a G and T.'

To Mr Pringle's astonishment, his lady friend reacted to this unwelcome apparition with spontaneous pleasure.

'Charlie! Where have you sprung from?'

'From me sister's. I got a lift. It came to me this afternoon—why the heck should I put up with it? I don't even *like* her, I never have, not since we were kids.' He gazed round in search of support. 'I mean, how many of you feel the same about your family.'

'I don't know about my sister.' Punch had unloosed one wag's tongue. 'I couldn't stand the wife. That's why I left home.'

The Salvation major tried not to sound disapproving. 'Shall we continue in our praise of the Lord.'

'Hang on a minute, Charlie hasn't got a drink.'

The abstainers waited patiently. When the newcomer had been primed, they picked up their instruments once more.

'Number four on the sheet, ''The Holly and the Ivy''. In three—'

'Excuse me.'

The gradual realisation of why DC Cass might have appeared in their midst produced an uneasy silence.

The landlord asked, 'Yes?'

'Is Miss Posner about?'

Good cheer changed to hostility.

'She wasn't too well, she decided to stay at home. Lila's with her.' Mavis Bignell stared at Cass. 'Why do you want to know?'

'It's my fault, Mavie,' Charlie piped up. 'I told him I'd seen her at Ernest's place…the day he was…you know…'

Betty Fisher was firm. 'He knows that already.' She addressed the officer directly: 'You all do. God knows we've said so often enough. Becky went round to make Ernest's tea.'

Other voices joined in:

'She told you all about it.'

'It upset her, though, after. The shock.'

'She shouldn't be bothered any more, not at her age.'

From the back, one called out, 'She did her duty this morning, her and Lila. They helped you lot with that picture for the television.'

'All right, all right, I'm sorry.' DC Cass made a prudent withdrawal. 'If Miss Posner had been able to chat, I just wanted to check a couple of points with her.'

'We'll tell her,' Betty Fisher said coldly, 'and when she's feeling better, maybe she'll phone.'

Ordering a half of bitter, DC Cass faded to the back of the room and eventually departed. He had phoned the incident room and left a message. Out in the car park, he looked at the stars. It was a sharp night but none was brighter than the rest. If there had been one over Bethlehem, it would probably turn out to be a Scud missile, sent by Iraq.

ON THEIR WAY HOME, Mrs Bignell informed Mr Pringle of her intention to visit Becky Posner. 'We'll take her a cracker and a drop of sherry in the morning. Poor old thing, she's taken the whole business very badly.'

'Yet she had no particular affection for Ernest.'

'Oh, no. It's the shock, that's what's done it. Especially as she may have been one of the last to see him. You know what I think?'

'No?'

'Well...I was wondering if she and Ernest had had words.'

'Ah...'

'It's just guesswork but I don't think she was *keen* to do his tea. He could be rather obstinate and she is a fussy sort of person.'

Mr Pringle thought he understood. 'A difference of opinion over cutlery, something like that?'

'Nothing important. But if she had been a bit short with him... She is very sensitive, you know.'

'We'll visit her in the morning,' he promised, thankful it was nothing more serious, 'and if she seems troubled, no doubt you can put her mind at rest.'

Mrs Bignell hugged his arm. 'Ta, dear. We won't stay long.'

Mr Pringle had had more sherry than usual. 'Stay as long as you like.'

'We have to be back home by twelve. Charlie will be round by then.'

'What!' He'd stopped in his tracks. 'Tucknell?'

'Yes, of course.' In the moonlight, Mrs Bignell smiled cheerfully. 'We couldn't leave him on his own, could we? Not on Christmas Day.'

TEN

MARIE-CHRISTINE MARTIN was preparing for bed when she heard the outer door rattle in the restaurant downstairs. Her son and his girlfriend slept on the ground floor but it was no use expecting them to answer it. Anyway, at this hour, Marie-Christine was curious as to the identity of her caller. She descended slowly, bulky flesh newly released from its corset expanding softly beneath her robe. She swayed languorously on the half-landing as she enjoyed a good scratch. The knock was repeated. 'Hang on . . . I'm coming.'

The small restaurant was narrow with a minuscule bar at one end. The tables, stacked with chairs, were pushed to one side. Marie-Christine padded past them, images of her rotund shape and long grey plait reflected to infinity by the mirrored tiles which covered the opposing walls.

The sign outside, Les Deux Escargots, remained on throughout the night. Variegated yellow and green neon were reflected in the wet pavements and made ghastly shadows on the face pressed up against the glass. Behind Karl, blocking the narrow street, was the dark shape of his empty lorry.

Marie-Christine recognised him. She was not a sentimental woman. Facts about this customer were speedily recalled and systematically ticked off. He paid cash, was quiet and clean. Alexandre had once done a repair for him. In fact, there was nothing she could hold against him. Despite the late hour, if he could afford it, he could stay. An extra pair of hands would be useful tomorrow for she had no compunction in ordering her guests to help when necessary. Without opening the door, she mouthed, 'You want a bed?'

'Please!' Shivering hands were cupped in an urgent appeal.

'I have to charge you extra because it's Christmas.'

Karl stared.

She explained glibly, 'Municipal taxes.'

Bollocks, he thought. He mouthed back, 'How much extra?'

'Four hundred francs.'

Feverishly he worked it out. Over forty quid—bloody hell! He was about to protest when he caught sight of the grim smile. Marie-Christine had got him over a barrel.

'Three hundred.'

'Four.' She held up her fat fingers by way of emphasis.

'Three-fifty.'

She shook her head.

He would have to cash a cheque. He daren't risk offering one to her, she was far too fly. He would have to chance it at a bank as soon as they reopened. She still waited for his answer. He was helpless; the shivering fits which had begun when he changed the tyre had increased. He now felt too ill to argue further; he nodded. She unlocked the door, holding it against the chain.

'In advance. How long do you want to stay?'

'A few days, it depends. I've only got English money. I can't give you more than a hundred quid tonight.'

The rain had turned to sleet. The coldness of it trickled down Karl's spine, numbing him to the core. He was covered in mud after changing the tyre. Now he felt lightheaded. He knew he was in danger of losing his grip. The memory of Sharon refused to disappear, he couldn't fight it any longer. He wanted to curl up in a ball and howl.

Marie-Christine examined each ten-pound note, checking both watermark and metal strip. Only when she was satisfied did she point at the lorry.

'You can't leave that there.'

'I want to take it round to your son's workshop, Marie-Christine.' Karl's teeth were chattering so much he could barely get the words out. 'There's work I need to do on it before I can take another load.'

The jack had slipped in the soft mud. Karl wanted to remove the wheel and check beneath the vehicle for any possible damage.

'I'll get the keys.' She shut the door leaving him outside. With the same slow rhythmic pace she went through the kitchen into the storage area behind and opened the door to her son's room.

There was an interlocking human mound beneath the eiderdown. Marie-Christine took no notice. This girlfriend was a stop-gap who would satisfy Alexandre for the present. She tolerated her, effectively using her as unpaid help in the bar if she arrived in the evening before Alexandre had returned.

Come the New Year the girl would have to go. Her son was ready for marriage and his mother knew just the right fiancée: an only child whose father had an excellent cake shop. Marie-Christine had tested their products over a twelve-month period before reaching a decision.

Alexandre's only interest was the garage, he had no talent for the restaurant. This place would have to be sold and would probably fetch a tidy sum. Marie-Christine was not yet ready to retire. She intended to preside over the cake shop till. The pâtissier would be glad of Madame Martin's expertise and from there she could watch over her future daughter-in-law. Such an investment needed protection for the girl was pretty and Alexandre would be absent much of the time. Marie-Christine was deeply satisfied with her plan—from every point of view it should prove ideal.

Ignoring the figures, now frozen to immobility, she collected the garage keys from the bedside table. Back at the front door she demanded of Karl, 'You remember how to get there? Through the one-way system.'

'I remember.'

She began to wonder if she wasn't being too tender-hearted, the Englishman looked so ill, but she comforted herself: he was obviously exhausted. A good night's sleep was probably all that was required. It would be a chance for Alexandre to charge for the use of his workshop, too; she mustn't deny her son that opportunity. Seeing her keen stare, Karl over-estimated her concern.

'Any chance of something hot when I get back? I haven't eaten since the ferry.'

Her shrug was eloquent. 'It's too late.'

He made a feeble attempt to ingratiate himself. 'It's also Christmas, Marie-Christine.'

She feigned reluctance, remembering the left-over scraps in the kitchen.

'I might manage it. I shall have to charge, if only to cover the electricity.'

Bitch! He needed hot food, he couldn't stop trembling. 'Soup and a bit of bread will do. When I get back.' He heard her slam the door as he scrambled clumsily into his cab. He felt dangerously giddy, as if he'd been driving non-stop for days. His eyes were hot, he'd got double-vision. Ahead, the traffic lights were a blur. He had to shake his head fiercely before the colours would separate.

IT WAS 1:30 a.m. in the incident room before the last line of serious enquiry had been followed up and DS Bramwell declared there was nothing more they could do. They had responded to every likely phone call, alerting police stations up and down the country. Now they must wait for answers to come in. At the end of the trail, with luck, they would learn the identity of the Inkerman Street prowler.

Bramwell was weary enough to agree with the SIO: Gough was still their best hope, when the French finally tracked him down.

Bleary-eyed, the group wished one another Merry Christmas and disappeared into the night. The receiver sent up a guilty prayer that none of their queries would have been answered by the time he phoned in to the duty officer later. He wanted to spend the rest of the day like everyone else in a normal family Christmas. Then he remembered: he hadn't bought a present for his wife.

MR PRINGLE had returned to his home in a state of dudgeon. He hadn't exactly planned what was to happen tomorrow. His imagination had conjured up a pleasant and, until this evening, perfectly plausible sequence of events, beginning with Mrs Bignell unwrapping her parcel, continuing with her consenting to model those delicious garments and ending with her being in full agreement that he should assist in the removal of them.

There was one more possibility, not specifically detailed, more in the nature of an anticipatory roseate glow. But was any of that likely to happen with Charlie Tucknell around? No, it damn well wasn't!

Mr Pringle didn't normally swear but there was no other scope for venting his feelings. He had no cat to kick nor child to berate. Having vented, he fell back on his usual consolation, his pictures. In his study, he lit the gas fire and then went to fetch his cocoa. Upstairs once more, he fell to brooding.

Their presence began to soothe. The knowledge they were hanging there, old friends watching over him, brought peace. Each represented a part of an artist with whom Mr Pringle could feel affinity. Precious fragments purchased during rare rash moments in his life and which now were invaluable in consoling him.

There was one small watercolour of two women facing one another across a café table. The face of one was so animated and vivacious, it reminded him of Mrs Bignell. The other woman was older, more restrained. Mr Pringle took another look to remind himself.

With only the anglepoise illuminating the picture from below, the two faces took on a different aspect. The elder one had more personality tonight and was poised as if about to offer some rebuke to her companion. Both were dressed for summer but the elder wore a long-sleeved dress with a lace collar, the sort of garment Miss Posner favoured.

Mr Pringle guessed her wardrobe was purchased at charity shops. Lace collars were intended to disguise that fact. The extreme poverty which had been revealed allowed for no other choice. Of all of those in Inkerman Street, Rebecca Posner was surely the most impoverished. Not that one would ever guess; appearances were always 'kept up'. Nevertheless it behoved him to take some acceptable item when they visited her tomorrow.

He went below to choose a bottle from the wine rack and added it to the pile of parcels in the hall. Apart from the lingerie, he had of course bought other small tributes for Mrs Bignell: her favourite chocolates (Belgian), a bottle of scent (by Guerlain)—small, of course, but even that sized flacon had been exorbitant.

Had it been a picture, one which he could enjoy, he might have cashed in some of his savings certificates and been a reckless devil. He gave a guilty sigh and rinsed out his mug

at the sink. Mrs Bignell was not a connoisseur. On one of
the occasions when art had been discussed, she had admitted a penchant for crinoline ladies.

Mr Pringle had turned a deaf ear to that suggestion. Instead, he had bestowed on her a delightful eighteenth-
century French print of a girl in a swing. Mrs Bignell had
examined it under a strong light, and disapproved. The girl
wasn't wearing any knickers. Mr Pringle knew already: the
expression in the swain's eyes had told him so.

Before turning off the bedside light, he made a note on his
pad. The inquest had been scheduled for the day after Boxing Day. Mr Pringle intended to be there and needed to
know if it was for the morning or afternoon.

As he waited for sleep to overtake him, Mr Pringle remembered the news item asking if anyone knew the whereabouts of Karl Gough. Many in the Bricklayers were excited
by it. The fact that they actually *knew* the person in question was sufficient to raise the temperature.

He had listened for someone to identify the faceless
prowler but this brought uncertainty. Joe, the landlord,
suggested the identikit resembled Karl himself. Mr Pringle
agreed. It was, after all, the image and garb of a thousand
young men in London these days.

CHRISTMAS DAY had begun, and so far Mrs Berriman was
finding it a trial. Sarah had woken her at dawn, screaming
because of her dirty nappy. Her grandmother had changed
her and stuck a dummy in her mouth but the child spat it out
and continued to yell.

Mrs Berriman's plans didn't include a fractious toddler.
She would do what she had promised—what Sharon had
suggested—and deliver the child to the hospital. It wasn't as
if *she* had any further responsibility. When Sharon first told

her she was pregnant her mother had urged her to get rid of it.

But her efforts to rid herself today were thwarted. Two police officers, one of them the DPW who had been so cheeky, were standing in the hospital reception area. Mrs Berriman hesitated but they had already spotted her.

'Mrs Berriman...' DPW Tunnicliffe transferred her attention to the child. 'Hello... You're Sarah, aren't you?' She bent down, holding out her arms and the child staggered towards her.

Her grandmother watched sourly. 'You wait, my girl. You won't be doing that in a few years' time. Bastards!'

DC Cass introduced himself. 'Good morning, Mrs Berriman. We were about to interview your daughter, with the doctors' permission of course.'

'Oh, yes...'

'We'll go up together, shall we? Detective Policewoman Tunnicliffe and I can wait outside until you've finished.'

It wasn't the way she had planned it at all. She followed reluctantly, the cheeky young DPW carrying Sarah. The child continued to behave as though the policewoman were a friend.

It was worse on the ward. The nurses had tinsel in their hair, singing away as they made the beds. They had opened Sharon's curtains a chink, for her entertainment. Mrs Berriman hung back, not wanting to be seen. DPW Tunnicliffe set the child down and the toddler made a grab for the bedclothes.

Sharon gasped. 'Take her away. I can't stand that.'

The policewoman scooped her up again. 'Sorry, no, of course you can't. I'll wait with her out here, shall I? Until you've had your chat.'

DC Cass sauntered past the chink slowly enough for
Sharon to register his presence. Mrs Berriman went inside
and tugged at the curtains angrily to close them.

Sharon said faintly, 'At least he's better looking than the
last one. What's Sarah doing here? Or you? I meant what I
said, so get out.'

Daylight showed further physical deterioration. Bruising
had developed, the whites of her eyes had a yellow tinge and
the outline of Sharon's face was puffy and unhealthy. Hair
lay lank against the pillow. The only sign of life was in the
eyes.

'Why can't you leave me alone?' she hissed.

Further down the ward, DC Cass murmured to Tunnicliffe, 'Keep them occupied. I'll see what I can glean.' Nodding affably at those nurses who'd gathered to coo at the
child, he drifted back toward the curtains.

'I didn't come to wish you a happy Christmas, what's the
point?'

'Thanks. I asked you a question, Mum. Why is Sarah
here?'

'They made me come up with them. Anyway, I wanted to
know if you'd changed your mind. She kept me awake all of
last night—'

'So put her in a home like I told you.'

Her mother quailed. 'It's the neighbours . . . they talk behind my back as it is. What are they going to say when I tell
them . . . ?'

Sharon's face had crumpled into ugly laughter which
stopped as she began to choke.

Mrs Berriman panicked. 'Nurse! Nurse, come here quick!
Oh, it's you.' She had bumped into DC Cass outside the
curtains. 'Make yourself useful—find a doctor.'

It was unnecessary. Cass stood aside as the nurses converged. There was swift, calm activity: the sheets were

stripped back and the full extent of her daughter's injuries was revealed. Mrs Berriman promptly gagged. She found herself in a chair with Cass urging her to put her head between her knees.

'All those machines she's hooked up to—why is her body bruised like that?'

'Try not to worry. D'you want a bowl?'

'No, I do not!' Mrs Berriman sat up defiantly. There were three nurses beside the bed now. One was regulating the oxygen flow. 'Why are they doing that?'

'To help her breathe, I think.'

'Christ.' Mrs Berriman stared up at Cass, her mascara streaky. 'She looks worse to me today.'

'Why not talk to the doctors?' he urged.

Mrs Berriman immediately looked sullen. 'I didn't come for no lectures, I came to bring Sarah.'

'But what about your daughter?'

Mrs Berriman's eyes were opaque. 'What about her?'

'Mrs Berriman, surely you're concerned? People don't just *fall* and break their necks. Two of them in one day? And Karl Gough just happens to be in the vicinity?'

'What about that other man, the one with no face? It said on the telly you wanted to find him.'

'We do,' Cass assured her. 'We think he may have been an acquaintance of your son-in-law.'

She shrugged. 'Always a loner, Karl. More in love with that articulated lorry than he was with Sharon.' She stood up and tugged at her skirt. 'I'm off.' She indicated the cubicle. 'Ask her what you want to know.'

Cass said quickly, 'What about your granddaughter? You're not intending to *leave* her?'

Mrs Berriman refused to meet his gaze. 'Sharon said she was to go for adoption. You lot sort it out. It's what we pay our taxes for.'

'Gough's her father, he needs to be consulted.'

'Does he? Ask him, then. I expect he'll wash his hands of her as well.'

Cass shouted at her disappearing back: 'As you are doing, you mean?'

Mrs Berriman didn't bother to reply.

MRS BIGNELL welcomed him with such fondness, Mr Pringle's grumpy feelings toward Charlie began to fade.

'He won't be here till just before one,' she assured him, 'that's when we'll have our meal. He's bound to want to stay for tea but after that we shall have the whole evening to ourselves.' She cuddled up. 'Just you and me.'

'When are we going to have our presents?' Mr Pringle asked eagerly.

'Later...'

Did he detect a cautious note?

'When—later? Before Tucknell gets here?' Would there be time for what he had in mind? Mr Pringle thought not. At his age, to be under pressure did not help.

'We can decide when we get back. Leave your parcel under the tree. My word,' Mavis watched as he brought forth his gifts, 'you've been spoiling me.'

'I hope so.'

'Wasting your money?' she sighed happily.

'Oh, no!' Every penny would have been worth it, Mr Pringle felt confident. Seeing his expression, she gave him a squeeze.

'Come on. We'd better go round to see Becky before we change our minds!'

It wasn't far. Inevitably, during the walk, they discussed the television appeal. 'Lila phoned me this morning. They both watched last night. Becky was terribly upset.'

'Why? They knew what to expect.'

'I think it brought it home to her, what had happened. According to Lila she's frightened the police will try and make her identify the prowler. She's bothered at the thought of having to be there, at a line-up.'

'That could happen, I suppose. Once they have a suspect.' Mr Pringle thought it more likely they would ask Lila or Reg Wolfe. 'If it would distress her too much, I'm sure Miss Posner's doctor would suggest they ask the others.'

'You tell her,' Mavis urged, 'it might calm her down.'

As always, he was depressed at the sight of so many doorbells. Mavis spoke cheerily into the grill. 'Merry Christmas, Becky. We finally got here.'

The front door was released. Inside, Mrs Bignell led the way across the smelly hall and up the stairs. 'It's not very nice, is it? You haven't been here before, of course.'

'No. When Miss Posner consulted me it was at my house.'

'I feel sorry for her.' Mavis had lowered her voice as they passed by graffiti and scarred doors which concealed so many stunted lives. 'For all her airs and graces, she could never have imagined she would end up like this. She once told me her family had had a really lovely house abroad. Here we are.' She gave a smart rat-a-tat. 'It's us, dear.'

Mr Pringle was left with the invalid in the tiny bedroom while Mrs Bignell bustled away to prepare a tempting snack. He tried to make light conversation but Miss Posner was not in the mood. He decided it was better to let her talk. He sat back to listen to her incoherent meanderings.

'I do so dislike Christmas…it reminds me of…so many things. Were you happy as a child? I had an elder brother. I was his pet. Oh, the presents he used to bring when he came home!' Her hand in its ragged sleeve touched her neck as if searching for jewels. 'Then, just before Christmas one year, I heard he was dead. My parents also. That's another reason I hate it so.'

Mr Pringle recalled that her brother had died in a camp. She was obviously reliving the nightmare. He murmured, 'It must have been very frightening at the time.'

Miss Posner emerged from the past. To his sensitive ear it sounded as though she was forcing herself to be brisk. 'A long time ago. One should not dwell on bad things. I arrived with no baggage. Can you imagine what it is to be female and have absolutely nothing? If only I'd had the foresight to wear my fur coat, eh?' He smiled, as he was expected to. 'And boots! That first winter in England was so cold!'

'I remember during the war one bitter winter when none of us had enough coal,' Mr Pringle said.

Thin hands plucked at the blanket. 'But now we have a sufficiency so what does it matter? We survive.'

Mr Pringle wondered if he dare suggest Miss Posner apply for her supplementary benefit to be reviewed, but how to say that without offending her pride? The opportunity passed as Mrs Bignell entered and set before her a dainty tray.

'Just a snack to keep you going, till Lila gets here.'

'Oh, Mavis ... what beautiful china!'

Mr Pringle recognised it from the shelf in Mrs Bignell's glass cabinet.

'I thought you might enjoy using it ... I always say food tastes better from a bone china plate ...' Miss Posner was distracted by the design. 'Is this Spode?'

'To tell you the truth, I've never really looked.' Mrs Bignell had returned with a small electric fire. 'There we are.'

'Oh, I don't need that, Mavis. I'm quite warm.'

'You keep it on for today.' Mrs Bignell patted her hand, murmuring, 'It's all right, we've fed the meter.'

Miss Posner had flushed at the charitable gesture. Now she indicated the tray. 'There's far too much, I'm not very hungry.'

'Becky...' Mrs Bignell perched on the bed. 'I shall sit here and watch you eat every scrap, I'm warning you.'

Miss Posner veered between pride and humility and finally gave in.

'You're very kind. I had hoped ... a little bit extra ...'

She flushed but Mrs Bignell nodded she'd understood. 'You thought you might win a share of the bequest? I'm sure it was your turn. I heard several people suggest your name. That wretched young Karl.'

'No, Ernest Clare would not have included me.' Miss Posner had recovered her poise. 'He only gave money to lower-class people who were bound to be grateful.'

Mr Pringle stayed silent until he and Mrs Bignell had regained the street. There he commented, 'That was an astonishing remark. Do you realise, it's the first time I've heard anyone criticise Clare since this whole business began?'

Mrs Bignell declared the reason was obvious. 'I told you Becky Posner was la-di-dah. You have to be stuck-up to turn down generosity. By the way, you owe me three quid.'

'What for?'

'Half of what I put in her meter. Sinful the way landlords rig them, isn't it?'

ELEVEN

LATER THAT DAY, in the women's ward, DC Cass had taken over the task of persuading Sharon Gough to take medicine. His plans had gone awry. The 'relative' he'd been hoping to visit in Southend had moved in with a rugby forward who hadn't sounded particularly welcoming. Better stay here and make himself useful; the nurses didn't object.

The immobile figure was unnerving. Rigidly fixed within the network of cables and collar, the bloodshot yellow-white eyes were the only things which could move. These swivelled to watch him. Sharon's hands—one flopped palm down, the other dangling over the edge—lay as the nurse had left them, as if they were completely disconnected from the only living part, her head.

Cass lifted the left hand to a safer position, placing it carefully alongside her body. Her flesh was clammy. He hoped his reaction hadn't been noticed. Sharon gazed cynically as he took off his jacket, hung it neatly over the chair and looked round for a towel.

'Why stop there? Take off your pants, come on in, help yourself. If you can stand the smell. I shan't feel a thing, of course.'

He spread the towel beneath her chin to catch any spillage, saying breezily, 'Time was, I would've accepted that invitation.'

'Time was.' It was bitter. It was such an effort for her to speak.

He said harshly, 'Stop feeling sorry for yourself,' and regretted it immediately. 'The smell is barely noticeable.' He checked the level in the bag. 'There's scarcely anything in this, that's why. Do you really want them to change it?'

'Why bother?' she said slowly. 'I'm dead from the neck down, aren't I? I could see it when you touched me.' Her lip curled. 'You'd never make a nurse. They don't let it show.' She saw the feeding cup. 'What the hell's that?'

'Medicine. About five mil. Try and get it down.' She closed her eyes by way of refusal. 'Suit yourself.' Cass put the cup back on top of the locker.

Sharon waited for him to leave, but he didn't seem to be in any hurry. 'Piss off.'

'Not yet.' He settled himself on the regulation plastic chair.

'Get back where you belong, pig.' She opened her eyes and saw he was reading the medical notes from the foot of the bed. 'Stop that! You've no business...'

He replaced the clipboard unhurriedly. 'I was trying to find out what that stuff's called,' he indicated the cup, 'as you're interested. I'd ask a nurse but they've got their hands full. Crash on the A13. Two killed, four in Casualty. Some of them will be arriving in here after they've been patched up.'

'What do I care?' She changed the subject abruptly: 'Where's Sarah? What's that bitch done with her?'

'Your mother has gone home. She refused to take Sarah with her so Detective Policewoman Tunnicliffe took her up to the children's ward. There's a playroom there where the nurses can keep an eye... till we sort something out.'

'She'll have to go in a home.'

'So you keep saying. You're right, though. She might. As a temporary measure.'

'Temporary?'

'DPW Tunnicliffe has gone over to Leigh to see if she can persuade your mother to change her mind. If she refuses, is there any other member of the family we can contact?'

'No one.' An imperceptible hesitation before she said, 'We haven't got any *family*.'

Cass picked up the cup once more. 'Try a sip. It's not poison.'

'God, if only it were! I've told everyone I don't want any drugs. It's my life—I want out.'

'You'd better make a will.'

'Bastard!'

DC Cass leaned forward. 'Listen, Sharon, I don't give a monkey's what you or Gough want, whether you want to protect him, whether he comes back here to finish the job— but when we catch up with Karl, with or without your co-operation, he'll be put away. If you're not going to take any medicine, I'm sure your wish will be granted, too. Very soon. But where does that leave young Sarah, eh? With one old tart of a grandmother who won't even give her a home. So make a will. Give your child something to remember you by. Let her know you cared.'

She stared at him for a moment. The sick eyes were too difficult to fathom, he didn't know whether he'd made an impact or not. Part of him was ashamed for being so brutal.

'I'm getting worse, aren't I?'

He'd overheard one remark about incipient kidney failure. He couldn't be that cruel. Instead he said quietly, 'Where there's life, there's always hope. But you're bound to get worse if you refuse medication.'

He waited. Her eyelids fluttered down. Against the pillow, her face was defenceless to his scrutiny. Her breathing was so minimal, he wondered if she were already drifting into the coma they were expecting.

Should he call a nurse? The various traces on the monitors appeared to be holding their pattern but if she really had lost the will to live...? He bent close to her ear.

'Sharon, I'm leaving now. Before I go would you please tell me what happened? If you don't, one of us will have to keep coming back to pester you, we have no choice.'

'No.' Then, finally, 'There's no way I can tell you...I can't tell anyone.'

He didn't understand but he accepted it.

'OK. I'll see that the welfare people are taking care of Sarah before I go. They'll let you know what's to happen. By the way, were there any Christmas presents for her?' He waited for the eyelids to open. Perhaps Sharon hadn't understood? 'Had you bought her a toy or something? We could drive over to your place and fetch it?' Apparently, there weren't.

As he left the ward, Cass found himself wondering if she did manage to die, which murder Gough would be charged with, or whether it would be one murder and one manslaughter. Why the hell couldn't she say he'd attacked her? It wasn't as if it would make any difference to him.

MAVIS BIGNELL was regretting her impulsive gesture toward Charlie Tucknell. The temperature began to drop as soon as he arrived. It was perhaps unfortunate that he should have caught sight of Mr Pringle wearing her old pinny. Mr Pringle's Christmas task had always been to peel the potatoes and sprouts, it was only natural he should want to protect his best flannels. To spare his feelings further, however, Mavis had thrust her own apron at Charlie and demanded that he made the bread sauce. This had been a worse mistake—Charlie was not a domesticated animal.

She bit her tongue when he dropped the first bottle of milk and spilt the breadcrumbs over the gas flame, but when he broke her mixing bowl she banished him to the dining room. 'You can set the table for me instead.'

Charlie was unabashed. 'I can manage that,' he said cheerfully. 'In fact it's what I'm used to. My late wife wouldn't let me into her kitchen. Thank God for microwaves, that's what I say.'

Mavis showed him the cutlery drawer, gave him the mats plus her clean white cloth and returned to the kitchen. Mr Pringle, exuding martyrdom, was on his knees with the dustpan and brush. The air was suffused with the unpleasant odour of burnt crumbs.

'There are still one or two shards of pottery—'

'Don't bother about them now. It's not important.'

'It will be if you kick your shoes off and wander about in here,' Mr Pringle said grimly. 'I don't know what it is about port, Mavis. After a glassful or two, your shoes are seldom attached to your feet.'

'It is odd,' she agreed. 'Gin makes me want to cry. Port always goes to my toes. I need to wiggle them.' He made a mental note not to offer her any until Charlie had gone. They busied themselves with the final stages of the meal, their whispered conversation increasing in acrimony.

'I couldn't *not* invite him, could I? Not at Christmas.'

'Next year I shall buy him the rail ticket to Kingston-upon-Thames as a gift.'

'He's hoping his sister will be dead by then.'

'In which case, he can go over there to comfort his brother-in-law. Whatever happens, Mavis, I do not want him coming here.'

'It's my house—I shall invite who I like!'

There was a warbling call from the dining room. 'I've set the table. Do you two love-birds need any more help?'

Mavis called out, 'No, thanks. Just dishing up.'

'What a disgusting expression! I'm sure he'd had a few before he arrived this morning. I smelt it as you opened the front door.'

'Oh, pour yourself another sherry and pipe down. Is this enough breast for you?'

Normally he would have responded, 'For the time being!' Today he said curtly, 'Ample, thank you.'

'This is Charlie's helping. Don't let him pour the gravy himself. I want that cloth to last through Boxing Day.'

Mr Pringle was immediately suspicious.

'Why? Have you invited someone for tomorrow as well?'

'Never you mind.'

'Mavis!'

'Only friends,' she said defiantly, 'that's all. Now take the veg in and try and be pleasant. Charlie's making an effort. He did bring us a bottle.'

'Hock,' Mr Pringle replied dismissively. 'No doubt you can find a use for it in one of your trifles.'

The worry that had been dormant pushed itself to the forefront of Mrs Bignell's consciousness. 'We'll have our presents after he's gone, shall we?'

'Most definitely!'

But Charlie had other ideas. As they joined him in the dining room, he beamed. 'I saw the little pile under the tree. I've added my contributions. They're not much.' He shook his head at Mr Pringle. 'You're a difficult person to buy presents for but I had this box of hankies left over. Violet gave me them last year. I never opened the packet, they're quite fresh.' He smiled at Mavis in a far more intimate manner. 'I'd already got you a little something, Mavis. I forgot to give it you on Christmas Eve because of Ernest. That business really upset me, you know. When I got home yesterday I found I'd not paid the gas nor the electric. I hope they don't cut me off.'

Curiosity made Mr Pringle comment, 'How thankful you must be that Miss Posner was the last to see Ernest alive. Though frail, I don't believe she has grasped the significance, nor should she be worried. The police will obviously eliminate her. You, however, must have been concerned. Perhaps you thought the police might treat you differently?'

He waited for Charlie to react. To his chagrin, Mavis brought the conversation back to Christmas.

'You haven't said what my present is, Charlie.'

Rheumy eyes looked at her fondly as he eased out half a sprout from behind his upper denture. 'I want it to be a surprise. I'd like to watch you open it when you two have yours. Of course mine won't be anything like what he's bought for you...' Charlie jabbed his fork for emphasis. A morsel of turkey deposited itself on Mr Pringle's cuff. 'He'll have got you something really special.'

Mr Pringle's expression might have deterred a less loquacious person but Charlie was determined to spread a little more happiness.

'You're a lucky man. You probably don't realise but when you two leave the Bricklayers of an evening, there's usually a bit of speculation.' Mr Pringle cringed, hugely. 'When you first appeared on the scene, some of us thought you were taking advantage of a beautiful widow lady.' He paused to bestow a wink on Mrs Bignell and cackled, 'We'd all wanted to do the same, mind. I mean, who wouldn't?' and savoured the sight of his hostess, now nervously fingering an earring, as he raised his glass to her. 'The day she appeared behind that bar, there wasn't a man there who didn't think Ay-aye! and wonder if he stood a chance. But none of us did because you came along. And what I mean to say is'— Charlie was well in his stride now—'who would have thought *you* would have been the one?'

He waited but no one picked up the challenge.

'When you thought about it after, I expect you were surprised an' all. But there you go... there's no accounting for sexual attraction between the species. I saw this programme on the television, about the coypu—'

'More stuffing?' It was perhaps not the most felicitous of interruptions. Mrs Bignell felt extremely hot under her pleated silk dress.

'I don't mind if I do, Mavie.' Charlie's plate tipped dangerously. She took it from him and added two sausagemeat balls. These suddenly assumed a different aspect and she quickly veiled them beneath a decorous layer of gravy.

'So,' Charlie turned from one to the other, satisfied he had raised the level of enjoyment, and returned to the matter under discussion, 'you've neither of you any idea what's in each other's parcels? Ee, fancy being able to keep secrets at our age!'

Mr Pringle was furious: this fool was at least five years older, probably five and a half. How dare he include him in the same bracket!

Charlie, masticating with obvious relish, hadn't finished. 'Wait till I tell them at the Bricklayers. And I'll be able to tell them what those secrets were, won't I? Because you're going to let me watch you unwrap them.'

Mrs Bignell, increasingly anxious, managed to dimple palely. 'I'm sure, whatever they are, it's the kind thought behind them which counts the most...at least, I hope we all feel the same about that. Cheers, both of you.'

Mr Pringle was trying to decipher this enigmatic statement when he noticed Charlie gulping the wine.

It had been a particularly expensive claret, selected with loving care. The helping for Charlie Tucknell had, it was true, been on the mean side for Mr Pringle had anticipated a full half-share rather than a third and this thought had stayed his hand. He watched with dismay as the unwanted guest extended his empty glass, declaring, 'You two eat like fighting cocks and this is a bit of all right as well. I wouldn't say no to a drop more.'

Fifteen quid wasted, Mr Pringle thought with murder in his heart, poured down the maw of a bloody peasant! To compound his felony, Charlie burped.

'Pardon me,' he announced loudly. 'Better out than in, as they say.'

'There is hock, if you would prefer? The bottle you brought, in fact.'

'No, no. You two keep that. I wanted to express my appreciation. You can let in the New Year with it. To tell you the truth, I prefer the taste of this one. Beaujolais Nouveau, isn't it?'

Mr Pringle replied through gritted teeth, 'No, it's not.'

'It's the same shaped bottle,' Charlie observed innocently. 'Same colour. Joe got some of that in this year. I tried it. Tasted like paint-stripper. What d'you call this then?'

Because he could no longer control his feelings, Mr Pringle exhibited the label silently. Charlie took the bottle and put on an intelligent expression.

'Very nice.' He thrust the neck too close to a nostril. 'Got a nice pong as well.' He remembered the right word— 'Fruity'—and added a touch more to his glass. 'It's amazing how much less there is in a bottle these days.' And handing the remnant back, 'Personally, I blame the EEC. Your very good health, both of you.'

Mrs Bignell decided privately not to douse the Christmas pudding with brandy. She might need the restorative for Mr Pringle after Charlie had gone.

'I MUST GET UP. I must go and phone Lee—' Sharon woke with a start. She had been dreaming but she wasn't alone. There was no privacy in this place. The bossy staff nurse was back on duty, checking the valve on a new saline drip. Another nurse had pulled back the covers and was attending to the lower part of her body. Realisation of her situation was abrupt, humiliating and painful.

Sharon whispered, 'You can pull the fucking thing out of my arm. I want to die.' Speaking had become more difficult. Her imagination was playing tricks; it felt as though she had an enormous weight pressing down, squeezing the air from her lungs.

The staff nurse was offended. Hadn't she befriended this particular patient as well as defending her from the police?

'You will die soon enough—we all will. Meanwhile this stays in.'

'Where's the doctor? I don't want any more medicine.'

The staff nurse entered details of the drip and replaced the clipboard before replying, 'I'll make a note. You can see the doctor tomorrow, those on duty have got their hands full. There's plenty worse off than you today. Meanwhile, if you want to chat...'—she looked at Sharon speculatively—'there's always Father Gibson.'

'Fuck off!'

'He's been playing with Sarah upstairs.' Her professional eye had noted the various changes in the patient. Now she murmured something to her colleague and moved out of Sharon's line of vision.

Sharon whispered fretfully, 'What's going on?' The other nurse peeled off her gloves and began to replace the bedcovers. 'Tell me!'

'We think someone should come and have a look at you,' the second admitted.

Eyes glittered in the pallid, decaying face; not long now, thought Sharon triumphantly.

IN A SMALL chilly room above Les Deux Escargots, Marie-Christine Martin waited impatiently for her neighbour to finish his examination. 'Well?'

'Madame...' The gesture toward the figure on the bed was eloquent. 'I am a pharmacist. This young man needs properly qualified medical help.'

Marie-Christine, forced into a corner, tried persuasion. 'Monsieur Rueg, you've known us a long time, since I became a widow in fact, struggling to make a living for myself and Alexandre.' She paused but Monsieur Rueg was expressionless. 'These few rooms that I let occasionally. Very occasionally. When the drivers whose vehicles Alexandre attends to ask if he knows of any accommodation...' There were small signs of impatience from the pharmacist. She finished rapidly. 'The income from these rooms, minuscule though it is—'

'Has not been declared?'

Marie-Christine nodded reluctantly.

'Ah.'

'Dr Maquet—an excellent man—is not someone I feel I could trust.' Monsieur Rueg agreed; the doctor would see it as his duty to report his findings to those in authority.

They both listened to a crescendo of noise from below. Downstairs, those neighbours including Monsieur Rueg who had chosen to take their Christmas lunch here today, had reached a noisy stage. He experienced a spurt of annoyance that Madame Martin should involve him in this instead of allowing him to enjoy his meal.

He did a swift calculation. If she had been letting these rooms ever since she took over the restaurant—what, fifteen years or so? And if the authorities were to discover the fact... The knowledge began to warm the cockles of his heart. He could dine here free for months! Then he caught sight of Karl Gough and sobered up. 'It's a bad fever, maybe a virus, there could be complications. He doesn't look too good to me.'

'You can give him something to bring the temperature down,' she insisted. 'I know him. He's young, strong. It's only rest that he needs—'

'He needs qualified help,' Monsieur Rueg said acidly, 'but if that is not to be made available, I cannot take responsibility. I shall deny ever having seen the fellow.'

Marie-Christine nodded. The Englishman was obviously quite sick. My God, she would make him pay for this afterwards. Imagine having to risk her livelihood because of... Memory came back, of the contents of his wallet, examined this morning when Karl's delirium was obvious.

'Merde!'

'Madame!'

She tried to cover her gaffe with a smile. It wasn't successful. Coldly, Monsieur Rueg began to list the conditions for Karl's survival.

'You will need to increase the temperature of this room considerably, madame. It is far too cold. A feverish patient will toss aside the bedcovers, he must be kept warm twenty-four hours a day.'

'But of course.' She gestured at the radiator which hadn't been switched on. 'Such young men don't normally require...' Her voice faltered. Monsieur Rueg had her future in his hands.

'He will also need constant nursing. Liquids, plenty of them. I would also recommend a camomile tisane every four hours or so, to enable him to sleep more peacefully. His body must be sponged, his clothing changed, he can't be left to lie in his own sweat. He has become dehydrated. The balance of the body, the various salts, et cetera have become disturbed. Note the face, the rapid breathing. You say he has been delirious and shouting for his wife—this young man is seriously ill, madame.'

Marie-Christine didn't know whether to believe him but she couldn't risk ignoring his advice.

'Alexandre must come with me to the pharmacy immediately. I will give him the medicine but I will tell you the dosage, madame.' She understood. Nothing in writing to connect the estimable Monsieur Rueg with a possible corpse.

'I shall take full responsibility.'

'I fear, madame, you have no other choice, given the circumstances.'

The business with Alexandre didn't take more than a quarter of an hour. Monsieur Rueg was back at his table as the café-fines were being served. There was no bill and when he donned his coat to leave the second time, he found alongside it a litre bottle of cognac. He raised his hat gravely. Marie-Christine was now presiding from behind the bar which meant Alexandre and that girl of his must have been delegated to look after the sick man upstairs.

'An excellent lunch, madame. My compliments.'

'Au revoir, Monsieur Rueg. Come back soon.

Oh, I will, he thought. But not for a week or so. Give her time to rid herself of the problem, one way or another.

THERE WAS AN uneasy atmosphere in Mrs Bignell's living room. Lunch was over, they had washed up, watched the Queen, decided not to bother with James Bond and now all three stared into the fire. There was nothing left except the presents.

'If you two would rather be alone, I can take a hint,' said Charlie, who couldn't.

'Oh, no, no!'

'Not at all.'

But Charlie had begun to work things out. 'You'd planned to be by yourselves, I realise that. On your own.'

'We're very pleased you could come.' Mrs Bignell was utterly insincere. 'There was far too much turkey for two.'

But not enough claret! Mr Pringle's mouth tightened. Mavis nudged him. He forced himself to say the words: 'Why don't we open our parcels?'

Charlie brightened. 'I wanted to see Mavie's face when she opens mine.'

'I'm afraid,' Mr Pringle began awkwardly, 'that we have made no provision—'

'Yes, we have,' Mavis said quickly. 'I remembered I had the very thing put by.' She went out and returned bearing packages. 'This is for you, Charlie.'

'Ooh, I say!' It was wrapped in elegant paper, Mr Pringle guessed it had been intended for him. Mrs Bignell's expressive look confirmed it.

'I hardly like to open it, it looks so nice,' said Charlie, but he did and Mr Pringle was consumed with jealousy: dark blue pyjamas with red piping round collar and cuff. On one of their shopping excursions he had remarked how smart he would feel wearing those. Mavis had obviously gone back to purchase them—and they weren't cheap. Now this wonderful surprise had been sacrificed!

Charlie stroked them lovingly. 'They're really special, aren't they? Thanks ever so much, both of you. I shall think of you every time I put them on.'

Could he insist Charlie bequeath them to him? The fool had stuffed himself, had drunk too much, surely it wouldn't be long before he had a coronary?

'I shall cherish this as well.' Charlie ran his finger over the hastily scribbled, 'To Charlie, with all good wishes from us both, Mavis.' He leered at her, 'Will you open mine now?'

Mr Pringle steeled himself, rightly so, for when Mavis had unwrapped the parcel, inside was a pair of garish, frilly knickers. If it was the thought that counted, he was prepared to name both his seconds and his choice of weapon.

Aware of the delicate nature of her dilemma, Mrs Bignell did her best. 'My goodness, these are rather saucy, Charlie.'

'They told me Joan Collins has a pair, similar. There was a matching brassière only I wasn't certain of the size.'

Had Mrs Bignell divulged that most precious piece of information, Mr Pringle would have slain her as well. As an intimation of the strength of his feelings, he coughed.

Charlie said anxiously, 'You don't mind, do you, Mr P.?'

'Hrrm.'

'Just a bit of fun.'

'Harumph!'

'Got a tickle, dear?'

A surge of blood swept upwards as he gripped the arms of his chair.

'Where's one for you?' Charlie asked kindly. 'Pass one over, Mavis. There you are. From me.'

The handkerchiefs, bright red with an embroidered Santa in the corner, were in a cellophane pack. The price, plus the original message, had been obliterated with biro.

'I don't know where my sister finds them,' he sighed, 'they're always the same. Be careful in the wash. They turn everything pink.'

Mr Pringle's blood pressure returned to a safer level when Mavis unwrapped her perfume. She went into raptures over the chocolates. His sensitive antennae decided such an effusion excessive but when she offered them to Charlie, he felt bound to protest. That small box had cost ten pounds. With the lid off—without resorting to his slide-rule—good grief! Politeness disappeared.

'Those were *all* intended for you,' he said sharply.

'I'd much rather share.' Mrs Bignell sounded edgy.

'Isn't there another present for Mr P.?' Charlie was determined to be fair. 'He's had mine. Where's yours to him?'

They were surprised to see Mrs Bignell check her watch. 'Goodness, I hadn't noticed . . . I'll just pop the kettle on, shall I?'

'Shall I fetch it?' asked Charlie. 'Is it still under the tree?'

'It's in the hall cupboard.' To Mr Pringle, she sounded reluctant.

'It must be big then,' Charlie said happily. 'Let's go and find it.'

It was a heavy, oblong box.

Mrs Bignell hovered nervously. 'Perhaps you'd better open it out here.'

'Certainly. I must confess, I haven't the least idea what it can be.' Mr Pringle unknotted the string methodically.

Charlie was impressed with the size. 'I hope you didn't have to carry it far, Mavie.'

'Quite a long way, yes,' she said bravely. 'It turned out to be larger than I'd expected.' Mr Pringle caught the vibes through the back of his neck. 'It wasn't like the photograph, either.' His expectation was at an all-time low as he stripped away the paper and read aloud,

'"For the busily executive, to relieve him from stain, stress and crumple".' His voice rose in disbelief. 'Mavis, I was never an executive!'

'No, well . . . it's only words, isn't it?'

'Made in Czechoslovakia,' Charlie announced from further down the label. 'I think they must mean "strain", don't

you?' They removed the lid and he gazed at the contents.
'What is it, exactly?'

'It's a musical trouser press,' Mavis said weakly. 'I
thought it might be handy because you don't like pressing
your trousers.'

'Musical, eh?' Charlie was eager. 'Shall we assemble it,
Mr P.?'

Despite his misgivings, Mr Pringle was touched to think
his beloved had gone to so much trouble. However, when
the component parts were spread out, uncertainty returned.

'An unusual shape.'

'I've never seen one like it,' Charlie agreed. 'Sturdy,
though: solid metal. It's probably from one of those Warsaw part factories where they used to make tanks. Are these
the feet?'

'I'll get the tea.' Mavis retreated to the kitchen, calling, 'If
you want to try it out, there's an old pair of trousers upstairs.'

'The first thing we need'—Charlie had found the end of
the cable—'is a plug and a screwdriver. Has she got a spare
plug?'

'I used it for the fairy lights.'

He contemplated the Christmas tree. 'Yes, well, they
don't take much. We could wire them in on the same circuit. Where are the instructions?'

There was a single sheet of paper with short paragraphs
in Finnish, Japanese, Taiwanese, German, Spanish and, finally, uncertain English. Charlie was contemptuous: 'We'll
manage somehow.'

The screwdriver was too large. When the plug was finally
dismantled, Mr Pringle was a little disturbed by the cavalier manner in which he began to wind the various strands
together.

'I thought colours were supposed to be a European standard nowadays?'

'Well, yes...there you have it: European. This is Czechoslovakian. Blimey, this is a bit old-fashioned. How long has she had these lights?'

'Since before my time,' Mr Pringle admitted.

'Read me those instructions again?'

'"Attention must be paid comma to the earthing comma and the living wires."'

'In your European standard,' Charlie announced, 'your actual live wire is brown but here we have no brown.'

'Why not?'

'Because your Czechoslovaks have not got the right colour plastic presumably. However, we have got your black, orange and purple.'

'Purple?' Mr Pringle wondered if he'd had one too many sherries. 'Not exactly *imperial* purple.'

'Browny red?'

'Browny red.'

'So our yellow must belong with their communist orange.' Mr Pringle wasn't confident enough to dispute it. 'And their black with our brown. All that remains is to put the plug back together... Ouch! Hasn't Mavie got a smaller screwdriver?'

'She prefers that size because she can use it to open the cornflour tin.'

Charlie struggled and finally declared himself satisfied. He tugged at the two strands of cable. 'There we are, nice and tight. Where are those trousers?'

Mr Pringle went to find them and Mavis emerged to ask how many sugars.

'You can have the honour of switching on, Mavie.'

'You do it.' Relief that the gift hadn't been dismissed outright was enough to dispel earlier doubts. 'The musical box was a special extra. They had to send away for the tune I wanted. I knew he wouldn't like "Lara's Theme".'

'More a Richard Clayderman fan, our Mr P.,' Charlie suggested judiciously but Mrs Bignell wasn't having that.

'You wait and see.'

Mr Pringle returned brandishing his gardening cords. 'Wasn't there something about water?'

'Yes, here we are.' Charlie read the phrase carefully, '"For steaming comma add water to tupe."'

'Tupe?'

'They might mean "tube"?'

'In here, perhaps?'

'Just a little drop, to see how we get on. It's a pity they don't include an illustration.'

Mr Pringle poured a quarter of a pint into the chrome pipe. The trousers were threaded in, the wing-nuts tightened. Charlie plugged it in to the wall socket and asked, 'Do we have lift-off?'

The Christmas tree lights went out with a loud *Phut!*

'Oh dear. I'm sorry about that.'

'Listen, listen...' In the gloom, Mavis strained to hear. 'The musical box has started.' She began to sing along. '"My bonnie lies over the ocean..."'

Charlie sniffed suddenly. 'There must be mud on those trousers.'

'"My bonnie lies over the sea..."'

'I can hear water boiling—is the kettle still on?'

'No, it's coming from the machine. From the tupe—pipe.'

'"My bonnie lies over the ocean..."'

'Ought it to glow like that?'

'"Oh, bring back my bonnie—"'

The explosion blew the metal plates apart. Mr Pringle found himself sitting several feet from his former position. He could hear someone screaming. Above the electric socket, the wallpaper developed a long black snake following the line of the cable which then began to smoulder. Charred fragments of corduroy floated down from the ceiling, landing on the tinder dry tree which burst into flames.

Charlie Tucknell entreated them not to panic. He raced into the kitchen, grabbed the tray and hurled the three cups of tea on to the fire. Red hot metal hissed as steam rose upwards and Mavis Bignell finally lost control. 'Those were part of a tea set, you—you cretin!'

As he dialled 999, Mr Pringle felt a glow of happiness. With her own lips he had heard Mrs Bignell declare she never wanted to see Charlie Tucknell again. It might be a high price to pay—wallpaper and carpet were ablaze—but providing they survived, he would now have her all to himself.

THE FIRE SERVICE were extremely thorough. Thick foam covered familiar objects, carpeting squelched underfoot and the fire chief admitted his lads had been keen. As they trooped off into the night, Charlie was persuaded he could be of no further assistance. Torch in hand, Mrs Bignell retired upstairs to pack, leaving the rivals alone.

'I suppose she'll be moving in with you.'

Mr Pringle was not a man to bear a grudge. 'It would seem sensible until the power can be restored.' Charlie looked downcast, so he added magnanimously, 'It wasn't all your fault.'

'I know it bloody wasn't!' Charlie was incensed. 'It wasn't me wired those flamin' Christmas tree lights for a start.'

Wisely, Mr Pringle chose to ignore the jibe. 'I fear she may have invited a few friends round to tea tomorrow.'

Charlie pulled on his old anorak. 'I know, I was one of 'em. If I see the others, I'll let them know.'

'Thanks.'

'I'll just collect me pyjamas.'

In the living room, he found the soggy box. 'Were these intended for you? She didn't have time to buy me anything, did she?'

'She wanted you to have them,' Mr Pringle replied nobly. 'She's inscribed the gift to that effect.'

Charlie remained unconvinced. 'You're a lucky man, you know that, don't you?'

Amid the wreckage, Mr Pringle acknowledged the fact gracefully. 'Extremely fortunate.'

TWELVE

IF THE DUTY OFFICER was surprised to see DS Bramwell turn up on Christmas evening rather than phone, he gave no sign. He summarised the results so far.

'We haven't had much response. What one would expect, of course. Tomorrow should be better. Another report from France, though. A follow-up.'

'Thanks. I'll be at my extension if anything comes through.'

'Right.'

The incident room was dark, silent and, without human activity to disguise its sordidness, a squalid retreat; to himself, Bramwell acknowledged that's what it was. He switched on his desk lamp and studied the new document. Although the French had lost sight of Gough they had been thorough in their questioning. They had interviewed the depot manager and the driver to whom Gough had spoken. Both had identified the faxed photograph.

The Englishman had not been able to find a load. He appeared eager to depart in any direction but mentioned Spain in particular. He also appeared unfamiliar with the area around Le Puy and had been seen studying a map. Checks on southern routes out of the town had not produced further sightings. Regrettably, it was thought that Gough might no longer be in the area. Further instructions would be acted upon as soon as these had been received.

DS Bramwell was convinced. He picked up his phone.

'This trace is our man. He was seen again in southern France yesterday. He must still be over there, the ferries don't start again till midnight tonight, do they?'

'I don't think so, no.'

Bramwell glanced at the clock. He guessed the duty officer was doing the same.

'We'd better put out an alert to the ports. He could decide to come back but, judging by this, he's hoping to stay out of sight. What about our prowler, any more on him?'

'The usual rubbish. Nothing worth following up. D'you want the details?'

'Not particularly.'

'One woman from Barnsley swore blind the prowler was the Santa Claus who made an improper suggestion to her little boy on Christmas Eve.'

'He could be, he's versatile. Our three witnesses couldn't even agree what he looked like. I'm going to phone the SIO then I'm off. I'll be at my home number if anything does crop up.'

'Understood.'

The SIO was not at home. Bramwell delivered his report to his answering machine then switched off his light and walked downstairs, followed by the echo of his footsteps.

He hadn't needed to come, it was just an excuse. He gazed for a moment at the empty, silent office blocks surrounding the police station. Seven floors up there was a brightly lit window. Had that poor sucker forgotten to buy his wife a present? Had his mother-in-law rubbed his nose in it? 'Oh, forget it.' Bramwell tugged at his seat-belt in futile temper. Alison had known what was involved from the start, it was no good blaming him now. She, who was normally so clear-headed, why had she suddenly sided with her mother? A born trouble-maker, his mother-in-law had revelled in their quarrel.

It was pointless to sit here stewing. The situation wasn't likely to improve until New Year when the old bat went back to her cave. Forget it. Forget everything to do with Christmas—sod the aggravation. He clenched his teeth. If only it hadn't happened in front of the kids!

It was the worst time of year. The suicide rate went up, more babies were battered—wouldn't Ernest Clare still be alive if it hadn't been for Christmas and those bequest envelopes tempting Karl Gough? If that was stretching a point, Bramwell was no longer prepared to be rational; domestic tension had put paid to that.

He drove out into the silent wet streets, bound for home.

THE PRIEST SAT reading beside the hospital bed. A shabby elderly man, he usually had a book in his pocket, apart from his 'service manuals', of course. That was a private joke with the Almighty—his own description for the Bible and Book of Common Prayer.

There was a lot of hanging about in this job. People took time to come round from an anaesthetic and those who had asked him to be there, to stay with them when the prognosis was bad, expected him to wait. Hospital was the place where the friendless needed an anonymous hand to hold.

There were those who were an unconscionable time a-dying, too... Not tonight, thank goodness. The staff nurse was adamant. Sharon Gough would linger until her kidneys gave out. Unless she changed her mind and started taking the drugs, of course. Father Gibson sighed and tried to concentrate on the poems of another tormented soul, Wilfred Owen. What a monstrous cross all those young men had had to bear in 1914. Would his faith have stood up to it? He doubted it.

Could he offer any comfort here? The patient had stated her intention plainly. As usual, that had caused affront, yet what could *he* say to dissuade her? One could scarcely talk of the quality of life. According to the outraged staff nurse, she had even taken against her child, poor creature.

SHARON AWOKE. Regaining consciousness was different now. Before, in that mean bedroom she had shared with Karl, she had come to slowly, resenting the dawn because it presaged disappointment; another frustrating day. That world had gone. Here in hospital she was immediately alert, not knowing how long she would remain conscious, alive even; aware of smells, most of all, of pain.

Those bloody stupid doctors had told her she would no longer experience sensations yet every part of her body was sending frantic, screaming messages to her brain. Her head felt as if it would explode, it hurt so much.

The dark shape of a man sat beside the bed, a stranger with a different odour. It was odd, her world was so limited yet the ability to identify smells had become significant. This was a dusty, masculine aroma, with more than a hint of grubbiness.

Her eyes were slow in accommodating themselves to the dimness tonight. Sharon felt her throat constrict; was this the first sign of death? Fucking hell! The terrible pain had returned, blotting out everything else. She wanted to scream but hadn't the strength.

Father Gibson was aware of a change. He knew the patient hadn't moved. She couldn't, she was pinned to the bed like a butterfly. He turned to stare at the shadowy pillow. The eyes had opened. In the dimness they were dark hollows that didn't give anything away. Even so he braced himself against the inevitable rejection.

'I've just come to sit for a little while, Mrs Gough.'

Sharon had seen the dog-collar. 'Am I dying then?'

'Oh no.' It was depressing when patients assumed that was the only reason: death's herald. 'You don't have to die, you know. Not yet anyway.'

'Have they found a way to cure a broken neck?'

'No. That's still some way off, I fear.'

Relief that death was still beyond the curtains invigorated Sharon. Her voice rose above a whisper. 'Too fucking right, it is. Shove off.'

'In a little while.'

So much hate, he thought sadly. In their closeted space the air was thick with it. What had happened to bring such torment?

'I have something for you.' He held the instamatic photo close to her face, tilting it so the image could be seen. 'It's not very good. We had to use flash, of course. The nurses in the children's ward have a camera so that parents who have to leave their children—'

'Take it away.'

As he watched, those dreadful yellow eyes closed in a deliberate refusal to look at it. He'd been warned of the effect of bile. Let the poison not affect her sight, dear Lord Jesus, it was the only thing she had left. Apart from her soul, of course.

He said sadly, 'No, well . . . it doesn't do her justice. Sarah's a sweet child, isn't she? We've found a temporary place, by the way. A foster family who have accepted many children over the years. There's a lovely atmosphere. She will be well looked after.'

If Sharon heard or cared, she gave no indication. He eased his buttocks. These chairs claimed to fit the contours of the human body but they always succeeded in mortifying his flesh. He'd once thought of carrying a cushion but decided against it.

Wilfred Owen had had no cushion, nor the rest of those doomed young men. It looked like being a long night. He had settled to his book again when he heard her whisper, 'I said, shove off. Find somewhere else to sit.'

'Is it what I represent that offends you?' When she didn't reply, he sighed. 'You're one of a vast number, Mrs Gough. And I'm not here to persuade you otherwise. I should be, of course, it's in my job description but there you go... There are failures in every walk of life. Did you have an interesting job before you had Sarah?'

She ignored that, asking, 'Are you Catholic?'

'No. Common or garden C of E.' High Anglican, of course, with its share of bells and smells but he wasn't going to waste time explaining that. He could see she was considering him for some reason and awaited her verdict.

'Tell me something...'

'If I can. I'm not particularly clever.'

'Is there a hell?'

He prayed desperately for guidance. 'God be in my head, my mouth...'

'If you mean hell on earth, there's plenty of that.'

'No. After.'

'Men have always preferred the idea of revenge. I believe the Almighty will turn out to be much more tolerant. That could be the biggest disappointment of all for one or two.'

Her whisper was so cynical it made his toes curl.

'There's nothing, is there? Heaven or hell—it's all crap.'

He made a mistake. 'Today we celebrate the birthday of our Lord—'

'Crap!' No, he mustn't try that. Don't argue. After all, there had been plenty of times when he felt despondent enough to agree.

'You're very brave, Mrs Gough. It wouldn't help to offer you false promises. The truth is none of us really knows what is to happen.'

Sharon was silent.

'As for hell... You already know about that so why ask me? If I can't give you the answers you need, I can at least listen if that's any use.' He waited, apprehensive she might simply dismiss him, dreading that she might not.

WHEN HE EMERGED, the doctor was at the nursing station, waiting to speak to him. He took one look and offered the priest tea. 'You look bushed.'

'Yes, well... it is fairly late.' It was human degradation that had affected him. 'I won't bother with tea just now, thanks.' He asked the nurse, 'Have you the name and address of Mrs Gough's mother? She would be down as next of kin, probably.'

'Somewhere...' She pushed back untidy hair and ruffled through the files. 'Here we are...she's a Mrs Berriman.' She held the form under the light so that he could copy the address.

Father Gibson glanced at the wall clock. 'Perhaps I'd better leave it till the morning.'

The doctor laughed. 'You weren't thinking of calling to-night? There's no immediate cause for concern. Did you persuade Mrs Gough to see sense? We can give intravenous medication but as she has expressly forbidden it...'

The priest knew he was being asked to exert his authority. This doctor wouldn't act without it.

'I didn't persuade her, no. I'm very sorry.'

'But it is for her own good.'

For the medical man there could be no question about it but the priest was weighed down with mortal sin. His voice trembled. 'Not necessarily.'

'That's no answer!'

'Maybe not...' He apologised again. 'It must be galling for you but I fear it's the only answer I can give. I do not think Mrs Gough will change her mind.'

'There's still time,' the doctor protested.

Father Gibson shook his head. In his experience miracles didn't happen to order and on this occasion divine intervention would not solve a thing.

The nurse asked, 'Did Mrs Gough say anything about her husband, Father?'

He shook his head absently.

'The police need to be informed if she did. There was a twenty-four guard at the beginning. Now they seem to think he won't come after her but nobody can guarantee it.'

'Mmm?'

The doctor answered patiently, 'Karl Gough. Did she say anything? Is he likely to come back and attack his wife again?'

'Oh...no. No, I don't think so. It's very unlikely.'

Father Gibson pulled out a handkerchief. The photograph fell to the floor. The nurse bent to pick it up.

'Is this a picture of Mrs Gough's little girl? What a good idea—we can pin it to her bed.'

'No.' He blew his nose decisively. 'It'll only upset her. Put it in the wastepaper basket. Goodnight.'

He heard the doctor's accusatory, 'He's bloody useless,' and knew it to be true. He had failed yet again but what else could he have said?

'Help me, dear Lord...'

Plastic ward doors slapped shut behind him. He was alone.

MR PRINGLE WAS a supremely happy man. He had achieved his objective. He hadn't expected to, the day had not started propitiously yet what a happy chapter of accidents had re-sulted in this conclusion. Mrs Bignell had been—was—so deeply appreciative of his gift. She lay beside him in her new nightdress, the ripples of lace spilling on to the bedclothes like pink-grey foam. 'I've never had anything so beautiful in all my life.'

'Nonsense.' He said it in order that she might contradict and she obliged immediately.

'It's not nonsense and you know it. This is the most lux-urious, the most special, the most *heavenly* nightdress in the universe. It fits so well, too; makes me feel like a queen.'

'I knew which size to ask for.'

'Don't be so smug! Poor old Charlie. You are sure about my insurance policy? When it says "new for old", it means it?'

There was a time and place for discussing such matters but this wasn't it. 'I'm absolutely sure. Can we leave it till tomorrow?'

'Yes, of course.' Her natural optimism began to resur-face. 'To be honest, I was a little tired of that wallpaper. We can choose another colour scheme for the hall, something really bright.'

Happily chattering about 'a Chinesey pattern with birds' she caught sight of the matching negligé draped over the dressing table mirror and was overcome once more. 'Will you look at those sleeves. They're enormous! It's utterly impractical, of course. I can't possibly wear it to answer the door to the milkman.'

'I should hope not!'

She smoothed the ruffle about her shoulders. 'Poor old Charlie,' she said again. 'I hope he's not too depressed.'

'He won a very special pair of pyjamas!'

'I had to give him *something*. I'll get you a pair for your birthday, if you like.'

'Yes, please.' He still fancied himself in dark blue poplin.

'We ought to pop round and see how he is in the morning.'

'Charlie?'

'He looked very depressed.'

'I asked him to let your friends know what had happened,' Mr Pringle admitted. 'I thought after the shock of the fire, the state of your house, you might not feel up to entertaining tomorrow.'

'Of course I will!' Mrs Bignell was astonished. 'It'll be just the thing to perk me up. I'll phone them. We'll invite them over here instead. You'll enjoy that.'

'Will I?' His was not such a sociable nature.

Mavis listed them on her fingers: 'Becky, if she's well enough, Lila, John Hines, Reg and Betty—just for a cup of tea. How long is it since you threw a party?'

Mr Pringle couldn't remember: since before Renée's last illness, years ago in fact.

'It'll be a real treat,' Mavis promised blithely. 'You can show them your pictures.'

'Oh, now . . . I don't really think—' but she was carried away with the idea.

'I might even let Lila have a peek at my new negligée. I don't know . . . perhaps not. It's so very special.' She shook her head at him fondly. 'Perfume . . . super chocolates and Italian lingerie. Anyone would think you were trying to seduce me.'

He already had; this time he contented himself with embracing those ravishing, wonderful—

'Why slivovic?'

'Pardon?' It was the irritant his mind had been trying to disgorge. In his relaxed state, it had resurfaced unexpectedly.

'You said you kept a bottle especially for Ernest Clare?'

'Yes, we did.'

'Wasn't it rather an odd choice?'

Mavis shrugged. 'Maybe. It's strange, he didn't seem to like the taste—he used to toss it back in one go.'

'You always said he must have been Hungarian because of it.'

'Did I?'

'According to the dictionary, the drink is Eastern European.'

'No one really knew where he came from.'

'Not even his neighbours?'

Mrs Bignell was shaking her head. 'I've never heard any of them say so. People in Inkerman Street, they've come from all over the place, that's what makes it such an interesting crowd. They drift to this part of London and when they find how friendly it is, decide to stay. Some of them have been here for years. Ask Betty Fisher, she's local; she's been living in this area since she was born.'

'Miss Posner's remark—considering she had agreed to help Ernest—it sounded rather *hostile*,' he murmured.

'I told you, she's la-de-dah. Besides, she probably thought she was demeaning herself. It was the first time she had helped, anyway. Lila hadn't asked her previously.'

'Oh?' Mr Pringle was alert.

'Lila began giving Ernest a hand at Easter. Then with Christmas and her wanting to go up West so often, that's when Becky got roped in. She hadn't been inside Ernest's house until that night, which is another reason she was so upset by what happened.' Mrs Bignell leaned across and kissed him firmly. 'Try and sleep. You don't have to worry about it any more. The police are looking for that prowler as well as Karl, they know what's what. Goodnight, dear, and thanks ever so much for my lovely presents.'

Mr Pringle continued to brood. The police obviously had a reason but he wasn't convinced Gough was the murderer. That faceless identikit had been given equal prominence on television, the implication being the prowler and Gough were a team. Yet none of the Bricklayers' regulars found that credible and they knew Gough. Mr Pringle yawned. Everyone had agreed he was a loner.

Miss Posner had been tearful. The police had bombarded her with questions. She repeated what she'd told them. How Ernest had bolted his back door behind her and watched from his kitchen window until she had crossed the yard and closed the gate.

Lila had confirmed the habit. Ernest preferred any helpers to enter the back way, partly out of embarrassment.

'He didn't like to admit he needed assistance,' she had told Mr Pringle. 'Pride. There's one or two prefer that the rest don't know they have Meals on Wheels. I was thankful. It gave me a break from him three times a week.'

Wide awake, hands behind his head, Mr Pringle stared into the darkness. This morning, he and Mavis commented privately how frail Rebecca Posner had become. Being one of the witnesses to the prowler had meant further questioning and it was obvious she had suffered by it. Yet there were still so many incongruities: Mr Pringle tried to reduce them to a more logical sequence.

Miss Posner had seen the prowler on her way to the pub. Reg Wolfe had seen him earlier when he hurried home from bowls, and Lila had glimpsed him when she paused on her front door step to find her key. What an extraordinary length of time the man had loitered, particularly after committing a murder. Unless he'd been waiting for Gough, of course.

Yet why had Gough waited, as well as announcing his intention to stay the night. Surely stealing Lila's credit card had been the impulse of a moment, not part of a grand design?

And if Gough had been in Lila's kitchen afterwards, surely the prowler had known that? Why not wait out of sight in Lila's back premises? It also made sense to think the two of them had watched Rebecca leaving before entering Clare's house, but afterwards, why not remain hidden?

Had something gone wrong? Was the prowler hoping to contact Gough and explain?

Mr Pringle was exasperated. It was all so very unlikely. As for those bequest envelopes . . . hadn't Karl asked about the notice in the bar? Mrs Bignell didn't believe his ignorance was feigned. Unless being an accessory to murder turned a man into a consummate actor.

'Harumph!'

Mr Pringle fidgeted. He needed answers, whether or not the police were satisfied. Illogicality bothered him. It was what he'd been trained to reject during his time at the Revenue.

DPW VIVIEN TUNNICLIFFE was extremely angry. She'd been trying to interview Mrs Berriman for most of Christmas afternoon. She first visited the bungalow after depositing Sarah in the children's ward and contacting the social services. Mrs Berriman had been out.

The policewoman returned two hours later, on her way home from shift. She was aware of neighbours watching but when she'd gone to Connie at number 48, all she'd been given was an evasive answer.

Mrs Berriman had returned and gone out again. No, Connie didn't know where. The only extra piece of information concerned a car. Connie was reluctant to talk about it but Vivien Tunnicliffe charmed her way inside and the two stood among card-laden ribbons in the hall.

'That car belongs to a friend of hers. He's not from round here.'

The inference was that the stranger wasn't welcome, either. These bungalows represented comfortable retirement; their status mattered.

'What sort of car?'

'An old Ford. Big. Noisy. Blue. He makes it squeal going round corners, he's that sort.'

'D'you know his name?'

Connie didn't reply. Instead she said, 'My husband heard him shouting.'

'At Mrs Berriman?'

'Filthy language. It's not the sort of thing we're used to.'

'No.'

'Harold thought he was a cockney. He's very big.'

'How long has he been visiting her?'

'It was before Sharon was married. Then he disappeared again. Harold was pleased. Mrs Berriman was a widow when she came, then he turned up and we prefer it to be quiet.'

'If Mrs Berriman does happen to contact you—'

'I'll tell her you called.' The woman was eager for her to be gone; police cars were an unwelcome intrusion.

'One other thing...'

'Yes?'

'The night Mrs Berriman went to the panto—he called round while she was out. Before you lot turned up. I saw his car. I don't know how he got in. After a while I saw him drive away. Mrs Berriman didn't say he'd been but it was afterwards her phone wasn't working, so she couldn't talk to Sharon.'

The policewoman frowned. 'We assumed she hadn't paid her bill?'

'Oh, no, she's got money. No, we think he must have damaged it. Like I said, she never admitted he'd been in her house, she never does. She pretends he's Sharon's friend.'

'He must have a name?' The woman looked round nervously, 'Harold doesn't like it if I talk about him. Mrs Berriman once called him "Lee".'

'Thanks.'

THAT HAD BEEN earlier this evening. Afterwards Vivien Tunnicliffe returned home and her personal life was shattered. It was now 1 a.m. Her hands were shaking, she couldn't think straight, everything had blown up in her face. It was stupid to do anything in this state but sheer frustration meant she couldn't bear to remain in her parents' house.

Gordon had waited until she returned from shift in order to break their engagement. In front of her parents. Christmas had been the last straw, he told her solemnly, especially the disappointment over the cancelled dinner party. What should have been the most wonderful evening of his life had turned completely sour.

His life! 'What about mine!' she yelled.

Calmly, rationally, he had explained that a wife who was so committed to her work, one who could not even attend her own engagement party, was no asset to a man with his ambitions.

Asset? What the hell was that supposed to mean?

Anger blurred the road ahead. Vivien tried breathing deeply—she could have an accident if she went on like this. She needed a focus to distract her from her own shrieking emotions. That innocent little girl, Sarah...with a mother unable to care for her, dumped by her grandmother. She'd bloody well give *her* a piece of her mind for a start. DPW

Tunnicliffe yanked the steering wheel viciously and headed off toward Leigh-on-Sea.

Mrs Berriman was home, no doubt about it this time: the lights were on. The sight of them renewed Vivien's anger. She didn't stop to think, she banged on the front door. She'd give the neighbours something to talk about, never mind old blue Fords. 'Come on, open up, open this door!'

When it did, abruptly, she was caught off balance. The figure blocking out the light was big and muscular. Even so her professional training might have saved her had she re-acted quickly enough. Emotion muffled her instincts.

As she stumbled, a hand pulled her further inside. When the man let her go, Vivien spun round bouncing against the wall. Too late, she heard the scream, 'Lee, don't!' As she turned to face him, the man's fist crashed into her face. Far, far too late, she remembered her training. She tried to get a knee to his groin but her legs no longer obeyed her brain. She was on the floor, limbs splayed as the man kicked her inert body in fury.

THIRTEEN

IT WAS Boxing Day morning. In the incident room four officers were gathered round the receiver's desk. The SIO was in the chair and the atmosphere was edgy. They had, with the SIO's vigorous encouragement, been barking up the wrong tree. It had happened before, it would occur again but that thought didn't help now. The SIO was prepared to spread the blame wide. 'What I can't understand is why she went there, on her own, so late at night?'

DS Bramwell was equally unhappy. He was also angry. Apart from domestic misery, if his earlier warnings had been heeded they might not have been in this mess. He fingered the fax from Southend. 'DPW Tunnicliffe didn't realise Mrs Berriman had a visitor. She'd been trying to contact her all day. She simply knocked at the door and—'

'But why go there on Christmas Day in the first place—we didn't request that?'

'No, sir, we didn't. As soon as this arrived this morning, I phoned for more details. Tunnicliffe had been on her normal shift. She'd visited the hospital earlier in another attempt to persuade Mrs Gough to talk. There was some problem to do with the Goughs' child—I don't know whether that was the reason for pursuing Mrs Berriman. Her phone wasn't working, apparently.'

'As long as we aren't blamed...' The SIO stared unseeing at the screen in front of him. 'A ruptured spleen—that sounds nasty. Do we know what her chances are?'

Cass gave a polite cough. 'I rang the hospital, sir. Just after you called this meeting, in fact. DPW Tunnicliffe's condition was described as "poorly but stable".'

'Not much comfort,' grumbled the SIO but with considerably less anxiety. 'So long as no one points the finger at us.' He was experienced at protecting his back.

'Sir, various aspects of this latest incident . . . there are more similarities with the attack on Sharon Gough than the one on Ernest Clare.' DS Bramwell's career prospects were about to suffer but someone had to set the ball rolling. 'In that incident, we know the deceased was strangled before his neck was broken. What we have tended to ignore were the various professional touches on that occasion: the use of a gag, thumbs pushed into the wind-pipe to render the victim unconscious before the vertebrae were severed—'

'Thumb marks. Exactly.' The SIO endeavoured to re-establish authority by side-stepping awkward facts. Gone was the insistence that Gough must be the killer, however. 'Do we yet know to whom those belong?'

The SIO knew that they didn't. And Bramwell knew that he knew.

'We know they don't belong to Karl Gough,' the receiver replied shortly and paused. The next move was down to the SIO. He had to confirm the obvious: that Ernest Clare had been killed by one person and Sharon Gough attacked by another, without a doubt the same man who had half-killed DPW Tunnicliffe. Which, by implication, meant Gough had done little more than steal.

'Come on, get on with it,' whispered a voice inside. Bramwell's impatience could barely be concealed yet the SIO continued to maintain his silence. The receiver took a deep breath.

'I think it is safe to assume the attacks on Sharon Gough and DPW Tunnicliffe were by the same person, sir.' The silence was deafening. 'Both women were brutally kicked in the same area of the body and from what we've learned so far, if it hadn't been for the intervention of a neighbour, Tunnicliffe's injuries might have been far worse.'

'And have included—a broken neck.' This, the SIO's sole contribution, was produced like a rabbit from a hat.

Bramwell said woodenly, 'Exactly so, sir,' because it was expected of him.

The SIO smiled benignly. 'I'm glad we agree, Jim.' My God, thought Bramwell, the bastard really must be rattled. 'And our next course of action...' Here the SIO paused and let himself drift into a brown study. Bramwell was tempted to leave him there but the instinct for self-preservation made him pick up the cue.

'With your permission, I think we ought to concentrate on the known attacker rather than Gough. Despite her injuries DPW Tunnicliffe was able to give valuable information. Southend followed it up last night. They have the name Lee Andrews. If correct, he has plenty of form. His last GBH got him eight years. He was involved in a riot at Gartree so served the full term. He *could* turn out to be our prowler as well.' Bramwell added this out of politeness, not conviction. He knew the SIO was hoping mightily that Andrews could be fitted into that role. It would shift the focus away from previous errors of judgement.

The SIO was nodding sagely, 'He could indeed be our man.'

'Although he in no way resembles our identikit—'

But the SIO pounced at that. 'Elderly witnesses, confused, in shock... I don't think we should rely too heavily...'

Bramwell kept emotion under control. 'Southend are working on it but as at O-nine hundred hours, Andrews was still at large. I've got a call out to my contact there, the one who filled us in on Mrs Berriman. He knew Andrews in the old days. Unfortunately he'd gone fishing this morning but his wife is expecting him back for lunch.'

'Ah, yes... Mention of the time factor brings me to another matter.'

The receiver looked at him warily. 'Sir?'

'The time factor, Jim.'

Bramwell made him spell it out. 'Time, sir?'

'Correct me if I'm mistaken . . . this is the fifth day of our inquiry?'

'Fifth since—oh, since Clare's death. Yes, yes it is.'

'As usual, resources are not infinite.' The words lingered in the air. Bramwell knew what was coming: he fought against it, anger bubbling inside.

'There has been a second attack, sir. We have also had Christmas Day to contend with during that period—'

The SIO seized on that. 'I understand you came in here yesterday. Was that really necessary, Jim?'

The receiver still managed to keep his voice neutral. 'Coming in turned out to be more practical than phoning. There won't be any claim, I shall take time off in lieu.'

'Good.' It was a pat on the head to a naughty boy. 'Sadly, I have been informed that this inquiry cannot be scheduled beyond the twenty-eighth. As we know, the inquest is being held tomorrow at ten a.m. We shall have the rest of that day plus another twenty-four hours and that will be it. Unfortunately the number of man hours we will have clocked up by then . . .' He shrugged, implying if only he could, he would have prevented authority's edict.

'What if Sharon Gough dies?' Bramwell knew he sounded crude and cursed, silently. The SIO hadn't argued against the curtailment because the bastard wanted out from a situation he had publicly misjudged, but this wasn't the way to handle it. His superior now bolted down the escape route with ever increasing confidence, his voice creamy.

'I'm afraid if that sad event does occur, any inquest would have to be informed of Mrs Gough's refusal to accept medical advice. That plus her stubbornness over her attacker's identity would muddy any attempt to pin a murder charge on *anyone*. Besides, it's not *our* problem. It's on their patch

not ours. We have enough to do without worrying about
Mrs Sharon Gough. Leave that to Southend.' Which was
neat and made Bramwell more furious. 'Any news of her
husband by the way?'

'The French are still awaiting our instructions.'

Which way would the SIO jump on that? It was perhaps
inevitable he would avoid it altogether.

'I leave it to you, Jim. Use the remaining time to best advantage. I have full confidence in your judgement. Now that
we're all agreed Gough probably wasn't responsible for the
attack on his wife . . . and he certainly couldn't have been
involved in the one on DPW Tunnicliffe . . .' Confidence
wavered momentarily. 'He couldn't have returned by then,
could he?'

The receiver shook his head. 'Tunnicliffe heard Berriman identify Andrews. Besides, she had time to get a look
at him before he knocked her unconscious. She was able to
give a brief description before they whipped her into the
operating theatre—'

'Of course she did, I'm being forgetful.'

'Her description did not tie in with the identikit—'

'You don't need to spell it out. So, we have no positive
evidence to link Gough to Clare . . . apart from that one
blurred finger mark on the door jamb.' He looked round
triumphantly. 'We all know how quickly a competent brief
would demolish that.'

'Karl Gough had the opportunity.' DC Cass didn't see
why they should relinquish him entirely. 'He was in the area.
We know he stole Boyce's credit card. He was in deceased's
house—he may have taken the bequest money.'

'Hardly a matter for the French police, in my opinion.'

Cass reddened. 'No, sir.'

'Let us concentrate on Lee Andrews as being our prowler.
We might consider an identity parade for those three witnesses, once Southend have bagged him, of course.' The SIO

dismissed this as mere formality. 'Then again, we might not. We can't be sure those three weren't mistaken originally. One foot in the grave, not exactly *reliable*. It's something to think about. I suggest there must still be some *connection* with Karl Gough—it's up to us to ferret one out.' He directed this at Cass as he rose to leave. 'Above all, let us keep our fingers crossed Andrews' thumb prints match the marks on Clare's neck, eh? That should screw down the lid.'

Dutifully, they laughed. It was, after all, almost a joke.

THE RECEIVER WAITED until the door had closed before speaking. 'Right, Cass. How d'you fancy another trip to the seaside?' Not waiting for a reply, he grabbed the phone. 'Let's see if that dozy bugger is back from catching fish fingers . . . I'll get him to phone you at the hospital with what they have on Andrews. Go through the file for possible contacts but don't worry too much about Gough. What you have to make sure is you get from Tunnicliffe everything she knows—and check whether Sharon Gough has heard about this attack, see if it changes her mind about talking to us. Hello . . . Mary? Is George back? Great. If you would, yes . . . George? Listen, mate, forget it's Christmas, OK? I'll send you a cracker when this lot's sewn up.'

As Cass was leaving, he asked, 'What about that identity parade? Do we warn the witnesses they might be needed?' Bramwell said briefly, 'Forget it. I don't know who they saw but it wasn't Andrews. We're dealing with a fly old con. He might not let himself get picked up simply because we've only got two more days left to finish this inquiry. Just dig out all you can so we can leave it on file. That's the best you and I can hope for.' He shrugged at Cass's change of expression. 'Sorry, but you heard the man. He's not going to ask for an extension on this one. He's managed to avoid looking a wally and that's all he cares about.'

PERHAPS BECAUSE OF the heightened activity the previous night, Mr Pringle awoke very early indeed. He could see the clock beyond the curve of Mrs Bignell's shoulder. Another hour before the alarm would go off. He rose quietly, washed, dressed and considered whether it would be anti-social to call so early on Lila Boyce. He decided to walk as far as her house. If there were signs of life, he would, otherwise he would try again later. What he wanted to discuss wouldn't take long. He could be back in here in time to brew his beloved her morning cup of tea.

There was an unseasonal softness in the air. Mr Pringle inhaled the rain-washed pollution. He was nervous but curiosity drove him forward. Lila's bedroom curtains were pulled back. Through the coloured glass panels in the front door he could see a distant light on in the scullery. He rang the bell.

'Goodness...' In her shabby brocade dressing gown, Lila looked him up and down. 'I thought you must be Damien.'

Mr Pringle indicated the empties on the step. 'Not till tomorrow, surely?'

'My God, I even forget what day it is—what a Christmas, eh?'

'May I come in?'

'Of course.'

He followed her down the hall. She called over her shoulder, 'Coffee?' The smell was rich and dark.

'Yes, please.' Like Lila, it was exotic and the cup she gave him was bowl-shaped, without a handle. He watched her dunk pieces of roll, cradling her cup in stubby square hands. Her kitchen, with its dark green walls and coloured pottery, was vibrant compared with the anaemic shades favoured by Inkerman Street. Mr Pringle became aware of her scrutiny.

'I apologise for such an early call.'

She shrugged. 'I'm always up early. People of our age usually are, especially if they live alone.'

'It's about Miss Posner.' It wasn't but Mr Pringle had decided to use this as an excuse. 'As you know, she has consulted me in the past over her financial matters.'

Lila laughed. 'An extravagant way to describe Becky's pittance.'

He reddened: the approach had been a mistake, Lila Boyce was no fool.

'She may be entitled to more social benefits. As her friend, I wondered if you would make enquiries on her behalf because of her natural reluctance to do so. If you prefer, I can visit the DSS to obtain the necessary forms.'

'OK, why not? You want milk?'

'No, thank you.' He was glad of an excuse to gulp a few scalding mouthfuls.

'So...now we have dealt with Becky,' Lila leaned back in her chair, reaching for the inevitable cigarette, 'any other problems?'

'Karl Gough.'

'Ah...' She blew smoke at the ceiling. 'Poor Karl. Always so impulsive. So very stupid. One always has to feel sorry, no?'

'Do you believe he killed Ernest?'

'The police believe he did.'

'I don't think I heard them say so,' Mr Pringle observed mildly. 'But you?' he pressed. 'You knew Karl better than anyone.'

'Yes, and he did not do such a thing. Never.' She was emphatic. 'It is not in his character. Karl *thinks* he is so clever with his forgeries, always he is caught. But never any violence. When the policeman's hand comes down on his shoulder, Karl immediately gives up. He is a petty criminal, that is all.'

'Then who did kill Ernest?'

Lila raised her eyebrows. 'The prowler, of course. He was outside the house because I saw him. How could it be anyone else?'

'Of course.' He repeated after momentary hesitation. 'The prowler. By the way, I don't think Miss Posner should be forced to attend any identity parade. I'm sure her doctor would prefer that she didn't.'

'Of course. I fix,' Lila replied briefly. 'I ask for a certificate to give to the police.'

Mr Pringle rose and indicated his empty cup. 'Thank you for such a delicious start to the day.'

Lila stared curiously. 'Do *you* believe the police are correct, that Karl is a killer?'

'No.' Hadn't they also considered him as a possible culprit? 'They can make mistakes. As for me, I only believe what I know to be true. You heard about the fire? Mrs Bignell has transferred this afternoon's tea party to my house.'

'Sure. She phoned Charlie and he told me. We're all looking forward to it.'

'Good.' He bowed slightly. 'Please don't bother, I can see myself out.' He walked back along the passage to the front door, taking care not to trip over the step.

'ENGLISH? YOU AWAKE, English?' Karl Gough blinked several times to try and help memory return. His mouth was parched. He licked cracked lips, the dark-haired girl offered him a glass of water. 'Here, drink. You are nearly better, no?'

Karl sipped, retrieving the facts one by one. This room . . . he'd been in it for some time . . . one, two days? In this high narrow bed. He felt hot and sticky. He was at Marie-Christine's. He'd collapsed. He remembered her son helping him upstairs. He recalled the guy's name and now said confidently to the girl, 'You're his girlfriend, aren't you? Alexandre's?'

She looked as though she'd been slapped. Without denying it, she poured honey-coloured liquid into the glass and insisted he drink that as well.

'Medicine. You finish all.' It didn't taste too bad. Karl tried to reconcile the memory of this girl's arm round Alexandre's shoulders with her tight hostile face.

'Is my artic where I left it?' She hadn't understood. 'My *camion*. I drove it to Alexandre's workshop before I came here, didn't I? It is still there?'

She became animated. 'Yes, it is. Listen. I have plan. You are better, no?'

'Almost.' He felt weak as a kitten.

'You have the fever when you come. She bring a friend to see. He give her medicine.'

'A doctor.'

The dark hair swished to and fro. 'Not doctor. She not want doctor to know. She no pay taxes on this.' The girl indicated the four walls. 'This places, where people stay and pay her money. Here, English, look.' She handed him his wallet and when he fumbled, she took it and shook it in front of his eyes. 'No money now. She take all.'

'Bloody hell!'

'She take other cheques. For bank.'

Karl began to quiver, partly from fever, mostly from terror. Marie-Christine had got hold of the cheques and Lila's card. Memory returned of how he'd folded them and tucked them into the back of his wallet. Why the hell hadn't he left such damning evidence locked in his cab!

'Here, more medicine. To make better.' He drank again, obediently. 'She say you not same as Visa card name. She know what you do.' The girl took hold of his arm when she saw the shock. 'Alexandre has seen on Minitel number of *camion*—you understand?'

Karl nodded dumbly. He felt very, very tired. All that effort for nothing.

The girl sensed his mental slump. She shook him impatiently.

'No, listen. I help. I have plan. I show you where is more money. You drive, OK?'

It was all too much. He was weary as he tried to work it out.

'You help me?'

'Yes! I want to go from here. I get plenty money. We buy *essence*. You drive. We not tell *anyone*. OK?'

'OK... What about...?' It didn't make sense. 'Aren't you Alexandre's girl then?' This time he understood. Watching her lip tremble, it didn't take a genius to realise she wasn't any longer. As for any 'plan', he was too bemused by the speed of events to think about that.

'I'll have a little rest first...'

'No! We go now. You nearly better.' It was a command, not a question. Karl tried putting his feet to the floor and was immediately dizzy. 'I help.' She pulled on his clothes with complete disinterest, he might have been a lump of dead meat. Finally, when his trainer laces were tied, she repeated, 'So. We go.'

He said feebly, 'Look—I'm sorry, I can't even remember your name—'

'Geneviève.'

'Geneviève—I don't think I've enough strength—'

'You must! Marie-Christine come back soon. We go now, please.' She half-dragged him downstairs into the restaurant and left him draped over a chair while she fetched her own small holdall. She was carrying a duffel coat. 'Here, put this on, please.'

It probably belonged to Alexandre, Karl realised. He was helpless against her determination. She fastened the toggles, found the beret in the pocket and pulled it on, standing back to check the angle. She tucked in a scarf which partially obscured his chin. Finally, she handed him a pair of dark glasses.

'Until we are in the *camion*. Come. We find money.' Heaving his arm over her shoulders, she staggered with him through to the storage area behind the bar. Opening the large chest freezer and reaching below a stack of assorted ice-cream cartons, she pulled the lid off one labelled 'Glace à l'eau' and showed him the contents: wads of francs.

'Bloody hell!' Each was fastened with an elastic band and she answered his unspoken question.

'Is ten thousand each *paquet*.'

One thousand pounds, times...how many were there? He watched in amazement as she counted out five wads and stuffed them into her bag. 'I work here every night, waiting for Alexandre. Every night. For months. Marie-Christine *nevair* pay me.'

'But how did you know about...?'

She pointed to the door opposite. 'Is la chambre d'Alexandre. One night I go bathroom. When I come back, she is coming down the stairs. I watch from inside. Door open a little bit. She hide the money. I see where. She no see me. She do same often.'

Devious old bitch, he thought in admiration.

'She no like bank. Keep in here. No pay *les impôts*.' Geneviève took two more wads and stuffed them into the inside pocket of his duffel. 'Is enough, I think. What she take plus a little bit more. OK, we go now.'

She replaced the carton exactly as she had found it and closed the freezer lid. Together they staggered through the restaurant.

'It's not open for business today.'

'La fête légale de Noël,' she replied. Boxing Day was obviously Marie-Christine's day of rest. But this girl still hadn't answered one vital point.

'I thought you and Alexandre...?' he began.

Her lip curled. 'His mother—she know better fiancée for 'im. He say, "Yes, Mother." No argue! She say 'im—*I* must leave...' A suspicion of a tear was dashed angrily away. 'He say, "Yes, Mother. End of month, Mother, not before." He say, "Having too *good time* just now."' The words were almost a snarl but she immediately recovered and wiped the expression from her face. 'We hurry.'

It took all his strength to cover the short distance to the workshop. She propped him against the wall while she unlocked the small door, went inside and rolled back the main one. 'Come quick, English. You drive outside. I close door before we go.'

She had to find a box for him to stand on, shove from beneath before he could struggle into the cab. He could no longer heave himself up using the footholds. Once inside, Karl clutched at his chest.

'You OK, English?' She was concerned for herself, not him. 'You can drive, no?'

'Not really, no. Chest hurts!' The red-hot needles made him gasp. 'I'll have to sit for a bit, I can't breathe.'

'We drive first, then you rest. Alexandre may come. Marie-Christine is with friends but only for lunch.'

Each move was agony. Karl knew he was ill, bed was the only place but he had no choice. It took three goes before he managed to drive the lorry into the alley, scraping against both stone walls as he did so. He waited, sweating and shivering, while the girl locked up and climbed in beside him. Dully he asked, 'Where to?' She could make the decisions, he no longer cared.

'Dijon.' It was where she lived. Geneviève's objective was simple: home, then call the police. It was still possible there might be a reward.

Karl's vocal cords hurt like hell. 'You'll have to tell me the way... I can't read the signs.'

BRAMWELL'S LAST instruction had been to take some flowers. 'Poor girl... Guts smashed in as well as her face. She won't be eating chocs for a while. Buy her a nice bunch.' On Boxing Day it wasn't that easy nor was Cass happy with the result.

In Women's Surgical, he felt conspicuous. The nurse eyed him coolly. 'Are you family?'

He held out his card for her to read. 'We're involved in the same inquiry. How is she?'

'Poorly.'

'She's no worse? We phoned you this morning from the incident room.'

Her face relaxed.

'I remember. No, not really. She's had a real pounding. The spleen had to come out, blood was pouring into the abdominal cavity.'

Cass was extremely sorry he'd asked. 'Is there any risk?'

'Not now. She's a fine healthy girl and a spleen is something we can all manage without. She had another upset this morning, that's the problem. The ex-boyfriend showed up.' The nurse indicated the over-stuffed vases on every sill. 'Look at all this. Sheer ostentation. He's got a bloody cheek! He only chucked her over last night. Then this morning he waltzes in here with his bloody mother in tow, and d'you know why?'

'Tell me?'

'Because the telly people were here. That's what we think, anyway. He hung about until they'd begun filming—he wanted to be seen as a really *caring* person.' She giggled. 'Mind you, he didn't get away with it.'

An ex-boyfriend wasn't part of the brief and there wasn't much time. Cass indicated his etiolated daffodils.

'Could these go in water?'

The nurse regarded them disparagingly. 'You're sure they wouldn't prefer digitalin?'

She went ahead of him through the curtains. Bearing his offering, Cass followed. What he saw in the bed made him hold his breath.

Vivien Tunnicliffe's broken swollen nose stretched the width of her face. On either side, spidery stitches criss-crossed her flattened cheekbones. One eye socket was purple, the shadows beneath it almost black. The plastic tubes protruding from each nostril, plasma and saline feeding her veins plus the drainage pipes from each side of her abdomen took away the last vestiges of any femininity, turning her into a zombie.

Jesus wept! Did he have to do all that? The girl had put up no defence once she was unconscious. They must be dealing with a psycho.

'Here's someone to see you.' The nurse had obviously forgotten his name.

'Cass, CID.'

'That's right. Five minutes.' She disappeared. He set down his milk bottle amid the red roses on top of the locker and said awkwardly, 'Hi, there.'

'Got a mirror?' Tunnicliffe's top lip had scarcely moved; he had difficulty understanding but at least she was awake.

'I haven't, I'm afraid.'

'They've taken mine. Which means I look bloody terrible.'

He was clumsy. 'I'm sure there's nothing that can't be repaired.'

'Thanks. Something to look forward to.'

It was cruel to push questions at her. 'Your friend's done you proud.' Cass indicated the roses. 'The ward looks like Interflora.'

'He's a Rotarian. He asked his pal to open up his shop.'

'Don't try and talk if it hurts.'

She indicated the daffodils. 'Where d'you find those?'

'At a cemetery.'

'Grave robber.'

'From a flower stall!'

'Did they tell you? My ex has decided I am an asset after all.'

'Has he?' Cass made a mental note to ask about brain damage.

'His mother agrees.'

He didn't know what the correct reply was.

'I'm sure she's right.'

The blackened eyes stared accusingly. 'She's one of the most stupid bloody women on God's earth and he takes after her. I told her so, loud and clear.'

Cass produced a notebook. 'As we haven't much time...' She was obviously exhausted but she might get worse... 'Have you remembered anything more since your interview?'

'He was Berriman's boyfriend, you know that, don't you?'

'Lee Andrews.'

'She pretends he's Sharon's—I don't know why.'

'What about Sharon? Did you chat to her eventually?'

'She won't talk. I reckon she's scared.'

'Of Andrews?'

'Maybe. Not her husband... Not bothered about him.'

'The thinking is that Andrews was responsible for both attacks.'

'Makes sense... the bastard's strong enough to break a neck. They told me... in Gartree... when he wasn't kicking warders, he spent his time pumping iron.'

The effort had been too much. Her mouth fell open slackly. Blood was oozing from the cottonwool packing in one of her nostrils.

Cass stood. 'I'll leave you to get some rest.'

'Try the priest,' she mumbled. 'I heard one of the

nurses ... she could've talked to him.'

'Thanks.'

AT THE NURSING STATION, he said urgently, 'Someone ought to take a look. She's bleeding.'

The staff nurse continued with her filing. 'That's a good sign. We worry when they don't.'

'All the same ...'

She rose tiredly, 'All right, I'm going. Is it true what she said?'

'What?'

'One of your lot came to take photographs this morning. She told sister it was for a recruitment poster.'

Cass grinned. DPW Tunnicliffe might be down but she definitely wasn't out.

'It's our new policy, to encourage more psychopaths to join the force. Where's Mrs Gough? I thought she was up here?'

Professional shutters came down. 'She's been moved to a side ward, she's in isolation and she's not to be disturbed.'

'Could you tell me who the priest was who visited her?'

'I could but he'll not say anything, he's a good man. He found a place for that little girl, you know.'

'I'm sorry to have to press you ...'

She replied reluctantly, 'Father Gibson.'

'Is he on duty today? Where will I find him?'

She glanced at her fob. 'He's always on duty. In the staff canteen, I should think. If he is, tell him from me: no chips.' And she disappeared behind the curtains surrounding Vivien Tunnicliffe's bed.

THE SMELL OF stale turkey reminded Cass he needed refuelling. He spotted the dog-collar. The priest sat alone, reading. When Cass arrived with a laden tray the face that looked up, though elderly and drawn, immediately became bland.

'Join me by all means.' Father Gibson waited until Cass was settled. 'My name's Gibson. I don't believe I've had the pleasure...?'

The identification card flipped open. 'CID.'

'I'm glad you're not a newspaper man. They were swarming over the place this morning. The patients who are here at Christmas are all very sick, they didn't enjoy it. You'll have come because of that splendid young woman.'

Cass said cautiously, 'DPW Tunnicliffe.'

'That's the one!' Father Gibson beamed. 'She's a caution. Waited till the cameras started to record before telling that awful young man he was a slimeball. Wonderful word, that.' He saw Cass begin to choke and thrust a paper cup at him. 'Drink from the opposite side.'

When he recovered, Cass asked, 'Why call him that?'

'Because he was.' Father Gibson's hands spread wide. 'He turned up here, with a colleague, both laden with flowers, showing off, posing for the telly people, making sure the florist's name could be seen in close-up.'

Cass was beginning to understand. 'And DPW Tunnicliffe noticed this?'

The face opposite clouded momentarily. 'The poor girl was squeezing my hand to pulp because of the pain. They couldn't anaesthetise her while they changed one of the dressings, you see. But she noticed all right.'

Hungry though he was, Cass stopped chewing. He took another sip of water. 'I understand the two of them split up last night.'

'Yes, thank God. I'd hate to see that girl wasted. Mrs Slimeball was there too, you know. His mother. She tried to patronise the nurses. Always a mistake, that. Two of our dear Lord's mistakes, the Slimes. He has his off-days, you know; just like the Ford people.' Father Gibson savoured the scene once more. 'Whatever you do, don't miss the news today. On ITV as well as the BBC.'

He appeared to consider Cass as he reached into his pocket. 'Here... one of Miss Tunnicliffe's colleagues brought this in to show the camera people.'

It was the standard photograph taken when Vivien Tunnicliffe first joined the force. Her uniform was brand new, her expression eager. Cass said slowly, 'I doubt if she'll ever look like that again.'

'Does it matter?' challenged Gibson. 'So long as no one makes her feel that it does. A woman who doesn't waste time hating, even though she was in such pain. She made them hold off treating her until she'd given her colleagues the facts. Then she collapsed, of course. She's got *character*, Mr Cass. And if you want her, you'll have to hurry to beat the queue.'

'Me! I'm only here as part of an official investigation—'

'Oh, to blazes with that. And keep that photo, it's got her phone number on the back. Now, listen... I know the real reason you're here. Sharon Gough talked to me yesterday. But that stays in my heart, it is not part of any official investigation—ever. Besides, you have all the facts you need after what happened to Miss Tunnicliffe. You don't need to involve Mrs Gough.'

'It was the same man? Lee Andrews?'

Father Gibson simply looked at him.

Cass coloured. 'OK, even we spotted the likelihood but we need more than that to get a conviction. What was Karl Gough's involvement and what about Ernest Clare's murder? Was Andrews responsible for that as well?'

'You'd better ask him. I'm sure Mrs Gough can't tell you.'

'Oh, we shall, once we find him. Is Andrews likely to return here—at least tell me that? We've removed the twenty-four-hour protection on her.'

Father Gibson's face frowned. 'I don't think that is necessary any more. Andrews' only fear would be that she
might talk. We've let it be known that I'm the only one who
heard what she had to say. She can be left in peace, such as
it is.'

'If you fear that he might come after you—'

'No, no. That's not what I meant.' Father Gibson wasn't
entirely dismissive. 'I'm not a brave man, Mr Cass, so don't
waste time, will you? The sooner he's under lock and key,
the better.'

'If Mrs Gough dies, the charge could be murder.'

The priest said quietly, 'That event cannot be delayed
much longer, as I'm sure you are aware.'

Cass leaned forward. 'She's confided in you, surely you
can persuade her to change her mind and tell us what we really need to know.' But when he saw the anguish these words
caused, he wished he had held his tongue.

'She sees her life as a living death. She believes there is no
point in prolonging that. I haven't attempted to dissuade
her, after what she told me... I hope to God I was right.
Besides, there is another reason. Nothing to do with your
inquiry, Mr Cass, but your questions might bring it to the
surface. It should remain hidden, believe me, for the sake of
others.' Father Gibson looked much older as he muttered,
'I wish I could help her but she's too intelligent. I cannot
give her the right answers, I don't know what those are...
I've failed that poor girl.' He rose, abruptly. 'I must be off.
Come and visit Miss Tunnicliffe soon—don't bring flowers
whatever you do.' He pointed at Cass's plate. 'You shouldn't
be eating those either. Staff Nurse Brown says they're bad
for you.'

FOURTEEN

DESPITE LAST NIGHT'S exertions plus his early-morning visit, when he returned home, Mr Pringle declared himself ready to tackle anything. Mrs Bignell promptly produced a list.

'I'm glad you feel up to it, dear. What I thought was, if you could deal with the wreckage at my place, I'll tidy up here for the party.'

That sounded ominous. 'You said it would only be a cup of tea.'

'Plus the odd nibble. You wouldn't like it if they thought we hadn't bothered.'

'Everyone will be bloated after yesterday.'

'No, they won't. Eats like a bird, does Becky. She needs something to peck at for a start. And Betty Fisher gave me smoked salmon sandwiches last time I called.' It was obvious Mrs Bignell didn't intend to be outdone. 'The men will expect cream sponge as well as fruit cake. I'll set it out in the dining room, shall I, then people can help themselves?'

'Can't they manage with plates in the living room?' He seemed to remember Renée's friends balancing theirs on the arms of the chairs. 'They won't be here *that* long, will they?' The idea of his house being taken over by strangers made him shrink. He found himself being ushered into the hall. Mrs Bignell handed him her keys.

'If you could get the electricity back on I'd be ever so grateful. I don't like to think of my pipes freezing up. You remember where I keep the cleaning things? If the hall carpet's very damp there's a fan in the back bedroom cupboard. Lunch at one o'clock, all right?'

With his front door closing gently but firmly behind him, Mr Pringle had little choice. Slightly miffed, he set off. A small burst of sunshine and his mood began to lift. He recalled certain details of the previous night—my word, yes! He had succeeded in surprising himself yet again. Euphoria lightened his step. There was another reason: following his conversation with Lila Boyce, he felt a thrill of nervous excitement. If his theories were correct, this afternoon might bring an opportunity to put them to the test.

Arriving at the house, he discovered the damage was not too bad, not in his present mood anyway. What did it matter if the blackened hall wallpaper was peeling away in strips? Mrs Bignell had declared she was tired of it. He found the fan and, having reset the circuit breakers, switched it on.

The remains of the tree plus the twisted charred trouser press he consigned to the dustbin. He felt no sense of loss. Fate, which had spared him 'My bonnie lies over the ocean' every time he put on his trousers, could not be criticised. It then occurred to him, he might go a little further in his disposal of unwanted items. Through narrowed eyes he surveyed the ground-floor rooms and wondered if he dared. Mrs Bignell had invited him to 'tidy up'. This was his chance.

With his aesthetic eye, he had always longed to banish the dreadful souvenirs from southern Spain, displayed in deference to friends with bad taste who had brought them back. Mr Pringle knew which kitchen drawer contained spare bin liners. He located the dusters, the cleaning materials—and began a clean sweep.

After he'd disposed of every trace of Viva España, he hoovered away the remains of the foam. Rolling up his sleeves, he began on the walls. Clearing them of rubbish would reveal the plain classical lines of the downstairs rooms. Pictures of crinoline ladies disappeared in an instant. Ghastly fluffy objects were seized from the dining-room plate rack. Indeed, if the screwdriver had been the right size, he might have removed the rack *in toto*. He then rearranged the furniture to better advantage, especially in the living room, with those fiddly little tables stacked to-gether to give more space.

As for the kitchen, what more loving gesture than for Mrs Bignell to find all her equipment stowed away in cupboards and the work surfaces hygienically bare for a change?

Mr Pringle was astonished. All that energy expended last night yet today he felt a new man. Goodness only knew how long it would last. Perhaps this evening...if Mrs Bignell also felt inclined...could he surprise himself once more? All that remained here was to give the woodwork a darn good pol-ish.

By midday, he could no longer straighten his back. His varicose vein throbbed in reproach. With a groan, he slung the dusters in water and made himself a mug of coffee. They could be left to soak, he needed to do the same. He hob-bled into the re-vamped living room. If he could just close his eyes for five minutes...

The phone summoned him peremptorily. As he leapt out of the chair, his back reminded him how foolish he had been.

'Hello?'

'Are you all right? You sound peculiar,' said Mavis. 'Did you know it's twenty past one?'

It took twice the time to struggle home. He inserted his door key, walked inside calling, 'It's me, I'm back,' and wondered if he'd mistaken the address. Mavis emerged tri-umphantly from the kitchen.

'Joe had these bits left over at the Bricklayers. I thought we'd use them to brighten the place up.' Mr Pringle gazed at the virulent plastic holly wreathing newel post and banis-ter, the brewery's lurid version of the Laughing Cavalier above the hall table. Mrs Bignell mistook his silence for admiration. 'It is nice, isn't it? I always like the way the eyes follow you about in that picture. Come and see what I've done in the living room.' His heart sank, and, having seen, stayed sunk.

As he searched for the right word to describe the dangling baubles and seasonal encrustations, she said, 'Sit down a minute. I've something important to tell you.' He wondered what was coming next. 'It's about the murder. Joe heard why the police are so certain Karl was mixed up in Ernest's death.'

'Oh?'

'That same morning, Karl tried to kill his wife.'

Mr Pringle stared at her blankly. 'He—what? I don't quite follow?'

'In Southend. Karl pushed Sharon downstairs and broke her neck. Someone found her and called the police. They don't know whether she'll survive. She'll never walk again, she's paralysed.'

'Karl Gough did that?'

Mavis nodded. 'I couldn't believe it at first. I knew it wasn't a happy marriage but no one would have dreamed Karl would do a thing like that. It explains why the police weren't surprised though, doesn't it? They obviously knew about Sharon when Ernest was found and put two and two together. Joe heard it on the radio first thing this morning. They repeated it on the one o'clock. They explained then why they didn't include a mention of Sharon in the television item the other night. They wanted people to concentrate on the identikit picture instead.' She added, 'It's even more dreadful because the other man's struck again.'

Mr Pringle's eyebrows went up. 'The prowler has?'

'He's been back to Southend. They think he must live in the area. He's called Lee Andrews. Last night he attacked a policewoman outside Sharon's mother's house.'

'Was Karl in the vicinity when this happened?'

'They didn't say. I expect they would have done if he was.'

Mr Pringle allowed himself to be led to the kitchen while he considered these new facts.

'We'll have our lunch in here, if you don't mind. I've already laid the table for tea.' From her expression he knew more surprises were in store in the dining room but he had already received one shock too many.

'I'll see it when the others do,' he suggested.

'I found a pretty cloth, and some china tucked away. I hope you don't mind me using it.'

'You've worked very hard, I'm most grateful. I'm sure the party will be a great success.'

Mavis gazed about equably. 'All it needed in here was a few hundred-watt bulbs. It's made all the difference.'

'It certainly has.'

Under the floodlights he remained deep in thought, munching away without noticing what he ate. He handed his cup across automatically, consumed something sweet-tasting and asked finally, 'Remind me again who is coming this afternoon.'

'Miss Posner, if she's well enough. Charlie, Lila, John Hines, Betty Fisher and Reg Wolfe. I kept the numbers down, I knew you wouldn't want to feel swamped.' Mr Pringle doubted whether there had ever been so many at one time during the whole of his occupancy.

'Before they arrive, I think I'll have a hot bath.'

'I warned you not to overdo it last night.'

He was huffy. 'I wasn't overdoing it.' Not last night, he wasn't. All the same he began to have qualms about this morning's effort.

The bath soothed him. Mr Pringle let hot water lubricate his shoulder blades and used the loofah on the difficult bit in between. He added more water. Without his glasses and the room full of steam, nothing was in focus. He lay back and gave the problem his full attention.

Try as he might Mr Pringle could not reconcile the attack on Sharon Gough with what had happened to Ernest Clare. Mrs Gough had been born and bred in Southend. As far as Mrs Bignell was aware, the girl had never even been introduced to Ernest.

If Karl was responsible for his wife's broken neck and the prowler for last night's brutality, had the two of them teamed up to kill one old man? It seemed very unlikely.

Mr Pringle had already worked out a possible sequence preceding Ernest's death. Today's bombshell did not alter this orderly progression: his logical mind having examined the fresh evidence, rejected certain parts of it. What worried him was the apparent lack of any connection between the crimes, not to mention the lack of motive.

Why would Gough break his wife's neck? The radio had quoted a neighbour's innuendo about men who had visited Mrs Gough during her husband's long absences. If true, surely these days such behaviour would lead to divorce rather than violence.

'Hurry up! They'll be here in half an hour.'

'Coming, coming...'

WHEN THE ARTIC began to jack-knife, Karl didn't panic. He had no strength left. The pain had spread to his arms. He held the wheel but made no attempt to counter the skid. They were slewing sideways and with no action taken to prevent it the back of the vehicle was swinging around.

It was in slow motion, either that or his brain had speeded up; he could consider the consequence to every other vehicle, especially those heading toward him, frame by frame. It wasn't fear which froze him but the realisation he could do nothing to prevent the catastrophe.

However loudly Geneviève screamed, that wouldn't achieve anything. Her mouth was an ugly twisted shape. He couldn't understand the abuse, it was simply one long screech. She had hold of one wrist so tightly her nails gouged his skin. That hand lost its tenuous hold on the wheel and fell into his lap. Her face was so close, he could see the rigid oesophagus arch at the back of her throat.

That black AX in the fast lane was bound to collide with the trailer. A gleaming new car, two occupants; they didn't stand a chance.

Sharon. Her face suddenly filled Karl's mind, swelling and obliterating every other image, even the weasel features so close to his own. His attention switched away from what was happening. He could longer understand why he had told her, he could have left it a little longer: he began to say aloud, 'Why did I have to tell her—?' but he never finished the sentence.

The impact produced a silence in his brain. No screaming, no sound of tearing metal and splintering glass from the Citroën. When bone and flesh were sliced by the sides of the trailer and the wheel finished the job, crushing, compacting, smashing everything into a hard impenetrable mass with shivers of shiny glossy black flecked with red, Karl's mind slid away from the responsibility. This was happening to someone else.

The cab tipped forward. Springy umbilical cables snapped. The entire vehicle gave a jerk and the cab went horizontal. They were suspended above the central barrier. Geneviève was jammed up against the broken windscreen. Karl reached out to touch the trickle of blood on her cheek. It was warm. His hands were quite cold.

DC CASS, together with Bramwell's friend George, had borrowed one of the interview rooms at the local police station. The table was littered with newspaper cuttings. 'We kept an awful lot of stuff in those days. Some of these date back to 1967.'

'Which was the year Andrews cracked the security guard's skull. He was lucky to get off with manslaughter.'

'That's what we thought.'

Cass examined the official black and white photograph of Lee Andrews. He checked the date on the back. '1982? Got a more recent one?'

'I doubt it. That would be the last time he was sent down.' George took another look at the photo. 'From all accounts he hasn't changed. He's older, of course. Still violent. He's a keep-fit fanatic—and I mean fanatic. Exercises night and day when he's banged up. A hell-raiser, always in trouble. Doesn't know his own strength which is half the problem. Here you are, this is what *she* used to look like.'

Cass read the details aloud. '"Mimi" also known as Alice Berriman, a.k.a. "Marilyn". Busy lady.' He studied the sulky face beneath the peroxide helmet, the pale pout and hard pointed breasts poking through the blouse.

'Pencil sharpeners, we called those bras. Padded satin with reinforced lines of stitching. Terrible.'

'Not much of a come-on,' Cass agreed.

'Depends what else was on offer. You're young. In those days women like this could earn a decent living. Nowadays, unless you're unlucky, you can get it for free.'

'George, you are quite certain Andrews has no connection with Gough? His car has been seen outside their place although usually when Gough was away. According to the woman next door it started over two years ago. Which could support the theory of Gough and Andrews working together.'

'I know.' George removed his glasses and rubbed his eyes. 'Gough's a mystery as far as I'm concerned. I'd retired before he arrived on the scene. All I can tell you is Andrews always went back to Berriman when he was in bother. She used to live more centrally in those days, middle of town, handy for businessmen. We'd always check her place if we were looking for him.'

'What did her husband think?'

'God knows. He must have known what he was marrying. She used to get charged regularly. Two-quid fine and bound over, the usual thing. Some blokes prefer to turn a blind eye, I reckon. Anyway, Andrews was definitely Alice Berriman's regular bloke. Sharon wasn't even born then, he's old enough to be her father. Maybe *she's* taken over looking after him now her ma's turned respectable.'

'Could be.'

'I'm sorry I can't help.'

'You've done all right with the rest of it, thanks.' Cass glanced at his watch. 'Let's hope Andrews gets picked up in the next couple of days. At least we can leave things tidy.'

'He's not usually difficult to find. Mind you . . .' George shook his head. 'He could have made a whole load of new pals in Gartree. I gave the front office the names of all the ones I could remember.'

'They're still checking them.'

'Where are you off to next?'

Cass was on his feet. 'To introduce myself to Mrs Berriman. Maybe she'll offer me a cup of tea.'

'Watch yourself if she does. Harm could come to a young chap like you.'

There was a police Land-rover parked conspicuously halfway down the street of smart bungalows. Annoy the neighbours, Bramwell had suggested: if it's an area where posh friends come round for a Christmas drink, the locals will come across with everything they know in order to rid themselves.

Cass chuckled when he saw how well these instructions had been obeyed. He opened the rear door and climbed inside. 'No flashing blue light, gentlemen?'

'Afternoon.' They introduced themselves. 'We had it on when we arrived,' the driver told him. 'And we had the window open so they could hear the radio. We didn't want them to forget there's a mad man on the loose.'

'Any result?'

'One complaint from a gent who was pretending to walk his pooch. He said the noise was giving his wife a head-ache. Nothing stirring at Ma Berriman's. She hasn't switched her lights on but we know she's in there. Presumably she's hiding round the back.'

'Has her phone line been restored?'

The second officer turned to face Cass. 'We thought if it wasn't, that might help speed things up.'

'Good thinking.'

'We had a quiet word with BT. Perhaps we ought to check, though.' He dialled the number and held the re-ceiver so they could hear the unobtainable tone. Satisfied, he replaced it. 'It should help flush Andrews out, if he needs to talk to her.'

There was a crackle on the radio. He listened and ex-plained, 'One of his contacts lives in Billericay. Our lads went there but no dice, obviously.'

Cass asked curiously, 'If he does show up, what's the plan?'

'Orders are to call up reinforcements,' the second officer said seriously. 'None of us want to qualify for a posthu-mous award.' He turned again to stare at Cass. 'You've been to the hospital—how's Viv Tunnicliffe?'

'Remarkable, under the circumstances. I hope I don't miss her on the news.'

'My wife's recording it. Thank God one of the neigh-bours used her loaf. The woman in number forty-eight.' The second officer nodded toward the relevant bungalow. 'She's been minding the Gough kid, occasionally. Ma Berriman never could be bothered. The neighbour was watching from her bedroom window last night and saw Viv arrive. When Berriman's door opened, she saw Andrews begin to thump her. She phoned us then dashed across and raised one hell of a racket outside—which made him scarper.'

'Bright lady.'

The other was fervent. 'You can say that again. Viv stood no chance with that gorilla. You haven't met him but he's built like a tank.'

'How old is the kid?'

'What?'

The pieces were beginning to form a definite pattern. 'Sharon Gough's child, how old is it?'

'No idea.'

Cass had the door open. 'She'd know, wouldn't she? That neighbour. Any idea of her name?'

'Connie, I think she said.'

Cass was already heading toward number 48.

THE TEA PARTY GUESTS had arrived, all except Charlie who phoned to say he would be along later. Mr Pringle watched as Mavis made the rest welcome, installing Miss Posner in his own deep armchair beside the fire. He wished she had offered it to John Hines. The ex-sergeant looked most uncomfortable, his bulk perched on the edge of the spindly legged stool by the door. The seating in this room was insufficient, that was the trouble. Mr Pringle had never anticipated entertaining seven people simultaneously. Mavis came to the rescue.

'Why don't you take Reg and John upstairs and show them your pictures?' she suggested. 'I expect Reg is dying for a smoke.'

'If it's permitted,' Reg Wolfe said politely.

'Upstairs, it is. Not down here.' She lowered her voice. 'It might upset Becky's chest.'

Mr Pringle wondered if it had been wise for the lady to leave her sick bed. His chair emphasised Miss Posner's pinched, shrunken features. Her dress looked too large and the brittle hands emerging from the sleeves were like claws. These clutched at the shawl Lila had put round her shoulders.

He gave his attention to his two male guests. 'I don't know if either of you are interested,' he murmured, leading the way. 'It is a small collection, going back many years.'

Behind him, Reg Wolfe had paused. 'I like that one.' He was admiring the Laughing Cavalier. 'Now that's what I call a good picture.'

'It is a favourite of Mrs Bignell's,' Mr Pringle admitted. He mounted the stairs in silence.

Inside the study, his two guests relaxed. Here there were no women's touches, nor ornaments to trap the unwary. Reg Wolfe found an ashtray and stretched out on the window seat. 'I'd like a room like this. If things fall on the floor, it doesn't matter, does it? They just get mixed up with the rest of the rubbish.' Mr Pringle was dismayed to hear his filing system thus described but as John Hines was already examining the first picture, he joined him to explain the provenance.

'Did either of you see the news this lunchtime?' Reg interrupted, apparently carelessly. 'There was a piece about our prowler.'

'Really?' Mr Pringle paused, mid-sentence.

Hines stared at Reg intently. 'What did it say?'

'You knew he'd attacked a policewoman last night?' Reg Wolfe went on to describe the item, finishing, 'They showed the identikit picture again. I suppose the three of us may have to try and pick him out once they catch up with him.'

Mr Pringle felt his own pulse begin to flutter. Had the subject been raised deliberately?

'Will Miss Posner be up to that?' he murmured. 'Today, I thought she looked particularly fragile.'

'There's no need for her to be involved,' John Hines was vehement. 'A gentle old soul like that—surely you and Lila can do what's necessary, Reg?'

Reg studied his cigarette. 'It would be better, I agree. Let's hope the police see it that way.'

Hines moved on to the next picture and the subject appeared closed. With mixed feelings, Mr Pringle began to describe the history of the Manchester school, finishing, 'And this is my particular favourite.' It was the sketch of the northern market.

Hines examined it in critical silence. 'Not much detail.'

Mr Pringle took his courage in both hands. 'No, but enough to see what each person represents. His or her relationship with his neighbour. How each is a part of the whole...' He was conscious how both had gone quiet. He could hear the pattern of Hines's breathing change. He grew bold. 'Interdependent, one with another, so to speak.' Indicating a faintly pencilled outline at the back of the picture, 'This figure is a mere suggestion, with no facial details, yet I believe one could guess what his function was intended to be, if one thought about it.'

John Hines's hands were clenched. The ash on Reg Wolfe's cigarette grew long. It was he who broke the silence.

'And have you thought about it, Pringle? If you have, I presume you have reached a conclusion?'

Behind his spectacles, Mr Pringle held their gaze without wavering. 'I have, yes.'

'Would you care to tell us?'

To give himself time to recover, Mr Pringle went to sit at his desk. John Hines stayed where he was, large and menacing, the ham fists clenched even more tightly.

'My idea is based on knowledge of the parties concerned but one fact continues to elude me: the lack of motive. I reached my conclusion before the events in Southend were known but I find no reason to change my opinion. And I would like to make one thing plain: I do not consider it necessary to pass my observations to the police. Frankly, I doubt whether they would be interested. They prefer facts to supposition.' He waited.

Hines glanced at Wolfe. 'Fair enough?'

Reg Wolfe nodded.

'So... what have you deduced?'

Mr Pringle took a breath to steady himself. 'I believe the events leading to Ernest Clare's death began last Easter, when Lila first saw inside his house—'

But Reg Wolfe was already contradicting him, 'Oh, no. Much, much earlier. In 1939, in fact.'

'Ah, but that is background knowledge, known only to those who are closely concerned. I base my observations on what took place in Inkerman Street.' Nevertheless, he hoped these two would explain. Nervous though he was, Mr Pringle dearly wanted to know the rest of it.

'Whatever happened in 1939, it was last Easter when the first discovery must have been made by Lila Boyce. Clare was a recluse. He guarded his privacy zealously and that included keeping his doors and windows locked. When Miss Posner described how he would lock the door immediately a visitor left and watch until that person was off the premises, I felt sure she was quoting Lila. No doubt Ernest followed that practice but not last Thursday. That day, Rebecca Posner went to his house for the first time, to make his tea and, I believe, she let others enter privately, via the back door, before she left.

'It is inconceivable Ernest would have admitted anyone he wasn't expecting. Even Lila had to telephone before knocking at his door. The police stated the house had not been

broken into. It is the only way those three people could have
gained entrance.' He waited.

After a moment, Reg Wolfe asked, 'You say "three"?'

Mr Pringle nodded. 'Those who claimed to have seen the
prowler. Miss Posner did of course; the others were Lila
Boyce and you, Reg. I also believe ...' Mr Pringle's voice
began to wobble. 'I believe Miss Posner admitted you, John.
And the reason you didn't join in describing this faceless
person was because you...'

To be within three feet of a neighbour and then to accuse
him of being a murderer required a courage G.D.H. Pringle did not possess. '... was because you were more heavily
involved,' he finished lamely.

It took another long moment before John Hines confirmed it. 'Unless you'd been in the services, you wouldn't
understand. The problem was straightforward—a case of
identifying the enemy and then taking him out.'

'Enemy!'

Hines raised a hand. 'Or in this instance, vermin. You
exterminate vermin, Pringle.'

Mr Pringle looked at him in horror. He hadn't understood, he still didn't understand the reason behind this terrible crime but this justification he could not accept.

'You claim the right to be both judge and executioner? If
that is really what happened, I refuse to stay silent. I shall
tell the police all I know—'

'Listen a moment,' Reg said quickly. 'Before *you* start
making judgements we'll tell you what happened in 1939.
You need those missing facts, Pringle. Neither John nor I
would ever plead not guilty to what happened...' He looked
at Hines, who nodded. 'Nor would Lila or Becky, if it came
to it. You've guessed correctly so far but let us tell you *why*
before you decide whether we were right to do what we did.

'At that period, just before the outbreak of war, Rebecca
Posner and her brother were living with their parents in Po-

land, near the border with Germany. The family were Jewish. For various reasons their father couldn't get out but he was determined his son and daughter should. It was still possible to pull strings if you were rich or well connected. Posner settled half his fortune on each of them but he had left it too late. The family were arrested and shipped with other Jews to a camp. It wasn't very large, these were early days; no gas chambers. The Kommandant was about thirty. He was Viennese. He was also, as Posner realised, known to him.

'Posner requested a private interview. He explained Becky and her brother could pay for their freedom. Unfortunately, Posner also revealed what he knew about the Kommandant's own background. There followed six months of brutal treatment, the Kommandant using all the pressure he could to make Posner release the cash. When he realised there was no other way to get his hands on it, he agreed to Posner's plan. This was to put Rebecca on a train for Switzerland. Her father was no fool. He had arranged with the bank in Zurich that only his daughter—in person—could transfer her half of the money.

'This she did, into a new account. What should have followed was the release of her brother who would then go to Zurich and repeat the process.

'However, when confirmation was received—and the Kommandant had proof the account had been set up—he forced her brother to sign a letter, instructing that his half be transferred without the need of his presence. The bank had been given strict instructions but they disobeyed. War was everywhere by then, rules were being broken all the time.

'Posner, his wife and their son were executed. As were all the other detainees in that particular camp. Over six hundred people. No one survived.'

Mr Pringle moved stiffly in his chair. 'And the Kommandant?'

'That was quite ironic,' Reg's voice was matter-of-fact. 'You see, the Posners knew he also had Jewish blood. His real name was Klaar although he had managed to conceal it. Had it come out, it would have damned him.

'The Posners passed the information on before they were killed and the guards learned about it. They were quite prepared to tell the authorities so the Kommandant had to make a quick exit. By now he had the means, and the British were prepared to make use of anyone who was willing to provide inside information. In return they "facilitated" his escape. He reached this country, applied for naturalisation and anglicised his name. At that time, Becky was struggling to make a living in the East End. Klaar became Clare, moved here and immediately went into hiding. Becky moved to Inkerman Street later.'

'She must have recognised him?'

'For several years, she never even saw him. She never visited the pub in those days. In her way, she was as reclusive as he was. Both of them living within half a mile of one another but never meeting—that's how it was.

'Eventually, when she did catch sight of him, she wasn't sure. He had altered his appearance of course, he was that much older and she had tried to blot out the memory of everything to do with that camp. Remember, Inkerman Street was the last place on earth she *expected* to see him.'

'And when she finally decided it was the same person?'

'She told Lila. She wasn't one hundred per cent certain even then. Klaar was using a different Christian name as well. In the camp he'd been known as Helmut Klaar. You were right in your assumption, however. It was roughly last Easter, when Lila first started to help him, that Becky told her of her suspicions.'

'Is there any connection between Lila Boyce and Miss Posner?'

'Not in the sense you mean,' replied Hines.

'None of us have any connection,' said Reg. 'My parents got out of Bavaria before the war. Lila came much later. She knew what Becky had gone through. Her family were from Alsace so she had first-hand experience of what Occupation could mean. The Nazis were living in her family's house. Once the retreat began they wrecked it then set it alight with the family inside. Only two got out, Lila and her aunt.'

Mr Pringle looked at John Hines. 'You were—in the army.'

'I helped liberate one of those camps. It's something you never forget.'

'But after all this time? You said even Miss Posner was unsure.'

'Wait till you've heard the rest of it. We told you the Kommandant was known as Helmut Klaar. Lila found Ernest had written "H.E. Klaar" on the notebook he kept beside his bed. Old habits die hard.'

'Even so. . . you may have been mistaken.'

'There was only one way to prove it beyond any doubt. The Kommandant had a sense of humour. He gave instructions as to what number the new account should be given. No names were to be used, of course. When he put Becky on the train he told her they needed a number they could both remember.'

Before he could continue, Mr Pringle pulled open the top drawer and took out the scrap of paper. He handed it to Reg Wolfe.

'Where did you find this?'

'Under the step in Clare's house, when I was searching for the bequest envelopes.'

Without commenting, Reg Wolfe showed it to Hines before setting light to it. The scrap shrivelled in the ashtray.

'You know what it is, don't you?'

'I think I can guess... Miss Posner always wears long sleeves, of course.'

Hines cleared his throat. 'We had two reasons for doing what we did, Pringle. When you hear the second, you may condemn us but when I was told of Miss Posner's suffering and the disgraceful way her brother had been treated, I want you to know I volunteered for the job.'

Mr Pringle glanced at the capable fists; there always were, always would be, many applicants for the post of public executioner. Yet if he guessed right, their second reason negated the first.

'You wanted to get hold of that money.'

'You think we were wrong?'

'I believe it cancels out any moral justification.'

'Let me try and explain...' Daylight had faded. Reg Wolfe was a shape against the window. Mr Pringle switched on the desk light and tilted it; he needed to see his face.

'You know better than most how little Becky has to live on. You've seen her physical state. Her GP has warned her it won't be long before she has to go into a home. She's dreading the prospect. Lila told us she'd even considered suicide.

'All your talk about that picture... people depending on one another, you were right. None of us have any "family" but we take care of each other as best we can.'

John Hines cleared his throat. 'We'd already discussed what action we should take because of Miss Posner's brother. We had another meeting, just the three of us, we didn't involve her. We knew there must be some money. Whatever it had cost Klaar to escape, the way he's lived since he settled here meant there had to be a healthy sum remaining. We decided to give him a chance.'

Mr Pringle moistened dry lips. 'Hand over the money in exchange for his life.'

'That might sound cruel to you. It seemed a bloody fair offer to us.'

'We didn't know what had happened to it,' Reg went on. 'Becky wrote to the bank when she first arrived in England, telling them the whole story; they claimed no knowledge whatsoever. Perhaps they were within their rights: she had renounced all claim on it when she opened the new account. Alternatively, Klaar might have moved the cash somewhere safe over here.' He paused, stubbed out the cigarette. 'Lila—she's never got over watching her mother burn to death . . . We were all involved but she was the one determined to make him talk. He refused to tell us anything.'

Those stubby nicotine-stained fingers. Mr Pringle knew he would faint if he was told what they'd done. His murmur was barely audible.

'And sentence was duly carried out.' If Klaar had handed it over, would they have spared him? Mr Pringle doubted it. There was too much hate, too many memories.

'It was the same person,' Hines insisted. 'We didn't kill an innocent man. That's why Miss Posner had to be there on Thursday, to show him her arm. She's never had the branding removed. As soon as he saw it, and we saw his face, we didn't need any further confirmation. He was the same Helmut Ernst Klaar all right. Miss Posner left immediately afterwards. She wasn't there when we . . .'

'No. Quite.'

Mr Pringle was finding it difficult to breathe regularly. Hines, upright as if it were a court martial, declared, 'Vermin, Pringle. That's all he was. He had his chance. He refused to take it.'

Those fists had choked another human being to death.

'The rule of law has to be upheld. You should have let the authorities know, and left it to them . . .'

'At first, we thought the same,' Reg insisted. 'My God, Pringle, we're not barbarians! We waited to see if this government would act as they had promised but then they began shilly-shallying. Becky had been warned by her GP by then. She was in a dreadful state.'

'Those six hundred other victims,' Hines reminded him. 'Their families wouldn't have hesitated and neither did we.'

'It was justice. No doubt about it.'

Then why were they both striving so hard to justify themselves?

'What size was Mr Posner's fortune?'

'Approximately one million pounds. Half for each child. Whatever Klaar needed to pay for his escape, most of it must still be salted away.'

'One wonders why he continued to live as he did?'

Reg Wolfe shrugged. 'We decided he must still be scared of discovery.'

He looked at Hines who nodded. 'We believe, in his heart, Klaar had always been expecting it to happen one day. He knew he couldn't escape.'

'But not vengeance at the hands of his friends.'

'We weren't his friends. Were you?' Reg challenged. 'Was anybody?'

'Not that I know of,' Mr Pringle admitted. Mrs Bignell had wept but not from a personal sense of loss, simply the horror of it.

'Miss Posner could never forgive the treachery to her brother. She was far more concerned about that. It was Lila who wanted her to have the benefit of the money.'

Mr Pringle recalled the changes in the frail victim downstairs. 'I fear, however, Miss Posner will always suffer as a result of what has happened.'

'We had to have her there on Thursday,' John Hines apologised. 'Although we were ninety per cent certain, until we saw his face when she showed him her arm, we needed that final confirmation. After she'd gone, he only opened his mouth once. He said "Joachim"—her brother's name.'

They sat in silence. Three elderly men contemplating the deliberate murder of one of their neighbours. Downstairs, the sound of Charlie Tucknell arriving and an increase in the level of jollity couldn't be ignored. They would soon be summoned down to tea. Mr Pringle wondered if he could play the part of host after what he'd been told. His body felt as if it could no longer move, it was weighed down by evil. Could his pictures ever bring consolation again or had they been tainted as well?

'What about Gough?' he asked suddenly. 'How does he fit in? I never could work that out.'

'He doesn't. Nothing but a bloody nuisance—an accident,' John Hines said bluntly. 'The fool let himself in through the back door. We left it unlocked after Becky had gone, we planned to leave that way ourselves. We were upstairs, trying to find details of the bank account. We never thought to look under the step—Lila cursed like mad when she found you'd done that, Pringle.'

'We heard a rumour you'd found some of the money?'

'His building society book, which the police kept, and that scrap of paper. That was all.'

The other two nodded.

'We heard a noise—someone creeping about downstairs,' Hines told him. 'We didn't know who it was, of course. We just had to wait. We heard Gough yelp when he found Ernest . . . *He* didn't hang about after that. But when we came down we found he'd managed to steal the bequest money. The notes had been on the table beside the envelopes.'

'The trouble was, we didn't know if whoever it was had gone straight to the police,' said Reg. 'We slipped away as soon as the coast was clear. Lila realised it must have been

Karl when she saw him sitting in her kitchen. Thank God he never knew we were hiding upstairs.'

'Do you think he guessed?'

Reg Wolfe smiled briefly. 'That young man hasn't a logical mind like you, Pringle. No, once he'd disappeared in his lorry, we felt certain we were safe. Especially when we found he'd stolen Lila's card. That's why he disappeared once the police arrived at the Bricklayers... Goodbye, Karl. As for that other business in Southend...' He shrugged massively. 'We were as surprised as you must have been.'

'We'd no idea,' John Hines insisted. 'That news came as a complete shock. We'd been worrying about keeping Karl Gough out of it. We didn't want him blamed for Klaar's death, naturally. Then this happens.'

'Which is why you invented the prowler.'

Reg Wolfe looked at him curiously. 'We'd already decided to do that before Karl appeared on the scene. How did you know he was an invention? Because we were deliberately vague as to the face?'

'Not entirely, no. That confirmed it, of course.' Mr Pringle quoted:

> ' "As I was going up the stair
> I met a man who wasn't there.
> He wasn't there again today.
> I wish, I *wish* he'd stay away." '

'So what was it?' John Hines pressed him. 'Did we slip up?'

'You certainly did. All of us in Inkerman Street are about the same age,' Mr Pringle pointed out. 'Miss Posner wears even thicker glasses than you or I, Wolfe. Lila can't see further than her gate, yet all three of you described the man's clothing: jeans, running shoes and jacket. Given the level of street lighting, if he'd really existed, none of you would have known if he'd been sporting a kilt.'

There was a shout from below. 'Come and get it!' Mrs Bignell cried gaily. 'Tea's ready!'

'Coming.' Mr Pringle began levering himself upright. Listening to such horrors had brought back the ache in his bones.

'If there is an identity parade, Lila and I will pick different people,' Reg Wolfe assured him. 'If we're found out, we shall take the blame. If that happens my conscience is clear and I doubt whether any jury is going to find us guilty. We shall swear that Becky let us in, then went home. As for Karl Gough, he was something we couldn't have foreseen.'

'You also involved Betty Fisher,' Mr Pringle accused him. 'It must have been exceedingly unpleasant for her to make that discovery—'

'I'd have given anything to prevent it,' he retorted angrily, 'but we had to fit in with what other people had arranged. We had to wait until Charlie had collected the football money before we could go in through the back door. Betty had already told several people she and I would call for Ernest because of the damned bequest money. We couldn't afford to draw attention to ourselves by changing anything, it was too much of a risk.'

Mr Pringle looked from one to the other. 'What you have told me, I regard as completely confidential. I shall not speak of it to anyone.'

'Thank you.'

'Thanks.' John Hines insisted on gripping his hand.

Mr Pringle tried not to shudder. 'That reminds me, Pringle, about those bequest envelopes. We had to dispose of them, of course, but Klaar had already made the list of names. One was intended for Mrs Bignell.'

'Thank God they were never given out!' It was such a spontaneous cry of alarm, both looked at him in surprise.

'I thought you would be pleased to know she had been chosen,' said Reg.

'Mrs Bignell does not see herself as over sixty,' Mr Pringle told him gravely, 'and I very much doubt she ever will. Shall we join the ladies?'

FIFTEEN

'HELLO—JIM?' To Bramwell, Cass sounded excited. 'I'm phoning from Southend—'

'Leigh-on-Sea,' interrupted a voice, further off.

'Sorry, yes, Leigh-on-Sea. I'm with a neighbour of Mrs Berriman's.' He paused. Bramwell could hear the polite exchange. 'Thanks very much, Connie, I'm through to the incident room.'

'I suppose you want me to leave?'

'If you wouldn't mind. I'll pay for the call.' There was another pause, the sound of footsteps followed by a door slam. Cass spoke discreetly. 'Sorry about that.'

'What's up?'

'I think I've discovered the connection between Sharon Gough and Andrews. He could be the father of her kid.'

'Not Karl Gough, you mean?'

'I'm off to confirm the date of birth with Mrs Berriman. This neighbour isn't totally sure but thinks it was June of last year. Going back nine months would just about fit with the time Andrews left Gartree—at least, I think it would.'

'I'll check that this end. But what you're saying makes it more likely for Gough to have done it, once he found out what was going on. Why should Andrews be upset? He already knew presumably?'

'That's what worries me. I'll phone you again when I've spoken to Berriman. Any news of Andrews? They're still checking his contacts here.'

'Not a sausage. Nor Gough. He must be shacked up with some accommodating mademoiselle. No doubt he'll resurface once the money runs out.'

'No doubt.'

'How was George?'

'Fine. Sends his best. Asks when you're coming to visit.'

Sooner than he thinks, thought Bramwell, depressed. Any more aggro at home and I'll pack a bag. To Cass all he said was, 'Don't forget to pay for your call.'

IT WAS DIFFICULT to see traces of either Mimi or Marilyn in the face that opened the door to DC Cass. Without make-up, Mrs Berriman had lost any allure, and these days her figure was not so prominent. The sulky aggression was all that remained: 'I've got nothing to say to you lot.'

'I'm coming in anyway.' Cass shoved against the door, catching her off balance.

'You've got a nerve—I shall report it. I've got a right to my privacy. How much longer is that bloody Land-rover staying out there?'

'As long as it takes.'

'He's not coming here!' She was shouting now, red-faced. 'I'll swear an oath if you want—Lee Andrews is not coming back here!'

'What is your granddaughter's date of birth?'

'What?' She recovered quickly. 'What d'you want to know that for?'

'Come on.' Cass was belligerent. 'We know it was June. Tell me the date then I'll go.'

'The sixteenth.' Even that could be a lie, he thought, seeing the defiance.

'It doesn't matter. We can check. I thought you might like to co-operate for a change.'

'Why the hell should I? Why should any of my family—'

Cass had reached the front door and swung round accusingly. 'That's what Lee Andrews was, wasn't he? Family?'

She stared, speechless, face and body sagging. 'Who told you? Not—Sharon?'

'Sometimes we can actually work these things out for ourselves,' he taunted. 'Of course she didn't tell us. She still wants us to think Andrews is responsible for attacking her.'

'What?' Mrs Berriman was staring as though she didn't believe her ears. It added to Cass's irritation.

'Karl found out, didn't he? That his wife had been playing around while he was away. He suddenly discovered he wasn't Sarah's father and his mind blew. He went for Sharon in a big way.'

To his chagrin, Mrs Berriman began to laugh. His nerves jangled as she walked away, her loud contempt increasing behind him.

'Hey! Cass.' The blue light was revolving. The two inside the Land-rover were summoning him urgently. Cass shot across the road. 'It's Andrews. He's been sighted—'

'Right, I'll follow. What's the address? How far is it?'

'No need to get excited, it's here in Southend.' The driver was shame-faced. 'Where none of us thought to look— where she must've sent him.' He pointed at Mrs Berriman's bungalow. 'He's hiding out at the Goughs' place. The landlady next door, she spotted him. Makes sense when you think about it—Ma Berriman must have given him the keys.'

KARL GOUGH refused to accept the evidence of his eyes: he wasn't that ill! They were trying to frighten him but he knew better. It couldn't develop that quickly. There were drugs to combat it, good ones from America. If only he could get out of this place and find a decent doctor.

He had been numb with shock after the crash. The artic was badly damaged, it would be a long time before he was driving again so why get worked up about it?

The girl—Geneviève—he saw her revive the minute the police turned up. She'd stood here, blood spurting from the gash on her face, hurling abuse until they'd told her to shut up. They'd put him in a separate van, thank God. From there he'd had to watch them disentangle the two bodies from the Citroën. It was obvious they were dead, he didn't bother to ask. Increasing fever had made the whole scene unreal.

He was in a state of collapse by the time they brought him here. A doctor shone a light in his eyes, they'd taken samples of blood, urine, saliva; after that, he'd been wheeled along corridors. All Karl remembered was a series of ceilings ending with this one. He was in a high bed with metal sides, it must be some sort of hospital but where were the other patients?

When anyone entered, they were swathed in plastic as well as masks and gloves. No one explained—they were trying to scare him. They spooned in medicine and then left again without a word.

He clenched the sheet in agitation, summoning up a puny defiance. He had to tell someone what had happened, otherwise they might start believing it was all his fault.

Two nurses entered. Neither spoke, they treated him with complete detachment. One checked the drip, the other thrust a thermometer in his mouth. He waited until it was removed.

'Nurse... Will you listen, it's important.' The infirmière was concerned with the acute viral infection and further manifestations of deterioration, she paid no heed to the rasping sound from the patient's throat. She commented on the rise in temperature as she entered it on the chart. Behind her mask, her colleague pulled a face.

'Sharon... Thursday, morning... She told me about Sarah. I was so flaming mad, I told her about the clinic... I had to hit her, to stop her screaming. She wouldn't listen... I told her it might never happen. After she'd been ... so filthy... she'd no right. Andrews turned up... I left them to it.' Karl tried to focus on the nurse closest to him. 'It hasn't happened, it can't happen, not yet. I always

take a shower.' Satisfied he'd made everything plain, he
closed his eyes, ready to sleep.

'*Qu'est-ce qu'il disait?*'
'*Je n'ai pas compris.*'

OUTSIDE THE mean concrete house, the apparatus was
moving into position to trap one powerful, violent man.
Cass stayed on the sidelines—this wasn't his show. Next
door, the landlady appeared in the bay window gesticulat-
ing with what was obviously a tray of tea. He remembered
how thirsty he was. Why not? But the chain stayed in place
on the door until he'd held up his card.

'You can't be too sure these days.' She released it and let
him enter. 'D'you take sugar?'

'One, thanks.'

'I saw his car yesterday.' She stirred vigorously. 'It's difficult to tell the colour in the dark but I was nearly sure. He
leaves it out of sight, round the back. Then this morning,
while I was watching, he opened a bedroom window. Likes
to do breathing exercises, you see. I knew it was him. He
was wearing a T-shirt.'

'Thanks.'

She nodded, garrulous with excitement and tension. They
had moved into her front room and stood in the bay as outside an officer with a loud-hailer emerged from one of the
vehicles.

Cass commented on what a comprehensive view she had
of the Goughs' house. Before she could stop herself, she
agreed, adding, 'It's even better from upstairs. Not that I
waste my time watching.'

'No, of course not.'

'But you can see how badly their roof needs doing. It's
stupid having flat roofs in this country, isn't it, what with the
weather and everything.'

'No doubt.' Outside, the house next door was surrounded and the team were closing in. Cass leaned forward. This mob were well organised. He could hear the loud-hailer voice ordering Andrews to give himself up. Beside him, the landlady's chatter grew breathless.

'A pity your lot weren't here last Thursday, I kept saying so to that policewoman, the one he duffed up, you might have been able to stop it if you'd acted fast enough.'

'Oh, yes.' He was scanning each of the windows on this side. They had no way of knowing if Andrews was armed. There was already one police marksman in position behind a van.

'When I saw Mrs Berriman arriving I thought, thank God, that'll put an end to it. She'll go in and sort that pair out. He always listens to her, you see. Karl had driven away in his lorry. You should have heard the noise by then. And what does her mother do? She calls out, "What's going on?" and Sharon yells something, then all Mrs Berriman does is wheel the pram away. Didn't take a blind bit of notice. I know Sharon was f-ing and blinding but if it had been my daughter—'

'What?' Cass was staring at her. 'You're saying Mrs Berriman didn't go into the house?'

'That's right. She goes off with the pram instead. I was glad. It was a cold day and that poor little mite was crying. After a bit it all went quiet. He come and asked me to make that phone call but I didn't see him leave. His car wasn't there when I went to do my bit of shopping.'

'Why didn't you say so before? Bloody hell, woman—'

'Here, don't you go calling me names. It wasn't my business, I'm not her keeper. I said so to that cheeky policewoman—'

'I read your statement—you said Mrs Berriman called at the house and collected the child.'

'She shouted and Sharon called back, I didn't hear what she said, that's when Mrs Berriman wheels the pram away—'

'You made it sound as if Mrs Berriman went inside. She must have known it was Andrews if they were already having a row?'

'I never said she went in. I don't know if she heard him, do I? Oh, my God—look out! He's coming this way!'

Lee Andrews, fifteen stone of body-building muscle hurtled out of a side window and cleared the fence between the two houses. He dived up the front steps and began shouldering the now unchained front door.

As he moved to intercept, Cass could hear the screech, 'Don't let him in—he'll wreck the place!' but Cass was already in the hall as the door burst open.

An illuminated fire exit sign was at the top of the first landing. As he turned to face Andrews, Cass recalled the metal ladder outside, leading to the adjoining roofs. His job was to prevent Andrews from reaching it. Deliberately, he blocked his route to the staircase.

It was an uneven contest. By the time help had arrived and Cass was rescued, he wondered why he'd ever dared to criticise DPW Tunnicliffe.

IN THE Casualty department, he mumbled to the baby-faced doctor, 'I'd like to see Father Gibson.'

The youth's lip curled: so much for heroism. 'You're not that bad. If there's no skull fracture, you can go home. You'll need several appointments with your dentist but that's not our problem. Need any pain-killers?' It was almost a sneer.

But there was a hair-line crack visible on the X-ray and Cass had to be admitted. They agreed to let him make one phone call.

Bramwell was unsympathetic. 'What the hell were you doing, interfering? You should have kept well out of it. It was their show. If you're seen on the TV instead of one of their chaps—'

'Jim . . . please listen.'

'Speak up. I can't make out what you're saying?'

'He's damaged my jaw.'

'Serve you bloody right. You were supposed to call me after you'd spoken to Berriman.'

'Andrews did it. Not Gough. The woman next door heard it happening after Gough had driven away. And Berriman didn't go into the house. She shouted something to Sharon then collected the pram plus the kid from *outside* and took it away.'

'While her daughter was being hammered? Doesn't sound very likely to me, even for a mother like Berriman. Are you sure the landlady wasn't lying?'

'I don't know!' His head was on fire, his gums were like balloons. 'As of this moment, I don't fucking well care!'

'That is not the attitude, Cass. Will you be back for the inquest tomorrow? It's scheduled for ten o'clock.'

'If they let me out, I will. I think I was right about the kid. When I asked, Berriman didn't deny Andrews was the father.'

Beyond the end of his bed, Cass saw a familiar figure enter the ward and speak briefly to the staff nurse.

'If you hang on a minute, I can probably confirm it. Oh—shit!' The payphone was registering zero. Cass fumbled with a fifty-pence piece. 'Hang on a minute.'

'Here, let me.' Father Gibson pushed it into the slot. 'My word, you've been in the wars.'

'Thanks. Father, I'm on to the incident room. We need to have one fact confirmed—I know it's breaking a confidence, just nod if you'd prefer not to speak—but from what you've been told by Sharon Gough, is Lee Andrews the father?'

Father Gibson hesitated. 'Whose father do you mean?' And with that Cass knew everything.

'Oh... that's what it's about.' He could hear squawks from the incident room and held the receiver away from his ear.

'Does it have to come out?' pleaded Gibson. 'She hasn't long, only a few more days.'

Cass had never felt so weary. 'I don't think so. I can't promise but I don't see why it should.' The squawks were angrier now. He said into the receiver, 'I'll tell you when I see you, Jim. It doesn't affect the inquest,' and hung up.

Father Gibson placed his offering on top of the locker.

'It's a present from your colleague.' In the milk bottle, the daffodils were now completely moribund. 'She said to tell you next time, leave them to rest in peace, otherwise the charge could be manslaughter.'

THE FOLLOWING MORNING, Mr Pringle attended the inquest no longer out of curiosity but on behalf of the murderer and two of his three accomplices. Because he could not bear the thought of facing all four—his latest nightmare had featured John Hines operating an extremely efficient guillotine—Mr Pringle requested a quiet chat with Reg Wolfe alone. They met at lunchtime in a corner of the Bricklayers' saloon. Mrs Bignell was not on duty, she had returned home; he was due to see her again that evening.

The place was almost deserted. Mr Pringle and his companion waited for Joe to switch on the television news. In silence, the few customers gathered to watch. Nothing happened. They gazed at a blank wall inscribed 'Coroner's Court', with the words 'Live from outside the coroner's court' superimposed beneath.

A frozen-faced reporter bounced into shot and announced that eighty-four-year-old Ernest Clare had been murdered by person or persons unknown and that the proceedings had lasted less than five minutes.

Behind him, the SIO swept out of the court. Aware of the sudden rush of fellow media representatives and with his microphone held in front of him like a probe, the reporter dashed after them.

The SIO was in a sunny mood. He addressed the cameras confidently. Now that a certain person had been apprehended, he announced, the police were no longer making further inquiries into this particular investigation: the matter was in abeyance pending the resolution of certain other charges.

He agreed that the same apprehended person would be questioned on two related investigations and saw no reason why all three inquiries should not be brought to a satisfactory conclusion. When asked if the apprehended person's name was Lee Andrews, the SIO would not be drawn. He allowed himself to look pensive at the suggestion Sharon Gough might be seriously ill, and full of praise when DPW Tunnicliffe's name was mentioned. When one reporter demanded to know why Karl Gough hadn't been arrested following the urgent newsflash a few days ago, the SIO took a lofty attitude. Gough had in fact been recaptured, thanks to the assistance we had given to our French colleagues. He was now under arrest in a hospital near Dijon. Once he had satisfied those authorities as to an incident on a French autoroute, an application for extradition would be made.

However, the SIO felt confident, subsequent questioning might or might not link Karl Gough with the recently apprehended person in the matter of Ernest Clare's murder and until they could be satisfied on that point, the matter was, as he previously indicated, in abeyance. The frozen-faced reporter asked the one question everyone wanted to

know: 'Why was the identikit so unlike the person apprehended in Southend?'

The SIO replied circuitously. 'We have a lot still to do,
gentlemen. There are many questions as yet unanswered and
until we have got to the bottom of these, which we will, you
can be assured of that, I can answer no further questions
here today.'

Mr Pringle dabbed at his moustache. 'I'm not altogether
happy with his syntax.'

'Was anything else said,' asked Reg, 'anything—relevant?'

'Not really, no. That officer had obviously made up his
mind. He had decided Lee Andrews was responsible for all
three attacks plus the damage to that policeman last night.
He can't prove it until Karl Gough has been questioned.
That sums it up, I think. However it does seem much more
likely that it was Andrews and not Gough who attacked Mrs
Gough. Nevertheless . . .' Mr Pringle sighed: to him the
matter seemed fudged. Another example of rough justice;
he certainly wasn't happy with it.

Reg Wolfe said warmly, 'It'll be a relief for the others.
We've been so concerned for Becky. Let's hope she'll start
to pick up now this is more or less finished. Whatever happens, she's not likely to be involved. Once Andrews is behind bars, we can put it behind us.'

'Yes, but—'

Reg was nudging him. 'Looks like you're wanted.' Behind the bar, Joe was replacing the telephone and beckon-
ing Mr Pringle across.

'That was Mavis. She says to tell you she's had burglars
but you're not to worry. She's called the police and could
you get round there as soon as possible.'

A drowning man might review his whole life as the wa-
ters closed over his head: in a much shorter period of time,
Mr Pringle recalled the details of yesterday morning.

'Oh, my lord!'

IT WAS LATE, long after visiting hours, when Bramwell arrived at the hospital. Cass heard the indignant whispering at the nursing station. He watched lazily as the receiver, having won the argument, came to sit beside the bed.

'Good of you to call.'

'I had to take Emma to the Brownies' Christmas concert—she's playing an elf. My wife's taking her mother home a few days early. She can pick Emma up so I thought I'd come on here.'

Cass hadn't seen him look so relaxed in days. 'Has it all come together?'

'More or less. We've had another fax from Dijon. Apart from the viral infection, Karl Gough is HIV positive.'

'Ah . . .' The last piece fell into place.

'That's not some kind of sample?' Bramwell was gazing at the milk bottle.

'They are a token of mutual esteem.'

'I've seen livelier specimens at an autopsy.' He looked at Cass more closely. 'Did you realise most of your front teeth are missing?'

'I was there when it happened.'

'You'll need a teat for beer—didn't they teach you *anything* at training college?'

'Lee Andrews was Sharon Gough's father—'

'We know. You've already told us, remember.'

'But Berriman only confided that fact to Sharon toward the end of last week, as the result of a row. I have it from Father Gibson. He's the one Sharon spoke to. Which also explains, paralysis apart, why she's lost the will to live.'

'I don't get it. She's illegitimate, so what? These days there's no stigma, it's so commonplace people can't be bothered. I should have thought he'd be much more upset when Gough told her he was HIV?'

'She was devastated by what her mother told her because Lee Andrews was also the father of her child, Sarah.'

Bramwell absorbed this in a long moment of silence. 'What a bloody terrible thing. What an animal! He must've realised she didn't know... And you think that was when Gough...'

'I don't know. She could have kept it to herself, there's no way of telling. But I do think last Thursday morning may have been the moment when Karl Gough decided to break his news. According to the landlady, he and Sharon were shouting at one another. We know Andrews called there shortly afterwards and when Berriman went to pick up the child, a terrific row between Sharon and *him* was going on inside. If she had just told Andrews she might be infected...'

Bramwell was nodding, his eyes bleak. 'What a bloody awful mess.'

'I dropped a hint to one of the nurses. I reckon she is. They clammed up about her but I know she's now in an isolation unit, with barrier nursing.'

Bramwell nodded thoughtfully. 'Andrews would want to break her neck. It wasn't her fault but he'd never see it that way. We know for certain it was Gough who infected her.'

'We do?'

'As a result of researches into possible contacts he may have made in prison... that old bugger he used to share a cell with—he's the culprit. He's infected six other people as well. Marvellous, isn't it, what you can collect along with a prison sentence nowadays?'

'Great.'

'We checked with the prison doctor. He claimed Gough pretended it would never happen. There was going to be this wonder drug which would stop his AIDs developing. Which probably meant he didn't bother taking precautions.'

Bramwell looked at his watch. 'Mustn't be too long. I want to be home before Jean gets back.'

'I appreciate the visit.'

'I haven't finished bringing you up to date We finally got the bank to cough up Clare's statement. You'll never guess, he was loaded. About two thousand in a current account plus another fifty thousand on deposit. With that other fifty thou in the building society, makes for an approximate total of one hundred and two grand. And we've still got to squeeze the info out of the Austrian bank.'

Cass was about to whistle but remembered his lack of teeth. 'If we'd known that before...'

'Exactly.' Bramwell nodded vigorously. 'We'd have seen things from a different perspective altogether. Assumed it was attempted robbery from the start. The SIO melted the wires when he spoke to the bank manager.'

Cass sighed. 'I was remembering those poor old freaks at the pub, grateful for their bequest handouts. Clare could've given them a thousand each without noticing it.'

'You're missing the point. The SIO believes, and, I must say, I see no reason to disagree—this murder was an attempted robbery which went wrong.'

Cass lay back against the pillows, his head beginning to throb. 'By Andrews, you mean? Did he travel to Inkerman Street with Gough? It seems bloody odd after attempting to murder the man's wife but nothing would surprise me any more. I presume the two thumb prints matched?'

'No, they didn't.'

'What?' Cass's eyes widened. 'Then on what possible grounds can we pin Clare's death on Lee Andrews?'

'We can't. It wasn't Andrews who was involved in that murder, it was Karl Gough all along, plus the prowler of course. However we can use the suggestion that Andrews *was* involved without fear of contradiction from Gough meanwhile. Didn't you listen to the SIO on the news? It was a neat solution, you have to admire him for it.' Bramwell forced himself to be honest, 'It's the reason he'll end up Commissioner unlike you or me.'

'You've lost me?'

'We are not going to charge Andrews with Clare's death—because we know he didn't do it—but we are going to announce, as the SIO did several times this morning, that our investigations are "in abeyance" while we press charges of malicious wounding and GBH to Tunnicliffe—after releasing plenty of before-and-after pictures—which we hope will incite the sympathy of both judge and jury—'

'Was that why one of our blokes turned up here to take snaps?'

'Presumably. Once he gets an idea, the old bastard goes into action and tells me afterward. We are also going to charge Lee Andrews with Sharon Gough's death when it happens, although we know we can't make a murder charge stick.'

'Father Gibson will refuse to testify about the double relationship.'

'So we'll use the HIV factor. Or rather we'll threaten to. Andrews won't want it to slip out, other prisoners would crucify him. We'll keep it up our sleeves to put pressure on with his brief, if we have to. We are also announcing, in conjunction with these two charges, that Ernest Clare's murder will remain on file.' Bramwell sat back with a smile. 'Neat?'

'So it's implicit that Andrews has a murder charge pending, one which *we* know he didn't commit.'

The receiver wagged a finger. 'Stop being so finicky. It may well appear that way to a jury, I agree. In fact, it had bloody well appear that way to a jury otherwise we're wasting our breath. Look, the SIO wants to make sure Andrews is put away for a nice long stretch—which, you would agree, is both right and proper?'

'But not by means of a deliberate lie.'

'Hang on, hang on. Clare's death will have to remain on file anyway because Karl Gough might well be resident in a

French prison hospital for some time. His artic caused two deaths in that pile-up.'

'And?' Despite his throbbing head Cass was becoming even more impatient.

'Something else turned up from the bank this morning. I told you we'd decided it must have been an attempted robbery which went wrong. Gough obviously found Clare's cheque book and he's been up to his old tricks, cashing at least one with the help of Lila Boyce's plastic. But it was only for a tiny amount. He obviously had no idea how much was in that particular account even though he knew there was money. We now believe Gough did have another accomplice after all. Someone other than Lee Andrews.'

Cass tried to grapple with this new idea. 'You mean the thumb prints? Because Gough knew about the old man and therefore could have heard about the money stashed away.'

'Exactly.' Bramwell looked complacent. 'Why not? There must have been rumours flying about in that tight little neighbourhood. Over eighty thousand nicker? Even if Gough didn't know the total, with his habit of sniffing out cash, he must have heard the odd whisper. You know how people hint, "That rich old bugger, he keeps it in his sock under the mattress." '

'Only he didn't, he was sensible,' Cass insisted, 'he kept it in the bank.'

'But Gough didn't know that. So he took someone else along to apply the necessary pressure to reveal the hiding place. We know from his records Karl Gough isn't a muscle man; he'd need a helping hand. Sadly, the old man didn't cough and too much pressure was applied, with the inevitable consequence. He must have been a right brute, whoever he was, to break Clare's neck as well as strangle him. We've been checking prison records. We're hoping to have a few names to try out on Gough when we nip over to Dijon. The SIO and I are off to have a preliminary chat.'

'Poor bastard,' said Cass suddenly. 'Gough may not know that his wife is dying, or that his daughter's in care.'

'Or even that she's not his daughter.'

'I still think it's dodgy, I mean—it is immoral.'

'Possibly.' Bramwell tucked the chair tidily beside the locker. 'In the good old days, we could have relied on a confession.'

'Oh, sure!'

'Tut-tut-tut . . . Where's your common sense. Today was our last chance to wrap things up. This way Andrews gets what we *know* he deserves. And if Karl Gough has the sense to finger whoever he took along—"the prowler"—he'll have something to bargain with when his trial comes up over here.'

'If he survives.'

'Ah, well,' Bramwell shook his head, 'at least he's got something to look forward to.'

'He has?'

'Whether he does or he doesn't survive, at least he won't be seeing his mother-in-law for a very long time.'

SIXTEEN

'"THE SMILING FACE Of Happiness".'

Mrs Bignell's choice of tabloid often caused pain to Mr Pringle. 'That's tautological.'

She replied absently, 'Is it, dear?' and continued, '"The new face of DPW Vivien Tunnicliffe as she finally emerged from hospital today, carrying a daffodil and hand-in-hand with her new fiancé, CID hero Colin Cass. There to congratulate the happy pair was the senior investigating officer who first brought them together, Detective Inspector Kevin Crombie. DI Crombie was quoted as saying, 'It is young officers such as these who are a shining example to the rest of the force.'"' Well then?'

'Well, what?'

'It says they ended up in the same hospital because of that Lee Andrews.'

Mr Pringle rustled his copy of *The Guardian*. 'I trust in future, both will learn to be more careful.'

'"See page three."' Mrs Bignell read the next item for a second or two. 'Oh, I say! Oh—here, listen to this!'

'Mavis, in view of the current financial situation, this leader is particularly—'

'No, listen!! "Late yesterday, following publication of the estate of the late Ernest Clare who, readers will remember, was the OAP brutally murdered at his home in Inkerman Street, London, at Christmas, DI Kevin Crombie, the senior investigating officer in charge of the case issued the following statement: 'Following the death from AIDS of Karl Gough in a hospital in France, the file on the unlawful death of Ernest Clare has been closed.' Gough was awaiting trial after an incident on an autoroute involving his articulated lorry and the passenger and driver of a Citroën AX. DI Crombie confirmed that he and his colleagues had been hoping to question Gough further once he had served his sentence and been extradited back to this country. Lee Andrews, an accomplice of Gough, is already serving a twelve-year sentence for the attack on Mrs Sharon Gough, aged twenty-eight, who later died from kidney failure, also DPW Vivien Tunnicliffe whose engagement picture we publish today.

"'Neither Gough nor Andrews was prepared to reveal the identify of the third man who assisted with that attempted robbery and murder, commonly known as the prowler. It will be remembered that Lee Andrews continued to protest his innocence of the Clare killing and was one of seven men involved in the recent rooftop protest at Albany prison in the Isle of Wight. See also page seventeen." What about that?'

Mr Pringle had an unhappy memory of Karl Gough drinking beer. 'Does Joe always remember to use sterilising tablets in the glass washer?'

'Is that all you can say?' Mavis went back to searching her paper. 'Here it is, page seventeen: "Further revelations of recluse Ernest Clare from our financial correspondent"... Oh, my godfathers! Six hundred and seventy-seven thousand, six hundred and forty-eight pounds!' Mrs Bignell's voice rose to new-found heights.

'What is?'

'Ernest Clare's estate. He left *all that money*!'

'Ah.'

She stared at him, mouth agape. 'Surely you can say something more this time? Aren't you a *little bit* surprised?'

Belatedly, Mr Pringle remembered it behoved him to be so. 'It is a great deal of money,' he said weakly. 'I suppose it must have included the sale of his house—'

'That house went for thirty-nine thousand five hundred pounds and not a penny more. I know because Lila came and told us in the Bricklayers. I said so at the time. She was really depressed. She was thinking her own couldn't be worth much more, naturally.'

'Yes, well...'

'Well? Where did the rest of it come from?'

He was at a loss to know what to suggest. 'What does it say in your newspaper?'

' "This astonishing fortune came to light when DI Crombie and his team began examining the possessions of Ernest Clare following his murder. A thorough search produced a building society book and bank account at a local branch of Lloyds, but the bulk of the fortune was with an Austrian bank, whose secrecy laws are second only to those of Switzerland. Only one docket was found at the scene of the crime. This gave the vital clue, however, to both the bank and the account number. It was DI Crombie who made the breakthrough when an assistant realised the name on the docket might be that of a foreign bank and the number that of the account. DI Crombie then put two and two together. No spokesman was available in Vienna to offer an explanation as to how this humble, reclusive old man amassed such an incredible sum. In the words of DI Crombie, it has amazed us all." '

Mavis flung down her newspaper. 'I'll give them "humble" and "reclusive", I could wring Ernest's neck, the way he's fooled us.' Mr Pringle held his tongue. Her anger increased. 'You do realise, for the last eight or ten years, ever since he began popping into the Bricklayers, I have been standing that man drinks? He never bought me a single G and T. Not a port, not a measly tomato juice, nothing.'

Mr Pringle wondered if he dared suggest her reward might be forthcoming in Heaven? Perhaps not. Mrs Bignell didn't care for strange drinks.

'What will happen to it?' she asked eventually. 'It says here he died intestate.'

'Ah!' Light shone in Mr Pringle's eye as he prepared to launch into his favourite subject but Mrs Bignell cut him short.

'I don't mean how much tax will he have to pay, what I mean is—who gets it?'

'The state,' he said flatly.

'What—all of it?'

'Once the probate office have taken their considerable cut, which proves how essential it is to make a will.'

'You needn't worry, I've left you everything.'

'How very kind—'

'After my funeral expenses have been paid and that includes a knife and fork champagne party at the Bricklayers. You make sure Joe doesn't cheat with sparkling wine or rubbish like that. Don't let him hide the labels.'

Mr Pringle promised he would do his best adding it was his sincere hope the sad task would fall to another. 'In which case, I have named you as my sole beneficiary,' he added.

'Yes, well that's enough mournful talk.' Mrs Bignell still simmered. 'Wait till the rest of them find out about this. Lila, helping him like that, even Becky Posner did her little bit. You'd think he could leave them a few bob. And when I remember that bequest money... He could have stuffed those envelopes with thousand-pound notes and never noticed the difference...' She began to calm down. 'What d'you think made him do it, keeping it in a foreign bank? Why not spend it on himself? He could have been a bit more comfortable in his old age.'

'Goodness knows.' Mr Pringle genuinely did not know the answer but then he had not spent his entire life trying to conceal his identity.

'I hope when I die, there's enough left for that party and not a penny more. Come on, get your coat on.'

'Where are we off to?'

'To choose the wallpaper now the insurance money has come through. I've seen a lovely pattern in a magazine with big blue azaleas. It would mean changing the hall carpet but what the hell—you're a long time dead.'

IT WAS A battered Morris traveller that drew up outside the smart converted coast house in Kent. Like his car, Father Gibson looked out of place. The lady of the house was on the lookout for him. Her welcome was gracious.

'Come in . . . how nice to meet you. We're in the morning room. It gets the sun at this time of day. Nanny and Sarah are reading *Thomas the Tank Engine.*'

'Reading already? I always thought she was a bright little girl.'

'Well, not actually *reading* but I'm sure she recognises several letters. You'd like to see her?'

'I would indeed. If it's no trouble.'

He hovered on the threshold of the room rather than intrude on the pair on the sunlit rug. The child, surrounded by toys, was absorbed in trying to detach a page from her book. He noted the uniform worn by the nanny. A respectful distance away sat an elegant spaniel thumping the floor with a stubby tail. It was all as glossy as a magazine.

Beyond the open door to the kitchen was another woman, presumably what he would refer to as a 'daily'. His came once a week. This woman looked as if she was a permanent part of the household.

'Hello—Sarah.' He spoke softly. He was part of the old life, out of place in the new. The lady of the house laughed a little self-consciously.

'She's awfully good with strangers. You can go closer.'

'Thank you.' Father Gibson crouched beside her. 'I brought you a gift . . . not that you need it, you've got so many new things and this one's definitely seen better days.'

As the child stuffed the rag doll in her mouth, he added quickly, 'The nurses gave it a thorough wash in carbolic. They wanted her to have it. Sarah played with it at the hospital, you see.' But from the adults' faces, he could see the doll would be put in the bin the minute he left.

'How very kind.' The voice was cooler although the smile was still in place. 'I'm sure you'd like a cup of coffee. Shall we go through? Coffee, Agnes.' The woman in the kitchen nodded.

Father Gibson followed his hostess across acres of polished golden wood into a room which overlooked a pleasant fecund valley. A Siamese cat was curled up on the most comfortable chair.

His hostess opened a window on to the full-length balcony. 'Timothy and I often have our coffee out here. If it's not too cold today... ?' It was but he joined her obediently. Out here, no one could overhear. He also waited until Agnes had come and gone, leaving the silver tray.

'I understand you were instrumental in arranging Sarah's adoption?'

'I was, yes. Her mother entrusted me with the task. Of course the adoption society took over officially; I've really no business coming here today.'

'I'm glad you did.'

He wondered how much of the carefully laundered background had been divulged. Out here, spring sunlight was cruel, it showed the deep lines on forehead and chin. She was several years older than her husband. He began to worry: had the child been adopted as a sop to a failing marriage? One never could tell with clever people like these. 'It's very kind of you to let me have a peep at Sarah. I wanted to satisfy myself, as I'd promised her mother I would.'

'Stay to lunch, you're more than welcome.'

'No, no... I've seen all I need. When I've finished this excellent coffee, I'll be off.'

The woman examined her rings, studiously. 'Sarah's mother died extremely young.'

'She did. She slipped away very peacefully, if ever Sarah should ask.'

'Timothy told me it was kidney failure. Really, people should be made to understand how important a donor card can be: literally, the difference between life and death. Timothy and I carry them all the time of course, so does Nanny.'

'Uh-huh. Very, very true. But out of a tragic situation, I can see nothing but happiness ahead for dear little Sarah.'

The brittle tension relaxed an inch or two. 'Thank you so much. We do our best.'

'Promise me one thing...' He could see she feared he was about to request regular attendance at church. 'Will you give me your word not to spoil the wee girl?'

Her relieved laughter confirmed it. 'But of course I will! It will be difficult. Timothy and I tried for years, you know. We went up and down Harley Street: in vitro, A. I. D., everything. Nothing worked. Sarah has come as a godsend.'

'Indeed, indeed.' Father Gibson hesitated but there was no way of wrapping it up. 'There's no chance you'll ever grow tired of her? Children can be very tiresome. Argumentative, too, as they grow older.' He got a glimpse then of the passionate desire the woman had had for one of her own.

'Never! I *prayed* for a miracle. When Timothy came home with Sarah's photograph, I knew my prayers had been answered.'

'Uh-huh. It's good to know miracles still happen.' *His* prayers had been answered when he learned Sarah had not been infected with the terrible contagion. 'I've a photograph for her, by the way.' He fished it out of his pocket. 'It's Sarah's mother, if ever she should want to know what she was like. Taken a long time ago, as you can see; long before her last illness.' He sighed, the difference at the end had been so great. 'Such a beautiful girl, wasn't she?'

Opposite, hostility had returned. 'I don't know whether I should take it.'

'Please,' he urged. 'Sarah's bound to ask one day. All of them do, believe me. Not to answer those questions, to hide the truth, will do more harm than good. Please, let Sarah see this. It will not affect her love for you. This poor creature is dead, so is Sarah's father'—dear Lord, forgive that one— 'neither of them could ever be a threat.'

'I assure you, I wasn't thinking of *that*.'

She was, it was her greatest fear, poor woman. To comfort her, he said, 'I know. You are far too kind-hearted to entertain such thoughts.' He replaced the expensive cup carefully, and rose. 'There was another reason why I asked if I could come. That was to thank you on behalf of Sarah's mother. From the love of your heart, you have given a home to another woman's child, which cannot be easy. And I'm asking one further act of charity, the most difficult of all: that you don't deny Sarah the knowledge of her parents, such as it is. A couple of decent young people who had all the bad luck in the world, except they were blessed with a child, of course.'

She was fidgeting wildly with those big rings. 'Of course I won't deny it to her. And thank you for this. Have you a photograph of her father? Richard told he he'd been killed in a motorway accident in France.'

'I'm afraid not, no. I'm sorry.'

The woman repeated, 'And her mother's end really was quiet and peaceful?'

'Oh, very quiet.' It always was when Father Gibson described it, he hoped his employer would understand. As he recalled the bloated face and putrid flesh he said, 'Her beautiful yellow hair was spread out on the pillow... She was holding my hand, she didn't speak, just slipped away into eternity.'

His hostess's eyes had filled with tears. 'None of us could ask more than that, could we? Thank you. I'll be sure to tell Sarah, when the time comes.'